They stayed in the main room and talked for hours. Rilla sat on the sofa next to Candace. He stared into her eyes and smiled a lot, telling her how beautiful she was a few times. Rilla told war stories about his hometown, Overbrook Meadows. Candace had never been to Texas. She thought it sounded like a pretty rough place. Rilla told her there were beautiful sights there, too. He asked if she might like to see his city one day, and Candace eagerly said that she would.

Around three in the morning, Rachel was nodding on the suite's love seat. Rilla kissed Candace for the first time and asked if she wanted to go to the bedroom with him. Once there, he asked her if she was sure about what they were doing. He asked again right before insertion. Candace had never experienced anything like it. When he mounted, Candace found out what an orgasm was.

And she loved it.

A GOOD DUDE

KEITH THOMAS WALKER

Genesis Press, Inc.

INDIGO LOVE SPECTRUM

An imprint of Genesis Press, Inc.
Publishing Company

Genesis Press, Inc.
P.O. Box 101
Columbus, MS 39703

ISBN: 13 DIGIT : 978-1-58571-431-5
ISBN: 10 DIGIT : 1-58571-431-3
Manufactured in the United States of America

First Edition

Visit us at www.genesis-press.com
or call at 1-888-Indigo-1-4-0

DEDICATION

This book is for Mama. Thanks for letting me read Stephen King when I was young. I had a few nightmares but they were worth it.

When you're next to me
All I feel is ecstasy
Your parts connect with me
You a dime piece?
Come here baby
Let me see

Rilla
Tasty Lady

CHAPTER 1
RILLA TIME

The music was deafening. A thudding bassline reverberated off of the walls in the small club, making Candace feel like she was trapped in the darkness of Rilla's car trunk.

It was hot, too. Candace dotted her forehead with a paper napkin and sucked on the straw poking from her Long Island iced tea. There was only ice in the glass. The teenager barely got a teaspoon of liquid, but it was enough to satisfy her dry mouth for the time being. What she really wanted was another round. She could have one if she asked, but this was already her second drink. Candace knew she really shouldn't partake at all (truth be told).

The atmosphere in Club Tron was ripped. Busty broads with tight jeans and belly rings crowded around the stage and cheered for the featured artist. Candace watched them from a distance with a smug sense of satisfaction. These women, with their thick thighs, coochie cutters, and lip gloss reminded Candace of how she must have looked eight months ago when she saw Rilla in concert for the first time.

Candace scanned the crowd, finding it funny how the women carried on like Lil' Wayne was up there. Their moody boyfriends watched casually from their tables, or they hung out on the walls and near the exit. They were excited, too, but black males have to be careful of the amount of praise they show each other, lest they be accused of *dick riding*.

And it wasn't that the men here tonight would never dick ride. Candace knew these same Negroes would pump their fists and yell out just as loud as the females if it really was Lil' Wayne up there. But Club Tron didn't have the clout to bring in big names like that. Club Tron was lucky to book local rappers like DJ Get Busy and MC Smurf and Rilla.

Rilla lived right around the corner, which is why he was being hated on. Most niggas aren't apt to get starstruck by someone they run into at the convenience store a few times a week. Especially when this particular rapper was Puerto Rican.

And that was a shame. Raul Canales, aka Rilla, was arguably the most famous entertainer to hail from Overbrook Meadows. His first single, "Traffic Stop," got national radio play, maxing out at number thirty-seven on the U.S. charts. His music video was a constant on BET for months, but that was two years ago. Since then, Rilla learned something every recording artist has to accept sooner or later: The music industry is a fickle beast. Having talent doesn't automatically guarantee you a contract, and it doesn't guarantee you can put food on your table, either.

Rilla's debut album, *Rilla Time*, sold only 27,000 copies nationwide, and he was unceremoniously dropped from his label. He was then schooled on the financial side of the music biz. Twenty-seven thousand copies at ten dollars a pop sounded like a quarter-million dollars to Rilla, but he was still getting bills from BMS Records six months after being released. No other label was willing to take a risk on the 25-year-old rapper, so Rilla took full advantage of every opportunity.

Club Tron was basically a hole in the wall. On Sunday nights, old men gathered in the back to throw dice on a dusty pool table. The drinks were watered down, and the place could only hold 150 people, but Rilla performed like he was at the House of Blues. He performed like there were cameras there and this might be telecast live. He dropped to his knees while singing *Mama Canales* and put a hand over his heart. He closed his eyes and the words dribbled from his lips like a condemned man's last wish:

> *I saw yo strength when Marcus died*
> *You was there*
> *You held him close*
> *You had his blood stains in yo hair*
> *And two months later when they got me*
> *Nobody cared*
> *But you was there*
> *You held me close and got blood in yo hair*

The Grammy people didn't think those lyrics were too special, but Candace did. She watched Rilla perform from a seat adjacent to the stage. Butterflies danced in her belly and she giggled and reminisced. Candace had these same butterflies eight months ago when she caught a Rilla concert in her hometown, Brooklyn, New York. Rilla didn't have a large crowd on that night, either, but his performance was the same whether there was thirty or three thousand in attendance.

꒰꒱

Candace was one of the girls at the front of the stage back then. She screamed and danced and threw her hands up when the hype man told her to. She got caught up in the magic of the evening. She wasn't expecting more than a fun night out, but an odd thing happened at that New York Summer Jam. While singing his song *Tasty Lady*, Rilla looked out into the crowd and asked if there were any tasty ladies out there. Of course Candace raised her hand, but she wasn't alone. At least a hundred other girls proclaimed their tastiness, but Rilla only wanted *one* girl to get on stage with him.

"Mmm. I need a *tasty lady* to come up," he boomed through the microphone. "Who wanna let me sing this song to them?"

"Me! Me, Rilla! I'm tasty!" cried the multitude.

Rilla put a hand to his forehead as if shading the sun. He was just as handsome then as he is today. His skin was darker than most Latinos, the color of coffee with one cream. He had warm eyes and thick eyebrows. Rilla had a perfect complexion; not one scar, dimple, or pimple. A neat goatee framed his platinum-laden mouth. His hair was short. Rilla wore jewelry, but not as much as you would expect on a rapper. His watch wasn't custom made, and his necklace wasn't extravagant, either.

"I think I see her," Rilla had said. "Yeah. I see her. She got pretty eyes, long hair, brown skin . . ."

All of the light-skinned women in the audience groaned in defeat, but caramel-colored girls like Candace felt reinvigorated. *Maybe he's talking about me*, she thought.

Candace was only seventeen years old. She had a nice figure, but some of the ladies at the concert were seriously stacked. The girl standing right next to her had an ass you could set a dinner tray on, but in the back of her mind Candace kept a little hope. She thought Rilla was looking right at her. What he said next erased all doubt.

"I see her, y'all. Yeah, I see her. I think she got on braces. Say, let me get some light over here. I think that's my girl right there."

Rilla pointed, and a huge spotlight spun in that direction. About twenty girls were bathed in the brightness, but Candace was in the middle. She was the only one wearing braces, too.

"There she go right there!" Rilla announced. "Come on up here, girl. You perfect! Can I sing my song to you?"

"Me?" Candace asked and put a finger to her chest—fully aware he couldn't hear her above the uproar.

"Yeah, you! With the pink shirt! Come on up here. Y'all let her up."

Candace felt like a princess as the sea of people parted to let her pass. In the back of her mind she still felt there was some mistake. When she got close enough, Rilla would shake his head and sneer.

"Naw, not you!" he would say, and everyone would laugh, and Candace would flee the scene with her head held *way* down, but each nervous step got her closer to the stage. And no one was laughing. They cheered her on, and when she made it to the front a bodyguard hefted her onto the platform.

Candace never felt more insecure, but Rilla and his hype man looked at her like she was the best thing they'd seen in New York. Candace stood five feet, three inches. She had large eyes and skin the color of a Snickers bar. She had a big smile. Her dimples made her appear younger than she was, and her braces furthered this effect.

She was thin and young, but Candace had the shapely bulges of a grown woman. In fact, her mother always warned that her body would be her downfall if she wasn't careful. Candace had a good head on her shoulders, but her mother said some men wouldn't see past her supple breasts and protruding hips. These men would ogle her openly and undress her with their eyes. They would look at her much like Rilla was looking at her at that exact moment, but Candace's mom was the last thing on her mind. This man, this *famous rapper*, had chosen her out of all the women in the building. Candace never felt more special.

"Damn, baby. You look good. What's yo name?" Rilla asked.

He thrust the microphone under her chin and she said, "Candace."

"I was right about you," Rilla said. "You're definitely a tasty lady." He looked her up and down and licked his chops. "*Candace*. Sweet like *candy*."

Candace wore a tight pink T-shirt with a denim skirt and leather sandals. The skirt didn't go past mid-thigh. It rose to ridiculous heights when she sat down, but Candace wore pink panties, too. She figured she was coordinating.

"Sit down, baby, I want to sing to you," Rilla instructed.

Candace looked around, surprised to see that the hype man had brought out a folding chair. With the audience screaming behind her, Candace took a seat and crossed her legs and listened intently as Rilla rapped "Tasty Lady" just for her. He stared into her eyes and held her hand most of the time. And although a big pair of panties came flying very close to Candace's head halfway through the set, she felt like it was just him and her there.

Close yo eyes, baby
Let me take you there
Let me smell yo hair
Kiss beneath yo underwear
Look in my eyes, girl
Feel my heart
You got me sprung
I'm sucking toes tonight
I'm licking thighs and pearl tongues

By the end of the song, a good number of the women in attendance were turned on, but no one was as moist as

Candace. Before he showed her off the stage, Rilla leaned in close for a conspiratorial whisper.

"You sho look good, girl. Yo name Candace for real?" His accent was barely discernable.

"Yeah."

"Check this out, I only got *one night* in town. I know that sounds shady, but I'm for real. No bullshit. I wanna kick it with you tonight. Can you stay out for a while?"

"Yeah," Candace lied.

"How old is you, girl?" Rilla wanted to know.

"Eighteen," Candace lied again.

"We having a little party in my room after the show, in about an hour. Can you come?"

"Yes. Where?"

"We stayin' at the Renaissance. Room 234."

"Okay."

"You gon' remember that, Candace? I really want you to come."

"I'll remember," Candace promised, and she did. Rilla wasn't necessarily the biggest name out there, but he appeared to be on the rise. His "Traffic Stop" video was always ranked in the top five on BET's 106 and Park. His *Rilla Time* tour took him all over the country. Candace was a devoted fan, but her girlfriends thought she was sliding into groupie territory.

"You're not going, are you?" Shannon asked. Shannon was tall, blonde, and about as soulful as Barbara Bush. Why she went to the concert in the first place was a mystery.

"Yeah, I think I'm going," Candace told her.

"You father's going to kill you," Shannon noted. And she was right about that. Candace graduated high school two months ago, but her stepdad was nowhere near ready to push her from the nest. He barely let Candace date at all, and he couldn't stand rappers. He would have had an aneurysm if he knew Candace betrayed him and sneaked to Rilla's concert.

"They're gonna treat you like shit," Rachel said. She was Candace's best friend. Rachel was in Candace's graduating class, but the private school never corrupted her free spirit. "They just want sex," Rachel went on. "You're not going without me!"

"That's what I'm talking about," Candace said.

Shannon was mortified. "Your dad thinks you're spending the night with me! What if something happens to you over there? You're my responsibility!"

"Stop being so melodramatic," Rachel said.

"Come with us," Candace offered.

"I'm not going. And you shouldn't, either."

But Candace did go. She and Rachel spent their last few dollars on a cab and made it to Rilla's hotel ninety minutes after the concert ended. Candace's life was never the same since. Rilla was an amazing guy, full of surprises. The first surprise came when they got to his room. Candace expected a party atmosphere. She expected a large entourage and loud music and groupies as far as the eye could see, but there were only three people in his suite. Rilla answered the door himself wearing jeans and a T-shirt. His platinum grill was removed, and his other jewelry was set aside somewhere. He looked like a regular person.

9

Candace had been in love before, but never swept off her feet. And she didn't think a guy like Raul "Rilla" Canales could do it. He was too much of a roughneck. Candace grew up on the other side of the tracks. Her mother was a college-educated social worker. Her stepfather was a retired naval lieutenant. Rilla invited her into his world of gunshots, broken beer bottles, and spilt blood, and Candace had never seen anything so amazing.

They stayed in the main room and talked for hours. Rilla sat on a sofa next to Candace. He stared into her eyes and smiled a lot, telling her how beautiful she was a few times. Rilla told war stories about his hometown, Overbrook Meadows. Candace had never been to Texas. She thought it sounded like a pretty rough place. Rilla told her there were beautiful sights there, too. He asked if she might like to see his city one day, and Candace eagerly said she would.

Around three in the morning, Rachel was nodding on the suite's love seat. Rilla kissed Candace for the first time and asked if she wanted to go to the bedroom with him. Once there, he asked her if she was sure about what they were doing. He asked again right before insertion. Candace had never experienced anything like it. The boys at her school were so eager. They wouldn't dream of giving her a chance to back out.

And Rilla was different in other ways. He was twenty-four, six years older than both of Candace's former lovers. Candace had never experienced *grown man sex*, and she took an immediate liking to it. When he put his head between her legs, Rilla knew exactly where to lick. He sucked her like he was trying to get meat off a neck bone. When he mounted, Candace found out what an orgasm was.

And she loved it.

Rilla left the city the very next day. He begged Candace to go with him, but that was ridiculous. Candace was a good girl. She graduated from a private school and had already been accepted to three universities. So he left by himself.

But he called her later that week. Rilla was in Michigan then. He told Candace there was no woman in the whole state who came anywhere near her beauty. He asked again if she wouldn't reconsider going on tour with him. Candace was so smitten by then that she actually asked her mother.

"Are you serious?" Katherine Hendricks asked.

"Mama, he just has another month to go before he goes back home."

"You want to ride around with some *dumb rapper* for a month? Candace, have you lost your godforsaken mind?"

"No, Mama. Rilla's not like the other rappers. He's sweet. He—"

"Your father would roll in his grave if he knew you were asking me this."

"Mama—"

"I know I raised you better."

"Mama, if you just listen—."

"There's nothing to listen to, Candace."

"You don't even know him."

"I don't even know *you*, girl! What the hell is wrong with you?"

"But—"

"You turn eighteen in six months. Even then you'll have to hook up with this guy *over my dead body!*"

Candace's mom was indignant, but her stepfather was livid.

"You went to that damned concert after I told you not to?" Gerald asked.

Candace couldn't come up with a response.

"You met this guy? Tell me you were with him. I'll have his ass locked up for statutory rape!"

"I'm seventeen!"

"Did you sleep with him? *I'll kill him! I swear to God!*"

"Daddy!"

"*Go to your room!*"

When Rilla called two weeks later to say he was in Jersey, Candace told him she would be on the next train headed that way. She squeezed what belongings she could in her school backpack and hit the road, becoming the most illogical runaway in New York. Most kids her age ran from abuse or suffering or some type of trouble. Against the advice of virtually everyone she knew, Candace ran straight to it.

Ꮒ

That was eight months ago.

Candace thought she would live a Hollywood lifestyle with Rilla, but he got dropped from his label at the end of the tour. The only thing he got from his record deal was plane tickets home. Candace was obliged to go with him.

Back in Overbrook Meadows, things got bleak. In a desperate attempt to fund his second album on his own, Rilla easily fell back into drug dealing. Candace thought of leaving him a few times, but he still had *some* money and a lot of clout. Rilla was a local celebrity in his hometown. He didn't perform often, but he could still pull in a thousand dollars a night, like this gig at Club Tron.

Candace sat back and watched the hoochies throw themselves at her man, knowing Rilla would never go for them. Ever since he invited Candace on stage at that Summer Jam, Rilla had never met a woman he wanted to be with more. He told her so almost every day.

CHAPTER 2
PIECE OF PARADISE

They stayed at the club for an hour after his set. A lot of girls lingered, too, so they could get some one-on-one time with the artist. This used to be cause for concern, but Candace respected and listened to her man. Rilla had a logical explanation for his interactions with the opposite sex, and if Candace wanted to be his girl, she had to accept certain things:

"See, when I write songs like 'Tasty Lady,'" Rilla once told her, "I do that for the bitches. I might have a steady girl, but I want everybody to feel me. You dig? If the bitches like me, the niggas will follow.

"I can't be actin' shady at my shows. If them hos wanna come and speak to me, I gotta be there for 'em. I love my fans. I *need* 'em. If I gotta kiss a couple broads on they cheek to sell my CDs, I'll do that. Is that gonna be cool with you or not? Let me know now."

Rilla told her that when it was determined they were a serious couple, and Candace said it was cool, but she never got used to it. She watched him now and a sneer marred her delicate features. An older woman wearing capris and a see-through blouse was getting a lot of one-on-one time. She pushed up on Candace's man, rubbing her old lady titties all over his chest.

Candace shook her head and then stood and went to the restroom. When she got back, Rilla was waiting for her.

"You ready?" he asked.

"You through?" Candace asked with a hint of attitude.

Rilla smiled. "That bitch was wild, huh?"

"She's old enough to be your mother," Candace replied.

Rilla's smile got bigger. The scant light caught his platinum grill, and Candace thought he looked majestic. For the show, he wore a huge Kobe Bryant jersey with dark blue jeans. He wore Polo boots and a bracelet tricked out with Lucky Charms. The only thing missing was his huge necklace, but that chain was property of his old record label.

"You know I don't want nobody but you," Rilla said, and Candace did know that. In the eight months they'd been together, she never heard rumors about his infidelity. Things might have been different if his career was successful, but Rilla was stable now. He and Candace had a home together. They had dreams together.

"You got lipstick on your face," Candace said. She found a napkin in her purse and wiped it away.

Rilla leaned back against a table. He grabbed Candace's hips and pulled her close. "Let me get some of yo lipstick now."

Candace smiled. "I wear lip *gloss*."

Rilla wrapped his hands around her buttocks and squeezed affectionately. "Well, let me get some of yo lip gloss then."

He kissed her and embraced her in a full body hug.

"You looked good up there tonight," Candace said.

"Yeah? I messed up that one part in 'Mama Canales.'"

"I know," Candace said, "but nobody noticed."

"*You* noticed."

"I hear *everything,*" she said. "I can't believe you can't get signed." Candace regretted the words as soon as they left her lips. Rilla's arms grew stiff around her. His smile faded.

"I'ma get signed," he said.

"I know you will, baby."

They smoked a blunt on the way home. Once there, Rilla took a shower while Candace put rollers on and stuffed her hair under a shower cap. They had a one-bedroom apartment. It was so small, you could stand in the hallway and see the whole place if you turned around a few times. Rilla sang Teddy Pendergrass as he bathed:

"*To be loved, and be loved in return, is the only thing that my heart desires.* What you know about that, shorty?"

"Huh?"

"I say what you know about that *Teddy P.*?"

"Who's Teddy P?"

"Yeah. That's what I figured. Bet you don't know nothing about no Marvin Gaye, either."

"I do know Marvin Gaye," Candace said as she undressed.

"Yeah? What you know about him?"

"I know he got shot by his daddy."

"That's just like a nigga to remember only the bad stuff. What about his music? Did you like any songs?"

"Didn't he sing 'Let's Get It On'?"

"Yeah. That's my boy. What 'bout Sam Cooke?"

"Quit trying to act like you all old," Candace said. "You're only twenty-five. You don't know all them people."

"Who say I don't?"

"*I* say you don't."

"Check this out," Rilla said, and then went into an impromptu karaoke performance. He was a nice singer, but Candace had never heard him sound so good, so deep and soulful.

Candace was speechless. She opened the shower curtain and slipped inside. Rilla turned to face her and marvel at her nakedness. Candace marveled, too. Rilla had never been to prison, but he had the muscular features of an Aztec warrior. He had the name of his old record label tattooed on one side of his chest, and *RILLA TIME* scrolled across the other side. He had *817 SCC*, the name of his old gang, tatted on his forearm.

Candace took the washcloth from him and wrapped it around a bar of soap. "I didn't know you could sing," she said and lathered up his chest.

"Yes, you did."

"You never sang like *that* before."

"I never sang Sam Cooke for you."

"You know some more Sam Cooke?"

Rilla smiled. His grill was gone now, and Candace was glad for that.

"How about this," he said. "It's old. Like Frankie Lymon old, but I still like it."

Candace didn't spoil the mood by telling him she had no idea who Frankie Lymon was.

Rilla put his hands on her hips and looked into her eyes. He softly crooned the words to an old song Candace had never heard before.

Again Candace was dumbfounded. This was the same guy who sold crack on the corner and penned catchy lyrics like, *Tell yo old-ass mama to stay out my business / Or I'ma kill yo little brother and rape your sister when I'm finished.*

"That was beautiful," she said.

"You liked it?"

"Yeah. I never heard it before."

"We can look it up on YouTube later if you wanna hear how it really goes."

"No, I liked it just like that," Candace said. "That was perfect."

❧

In the bedroom, she tried to put on a pair of boxer shorts, but Rilla told her not to. She sat on the bed instead with her hands in her lap. Rilla stood between her legs.

"Scoot back," he told her.

Candace inched back on the mattress, trying to keep her legs together.

"You uncomfortable around me?" Rilla asked.

"No," she said. "Not really."

"Ain't nothing wrong with being naked," he said.

Candace took in his nude physique, her eyes settling on the limp snake between his legs. "No, there's nothing wrong with that," she agreed.

Rilla looked down at her and grinned. "Open your legs," he instructed.

"Why?"

"I wanna look at you."

"You're looking at me now."

"No, I want to look at you *down there*."

She thought that odd, but did as she was told.

Rilla licked his lips, and that set off a fire in Candace's chest.

"Hey," she said.

"What's up, girl?"

"I'm a *tasty lady*," she announced with a wicked smile.

"Oh, yeah?" Rilla climbed onto the bed on all fours like a gorilla. He stopped when his head hovered over her belly. "How do *I* know that?"

Candace lay back and stretched her arms out. "I guess you have to taste."

Rilla lay flat on his stomach, and ducked his head for a sample. His tongue was warm and wet. Candace thought she could feel every taste bud as he licked her. When he came back up, he was the one with lip gloss.

"You are pretty tasty," he agreed.

"You sure?"

"Yeah."

"I don't think you got a good enough taste."

"Why you say that?"

"Cause your nose is still dry."

Rilla chuckled and went back for seconds. He could bring her to a climax immediately if he wanted to, but sometimes he didn't. Sometimes he licked and teased and pleased her for minute after wonderful minute.

Tonight the foreplay went on through two songs on the radio. When Rilla finally got on top, Candace could barely open her legs for him; they were shaking so badly. She only had two previous partners, and Rilla was by far the largest. When they first met there was a lot of pain involved in lovemaking, but now things fit perfectly.

Rilla was like a missing part of her own body.

When he was inside her, nothing felt more right.

She stared into his eyes and traced her fingers down his spine. At some point, these fingers became claws, inflicting light scratches that would be visible in the morning.

～

A knock at the door woke Candace, but not her boyfriend. She sat up and shaded her eyes from the light peeking through the curtains. It was already eight-thirty in the morning. She threw her legs over the bed and groggily dressed in sweatpants and a T-shirt.

Rilla sold drugs, but his customers rarely came by the house. Candace couldn't think of anyone else who would visit this early, so she shook Rilla's arm before she left the room.

"Uh-huh?"

"Somebody's at the door."

"Who? Who is it?"

"I don't know."

"What time is it?"

"It's eight-thirty."

He sat up quickly as if a firecracker went off in the room. "Shit! That's CC. I gotta go."

CC was Rilla's closest friend. They grew up together in Overbrook Meadows, attending the same middle and high school. They both dropped out around the same time and went into crack sales as a joint venture. When Rilla's rap fantasy became a reality, he left his best homey for a few years. When Rilla got dropped from his label and had to come home, CC was still there doing the same thing. Rilla got back in the game as if he'd never missed a beat.

"I kept them rocks warm for you," CC was fond of saying.

Candace didn't dislike CC, but he was definitely not one of her favorite people. She blamed him for Rilla's lackluster efforts to get his music career back on track. She didn't think Rilla would ever be hungry enough to give rap his all as long as he had a pocket full of dope and dope money.

"Why is he here so early?" she asked.

Rilla was out of bed now, looking for his pants. "He taking me to meet a new connection. I'm late. Let him in for me."

21

"What about your CD?" Candace asked. "I thought you were going to work on a mixtape today."

"I'll do it later. Let CC in."

Candace left the room and grudgingly made her way to the front door. CC was knocking again when she opened it.

"Calm down," she told him.

CC stepped by her without so much as a *hello*. "Where my nigga at?" he asked.

CC was tall, about five inches taller than Rilla. He was light-skinned and handsome. He wore his hair in an Afro, which was puffed out today rather than braided to his scalp. CC wore khaki Dickeys and a white T-shirt. He didn't have on any jewelry, but his arms and neck had enough decoration to catch anyone's attention; his tattoos looked like a wall of graffiti.

"He's getting dressed," Candace said.

CC went to the kitchen and opened the refrigerator. "How'd the show go last night?"

Candace walked to the living room and leaned against the back of the couch. "It was good. How come you weren't there?"

"I was in Oklahoma." CC came out of the kitchen chugging from a carton of orange juice.

"You're going to drink all of that?" Candace asked.

"Naw. I'm just gonna take a few swallows and put it back in there. What you think?" He turned the carton up again, and his Adam's apple bobbed like a fishing float. Candace wanted to punch the damned thing. She heard you could cause someone to choke to death with a well-placed blow to the throat.

"What's going on in Oklahoma?" she asked.

"Business."

She stared at him and twisted her lip. CC winked at her and took the last swallow from the orange juice. He placed the empty carton on the counter and burped loudly.

"There's a trash can in there," Candace informed.

"Where?"

"It's right next to the refrigerator. I know you saw it."

He grinned at her. "That's woman's work."

Candace was about to tell him where he could shove that damn carton when Rilla rounded the corner. He wore blue Dickeys with a blue T-shirt and white Chuck Taylors.

"What's up, my nigga." He greeted CC with a handshake and a quick embrace.

"You ready?" CC asked.

"Yeah. You talked to him already?"

"He's waiting on you," CC said.

Rilla patted his pockets. "Hold up. Let me get my pistol."

"You straight," CC said. "We already got this nigga waitin' on us."

CC headed for the door, and Rilla followed. He stopped to give Candace a kiss on the way out.

"You going to school today?" he asked.

"Yeah," she said, but something in her eyes made him linger.

"You okay, baby?"

"Where are you going?" she asked again.

"I'm just finna hook up with this connect. It won't take that long."

CC opened the front door. "Come on, old sprung-ass nigga."

Rilla kissed her again and Candace was left in the apartment alone. She wondered, not for the first time, if maybe she should call her parents. Rilla was talented, but his criminal lifestyle took precedent over his music career. Rilla had always been a drug dealer who wanted to be a rapper, but lately he'd been content with just the drug-dealing side of it.

Ruining her own life was one thing, but Candace had another life to look after now. She wondered if Rilla would still love her if he knew she was pregnant.

CHAPTER 3
THE CC CONNECTION

The gig was up two weeks later.

Rilla opened the bathroom door at 9:30 a.m. and found Candace on her knees, hanging on to the toilet.

"What you doing?"

"Nothing."

"You sick?"

"No," she said, but a fresh wave of nausea belied this. Candace thought her stomach was depleted, but no such luck.

"What's wrong with you?" Rilla asked.

"*Ack*—nothing. Close the door!"

"You got a hangover?"

"Leave me alone!" Candace tried to push the door closed with her foot. The knob banged into Rilla's forearm, but he didn't send it flying back at her like she thought he would. Instead he stepped into the hallway and closed the door behind himself.

"I'ma let you do that cause you sick," he called from the other side. "But you know I don't be letting nobody hit me."

"Kiss my ass," Candace mumbled and wiped her face with the back of her hand. She lifted her head and waited, but the nausea receded. She flushed down the mess and brushed her teeth. In the mirror over the sink, she thought she looked like an old hag. Rilla was waiting for her in the bedroom when she got out.

He lay on his back with his head propped on two pillows. "You all right?"

"Yeah," she said.

"Them burritos messing with your stomach? They had me feeling sick, too. I told you not to buy no food from a truck. Them people don't have no health license."

Candace walked to his side of the bed and put a hand on the top of his head. She ran her fingers through his hair. Rilla gave her a pleasant smile.

"So you okay?"

Candace lifted her T-shirt up to her breasts. "Do I look fat to you?"

Rilla stared at her belly and then reached out and rubbed it. "You got a little pooch. It's nice, though. I like it."

Candace put her hand over his. "What if it gets bigger?" she asked.

"Big like what? Mine?"

"No. Bigger than that."

"You plan to get fat on me? Is this, like a test? You wanna know if I would stay with you?"

"No, Raul. This isn't a test. I'm definitely going to get fat."

"What, you pregnant?"

She nodded and his eyes lit up like he took a hit of crack. He sat up.

"You pregnant?"

"I'm pretty sure," Candace said, her eyes welling with tears.

Rilla still had his hand on her belly. He stared at her stomach and rubbed it as if he could feel the infant inside.

"You sure? How you know?"

"I haven't had my period," she said, "in *three* months."

"*Three months?* You took a test?"

Candace nodded. "Two weeks ago. It was positive."

"Why you didn't tell me? Is that what's wrong with you? That's why you throwing up?"

She shook her head and shrugged. The tears streamed down her face. "*I don't know.*"

Rilla's smile faded when he looked up at his woman. "What's wrong?"

"*It's bad, Rilla. Everything's going so bad.*" She held her arms to her sides and sobbed uncontrollably. Her whole body shivered.

Rilla jumped out of bed and held her close. She put her head on his chest. "Why you crying?" he asked.

" '*Cause I don't know what to do.*"

"What you mean?"

"*I don't know how to take care of a baby. I don't know how to have a baby. I don't know how to go to the doctor. I don't know anything. I just, everything's bad. It's all bad.*"

Rilla looked like he was going to cry now. "You not excited?"

Candace thought that was pretty ignorant. What was she supposed to be excited about? She had no job, no family. Her boyfriend was a rapper-turned-drug-dealer.

They didn't even have medical insurance. In the back of her mind, Candace knew it was all possible, girls much younger and less educated than her had babies every day. They got government aid and lived off the system and everything was just fine and dandy.

But Candace knew nothing about that lifestyle. Combined, her parents made more than a hundred thousand a year. They taught her so much, told her so many times not to end up in a situation like this. Candace's body ached to call them, but how could she now? She knew how that conversation would play out:

Hey, Dad? Yeah, It's me. I know. I missed you, too. Hey, um, you remember that rapper I ran away to be with? Yeah, well, guess what? He got dropped from his label! Yeah. I know. You were right. But wait, there's more. He had to come home to Overbrook Meadows. Yeah, that's in Texas. Yes, I'm here with him. I know, but wait, there's more: He started selling drugs when we got back here, and now he's a full-time dealer again. And before you cut me off again, there's one more thing: I'm pregnant. Yeah? . . . Yeah? . . . Okay . . . Well, I kinda figured you'd never want to see me again, but I thought I'd check anyway. What's that? Okay, I promise I'll never call again. Well, thanks for listening. Bye—huh? Oh, yeah, I love you, too.

"What's wrong?" Rilla asked again.

"I don't know what to do," Candace whined.

"It's not gonna be that bad. We got some money."

"*I don't know nothing about raising a baby, Rilla.* I don't even know how to change a diaper. You're not rapping anymore. *You sell drugs.*"

"That's what it is? You think you not gonna be a good mother?"

"I don't think *we're* going to be good parents."

"Why? Cause we ain't got a lot of money laying around like yo daddy?"

"It's not that."

"Good. 'Cause my mama didn't have a lot of money, either, and I turned out just fine."

Candace would have laughed at that if her unborn child wasn't the butt of the joke. "Rilla, I don't want to bring a baby up in *this*. When we came back here, you said you were going to get your music back on track."

"I am."

"It's been eight months. All you're doing is selling crack."

"I gotta put a roof over our heads."

"I know, but—"

"Who put the food in the refrigerator? Who bought your car?"

"Rilla, I know you did."

"So all of a sudden I can't take care of you now? Is that what you saying?"

"No. I know you can take care of *me*. I'm not talking about me."

"I can take care of the baby, too. Candace, I'm excited about this. I always wanted a little Raul running around. You can't be happy, too? You ruining this for me. This ain't how it's supposed to go."

That brought on a fresh wave of sorrow.

"Candace?"

"*It's bad, Rilla.*"

"It's not," he said. "Look at me."

She did, but couldn't get her eyes to focus.

"Baby, I understand what you're saying," Rilla said. "You came from a whole 'nother lifestyle. And I know you're scared. But *I'm* not. I wanted a baby for a long time. You're not by yourself, Candace. I'm gonna be here for you. And Trisha can help, too. She got three kids. You know she knows how to change a diaper."

Trisha was one of few friends Candace made since migrating to Texas. She lived in the apartment complex across the street from them.

"And I'ma do right," Rilla went on. He cradled her belly in both hands. "I know I been screwing up. I ain't did what I said I would, but this, this right here is going to make the difference. I feel motivated already. I'ma get my shit together, Candace. I swear. By the time he come, I'ma have my rap shit straight."

Candace stared into his eyes, and she believed him. What choice did she have?

"It's a boy, right?" he asked.

"I don't know. I don't think they can tell yet."

"When can they tell? What the doctor say?"

"What doctor?"

"You ain't been to the doctor?"

The tears had slowed, but they were on the verge of spilling again. "What doctor, Rilla? I told you, I don't know anything about this. I don't know how to go to a doctor. *It's all messed up.* I told you—"

He smiled. "Calm down, baby. You all right. You prolly don't need to start going to a doctor right now anyway. How far along are you?"

"I don't know. At least three months."

Rilla sat on the bed and stared at her kangaroo pouch. "Six months. I'ma have my little soldier in *six months*."

"Or my little princess," Candace said.

He looked up at her, happy to see she wasn't crying anymore. "I'll take a little girl," he said. "But we still gonna name her Raul."

She pushed his head playfully. "You're not naming my little girl *Raul*."

"Well, what you wanna name her?"

"I don't know. I never really thought about it."

"You still scared?"

"A little," she admitted.

"Do you believe me, though? About how everything is gonna work out?"

She nodded.

Rilla kissed her belly button. "My little *vato's* gonna be straight. Watch. He's gonna have it all."

Someone knocked at the door.

"That's CC," Rilla said.

Candace's body stiffened, but he didn't notice. "You finna go?" she asked.

"Yeah. We gotta make a few runs. You gonna be all right? You want me to stay with you? I will if you want."

"No. Go ahead. I have classes today."

"You sure you gonna be all right? I want you to be happy, baby. This is *good* news."

"I'm happy," Candace said. She painted on a croco-
dile smile, and he seemed to be convinced.

"Cool. Can you let CC in for me?"

Candace went to answer the door. CC stepped in
looking a little scruffy. He was usually clean-shaven, but
today he sported a scraggily goatee and had a few stray
hairs on his cheeks.

"Where my boy at?" he asked.

"He's in there getting dressed."

CC looked her up and down. "What you doing
today? Nothing? I'm surprised you woke this early."

"I'm going to *school*," Candace said, unsure why she
was explaining herself to the likes of CC.

He nodded and grinned. "You learning something, or
you still taking your basics?"

"You been to school?" she asked.

"Naw."

"You graduate high school?"

"Naw, girl. I didn't have to. I learned my math,
though. That's all I need to count this money." He patted
his bulging front pocket and Candace rolled her eyes.

"Rilla's in the bedroom."

"Straight," CC said and disappeared down the hallway.

Candace sat on the couch, but she could still hear
their conversation through the thin walls.

"You ready, homey? We gonna lock the city down
when we get this shit." That was CC.

"Yeah. Hand me that shoe."

"Nigga, you need to get some more shoes. What you
doing what all yo money?"

"I know what I'm *gonna be* doing with it from now on," Rilla said. "It's time for me to get right, dog. I gotta get my music going for real. Candace pregnant. I'm finna have a little boy running around."

There was a pause. Candace's heart shot up in her throat as she waited for CC's response.

"Candace pregnant?"

"Yeah. She just told me today."

"You happy about that?"

"Yeah, cuz. Why? You know I want a little boy."

"Yeah, but . . ."

"But what, Cordell?"

"Nothing, Rilla. You happy, I'm happy."

"Yeah, I'm happy, man. I love Candace. You know that."

"Then we straight. We get a couple more big ones, and you can get yo music recorded. This yo restroom over here?"

"Yeah," Rilla said.

CC appeared again in the hallway.

Candace looked over at him, her heart thudding in her chest.

CC gave her an evil glare and shook his head. He disappeared again, and she heard the bathroom door close.

She exhaled a pent-up breath. Her fingers were shaking. She held her hands together in her lap. CC didn't tell him yet, but he and Rilla were going to be together all day. Candace figured he would drop the bomb at some point. She wondered if she should do it herself.

Rilla went to jail for a week about three months ago. He was only arrested for traffic tickets, but the judge said she was sick of seeing his face at arraignments. She made him do the time rather than allow him to pay the fine. CC came by the apartment often during that six-day stretch. His intentions were to look after his homeboy's girl, but one night he brought a lot of weed and a bottle of hard liquor.

Candace either passed out or fell asleep at three in the morning. When she woke up, her pants were off and CC was on top of her. He was *inside* her. She would have told Rilla about it, but CC wasn't the only one who made a mistake that night: When she awakened, Candace didn't immediately push him off of her. She eventually did make him stop, but after how much time?

CC said she was awake for at least ten minutes. Candace thought it was more like thirty seconds. CC said she took her own pants off. He said she initiated the whole episode, as a matter of fact. Candace didn't believe that to be the case, but how could she know for sure? If she told Rilla what happened, would he believe a girl he met at his concert five months ago or his best friend of ten years?

All Candace knew for sure was that her pregnancy coincided with Rilla's week in jail. Maybe she got pregnant before he went. Maybe it was after he got out. It was too close to call.

2

Rilla gave her a nice hug and kiss on the way out. CC didn't say anything to her, but that was pretty much the norm.

CHAPTER 4
MAMA'S BABY, DADDY'S MAYBE

Candace got dressed and went to school thirty minutes after the guys left. She drove a 2008 Nissan Sentra. It was champagne-colored, sitting on chrome sixteen-inch rims. She wasn't particularly impressed with big wheels, but Rilla put them on anyway. He said he wouldn't feel right unless his girl was riding in style.

Rilla's car was a 1994 Fleetwood Cadillac. He had twenty-inch rims on his flashy ride. Candace didn't like big, bulky cars, but there were advantages to rolling around in the Fleetwood. She once fell asleep in the back seat and found plenty of room to stretch her legs out. Rilla once joined her back there, and there was plenty of room for everything else, too.

Overbrook Meadows Community College was only a fifteen-minute drive from the apartment. Candace hit the campus ten minutes early for her first class. After being accepted to prominent universities like Syracuse, Cornell, and Columbia, she felt a little odd paying for classes at a Texas community college, but running away from home didn't mean Candace was running away from everything she believed in. Education had always been of upmost importance in her household. Getting drunk, high, and even pregnant didn't diminish this motivation.

She had two classes today. Government was boring. As always, they sat and listened to the professor lecture for the whole period. He didn't look up from his notes once. Her anatomy and physiology class was more interesting. They got to slice into baby pigs and label the colorful innards.

On the way back to her car, a familiar face approached Candace, but she couldn't place him.

"Hey, your name's Candace, right?"

She turned and watched a Hispanic man approach her. Actually, he was more like a boy; only eighteen, the same age as her. He was about Candace's height, too. He wore a white golf shirt with faded blue jeans and white sneakers. He toted an armful of books rather than carry them in a backpack. Candace thought he had a baby face. He looked like a young Joey Lawrence, with the long hair to match.

"Yeah," she said. "How do you know my name?"

"Hi. I'm in your Economics class," he said, producing a hand for her to shake.

She shook it and smiled. "Sorry, I remember you now."

"It's okay," he said. "A lot of people forget me. I was voted '*Most Likely to be Forgotten*' in high school." He smiled. It was a pleasant smile. He had nice teeth and pink lips. Candace grinned back at him.

"That's pretty sad," she said, "but I didn't forget you. I just never knew your name."

"I listened for yours when the teacher called roll," her classmate said. "I don't like to run up on people yelling, '*Hey, you!*' "

Candace giggled, still unsure why he approached her in the first place.

"Is this your first year here?" he asked.

"Yeah."

"Where are you from? Did you go to high school here?"

"No. I'm from New York."

"*New York City?*" he said, in an imitation of the Pace Picante Sauce commercials.

Candace laughed.

"So, you like it here?" he asked. "Met some nice people? Seen some sights?"

Candace was walking now, towards the parking lot. The stranger followed. He didn't have an accent at all. If not for his bronze skin, he could have passed for white.

"I've been to a few clubs," she said.

"Have you seen the stockyards?" he asked.

"No, but I heard about it. That's the '*Cowtown*' part of the city, right?"

He grinned. "The whole city is called 'Cowtown.' They used to do cattle runs right down Main Street. Back in the day, there were cowboys everywhere. The stockyards still look like that. Everyone's got on boots and big hats."

"You lived here your whole life?"

"Yeah. It's cool. Most parts. I'd love to travel one day. I've never even been out of the state."

"You definitely need to see more places," Candace agreed.

"I plan to," he said. "I know I don't look like much, but I'm going to be a doctor."

"You're pre-med?"

"Not till I get to Texas Lutheran. I'm working on my basics now. That place is expensive."

TLU was the largest and most prominent university in the city. Famed NFL running back LaDainian Tomlinson hailed from the prestigious school.

"Pre-med is hard," Candace said.

"What's your major?" he asked.

"Physical therapy."

"You wanna be a tech?"

"No. I want to be a physical therapist."

He smiled. "That's cool. Everyone wants to be a respiratory *tech*, or a dental *tech*. No one wants to do the real thing anymore."

They approached her car. Candace pulled her keys from her purse and disabled the alarm. The stranger's eyes grew big when he saw which vehicle chirped for her.

"This is your car?"

"Yeah."

"*Man.*" He shook his head. "I was going to ask you out, but now I know I can't afford you. You wanna know what I drive? Never mind. I'm not even going to tell you."

Candace laughed and blushed, glad to finally know what he wanted.

"Okay, I lied," he said. "I'm still going to ask you out. You probably won't want to go in my car, but we could get lunch in the cafeteria, after classes if you want to."

She chuckled. "I don't even know your name."

"I didn't tell you my name? I planned this whole conversation out in my head over and over. I can't believe I forgot that. My name is Celestino. Celestino DeLeon. My friends call me Tino."

The only time a Latin accent showed up was when he pronounced his full name. He sounded like Ricky Ricardo when he said that.

Celestino. Celestino DeLeon.

"You *planned* this conversation, Tino?"

"For weeks," he admitted. "That sound stupid to you?"

"No. Not really. It's sweet, but—"

"No. Please don't say 'but.' Nothing good ever comes after *but.* Well, some butts are good. Yours is—*God, did I just say that*? I didn't mean it. I promise I've never looked at your butt."

She laughed. "Tino, you're a trip—"

"Okay, I look at it sometimes."

"You're crazy."

"Okay, every day. *Dammit*! I can't help it. But I don't stare at it. I just, I just think you're awesome."

Today Candace wore a gray sweater with tight blue jeans. She wondered how long Tino had followed behind staring at her lady lumps before he spoke. She was devoted to Rilla, but couldn't help feeling excited about Tino's advances. This guy was handsome, smart, and charming as hell.

"Tino, I have a boyfriend," she said almost grudgingly.

His smile fell for the first time. "Damn. I knew you were going to say that."

"I'm sorry," Candace said. "Honestly, I think you're pretty cool. You make me feel special. If I didn't have a boyfriend, I would definitely go out with you."

"Really?" His smile was back now.

"For real," she said.

"Cool," he said and took a couple of steps back. "You'll go out with me if y'all break up?"

Candace giggled. "Sure, Tino."

"Will you tell me when y'all break up?" he pressed. "I want to be first in line. There's a lot of guys here who like you."

That was news to Candace. "Who?"

"I'm not telling you," Tino said as if this was common sense. "Some of them look better than me."

She laughed again. It felt good to be happy.

"All right. I'll see you later, Candace," he said. "We've got Economics tomorrow."

"I'll be there," she promised.

"I really look forward to seeing you," he said and turned to go.

Candace got into her car, smiling big. She was still cheesing when she made it to her apartment complex.

⌒

LaTrisha Turner was a twenty-four-year-old mother of three boys. Four-year-old Peter was the oldest. Little

Sammy just finished potty training, and Willie Jr. was still on the bottle. All of these children had different fathers. Petey and Sammy's dads were locked up, doing big time for dope pedaling. Willie's father found himself on the wrong side of a .44 Magnum two days before his son was born.

Trisha was unemployed and unmotivated to do anything to better her position. She was the woman Rilla said Candace should go to with her baby-rearing questions. She would also have helpful information on getting doctor visits and government aid. Candace never thought she'd be in need of such help, but, unless she called her parents, that was the only help she was likely to get.

Trisha thought she should man up and bite the bullet. "It's gonna have to be done sooner or later."

"Who says it has to be done?"

They sat in Trisha's living room, each girl with a baby in her arms. Candace held Little Sammy. He was too old to be running around topless, but such was the case. He was also too old to get toted around, but the two-year-old had a thing for Candace. Whenever she visited, he managed to get in her lap within minutes.

At one o'clock in the afternoon, Trisha still wore a nightgown and robe. Her hair was pulled back in a ponytail, but the roots were fuzzy and unkempt. She was dark-skinned with a red tint, the color of mahogany. She had large eyes, a pudgy nose, and thick lips. Candace didn't think she was attractive, but at least three guys felt differently.

Trisha breastfed Willie Jr. openly. Her boob was huge. The baby gobbled on her nipple so hard that Candace's were starting to hurt.

"*I* say you gotta call them," Trisha said. "That's they grandbaby. You know they'll help if they know you're pregnant."

"They didn't sound like they wanted to help last time I talked them," Candace reported.

"When was that?"

"I only talked to them once, when I first got here."

"What'd they say?"

"I talked to my mom first. She was crying, trying to get me to go home, but then my dad took the phone and started talking crazy. He's not even my real dad. He's my stepdad."

"What'd he say?" Trisha asked.

"He said I was stupid. I was disgracing the family. He said if this is the life I wanted to live, then so be it. Don't ask them for shit."

"You've been gone a while," Trisha noted.

"Almost eight months," Candace confirmed.

"Yo daddy said that long time ago, girl. You need to call them back. I'm telling you, it'll be different now."

"Why?"

"Cause they miss you more. Especially if they knew you were pregnant."

"I don't know," Candace said. "I wanted to call and talk to them when things were good. So I could tell them I was doing all right. I don't want to call with problems."

"Why?"

"Cause they gonna say, '*I told you so.*' I don't want to hear that."

"You don't want to raise a baby by yourself, either."

"I'm not by myself. Rilla's happy about it."

"You finally told him?"

"Yeah, this morning. He was excited."

"Girl, all men is like that. They be like, '*Ooh, I can't wait till you have my baby, my little Raul.*'"

Candace laughed. "That's *exactly* what he said."

"I already know. This boy's daddy," Trisha patted Willie Jr. on the head, "he called everybody he knew to tell them I was pregnant. And this was two in the morning."

"Rilla didn't do all that," Candace said.

"Did you tell him about CC?" Trisha asked.

Besides Candace and CC (and whoever else *he* might have told), Trisha was the only one who knew about the CC connection.

"No," Candace said. "And I sure as hell can't tell him now. You should have seen how happy he was."

"You shoulda told him when it first happened," Trisha said. In retrospect, that probably would have been the best course of action, but hindsight is 20/20. "Do you think CC's gonna tell him?" Trisha asked.

Just the thought of it made Candace's heart drop.

"I don't know. I feel like he won't . . . If he was gonna tell, I think he would have done it as soon as Rilla got out."

"He was probably scared to tell," Trisha ventured. "He would have had a lot of explaining to do."

"Not really," Candace said. "He could just tell him I came on to him."

"But you still not supposed to sleep with yo homeboy's girl. Even if they throw theyself at you."

Thinking about that incident made Candace sick to her stomach.

"Whose baby do you think it is?" Trisha asked.

Candace knitted her eyebrows. "How am I supposed to know?"

"You should know," Trisha said. "You should *feel it*."

"It's Rilla's, then," Candace said. "I feel like it's Rilla's."

"Then leave it like that," Trisha said.

But how impossible was that? Was Candace supposed to take her assumption and run with it like it was fact? The awful truth was she really believed CC was her baby's father. In the eight months they were together, she and Rilla had quite a few *accidents*, but never were there repercussions. After only *one night* with CC, Candace was suddenly with child. That didn't prove anything conclusively, but it was one hell of a coincidence.

Too much of a coincidence, in Candace's opinion.

⌒

Trisha was the only person Candace knew who didn't keep her doors locked at all times. This was because her hands were always busy with a bottle or a dirty diaper. She didn't feel like getting up to answer it, so friends were free to come and go at will, giving her apartment a television sitcom atmosphere.

As Trisha fed Willie Jr. and Candace cradled Sammy, a woman they both knew walked into the living room. The sight of her was enough to make Candace feel quite uncomfortable.

"What's up, bitches!"

Delia Johnson wore stretchy capris with a fashionable halter top that showed her whole stomach. She had a pearl, teardrop belly ring. She was high-yellow, with thick thighs, protruding hips, and ample breasts. Today her hair was auburn with pink highlights. She wore it pulled back in a ponytail with a bang hanging over her forehead.

Delia was tall for a girl, just a few inches under six feet. She had beautifully manicured nails and wore sandals to show off her equally sexy toes. She wore no makeup—didn't have to. Delia was the most beautiful woman Candace ever met in real life.

But that wasn't why she was uncomfortable.

The reason Candace felt like throwing Little Jimmy to the floor and fleeing the scene was because Delia's boyfriend was a big-time dope boy, none other than CC. Candace knew word would get out sooner or later. It was only a matter of time before the stallion would be in her face, claws at the ready, accusing her of sleeping with her man.

"Where you on yo way to," Trisha asked, "the Freaknik?"

"Don't hate," Delia said. She took a seat at one of the dining room tables. "Hey, Candace!"

"What's up," Candace said.

"Hey, Jimmy! Come here, baby," Delia said.

The boy's head shot up from Candace's chest. He jumped off of her lap and waddled to Delia, in search of more supple breasts to snuggle against, Candace guessed.

"Where Petey at?" Delia asked.

"He in there sleep," Trisha said. "And don't wake him up, either."

"You go to school today?" Delia asked Candace.

Candace actually jumped from the sound of her voice. Delia was thirty-one years old. She pulled out a lot of hair in all those years.

"Yeah. I only had two classes today."

"Girl, I don't see how you do it. I went to college for a little bit, but I could only take one class at a time. That stuff be getting all mixed up in my head."

"That's 'cause you stupid," Trisha kidded. "You gotta be smart to get through college."

"Go to hell. I'm smarter than you," Delia said.

"What's six plus eight?" Trisha asked. *"Quick! Quick! Quick!"*

Delia rolled her eyes. "Kiss my ass, bitch."

Trisha laughed and said, "Hey, I got some *news* for you."

"What?" Delia asked.

Trisha looked over at Candace. "Can I tell her? If you told Rilla, it's over with anyway. Everybody gonna know by tomorrow."

Candace couldn't help but laugh. Trisha was such a gossip, she would talk about you even if you were in the same room.

"I'm sitting right here," Candace said. "Don't you want me to tell her?"

"No! I wanna tell her," Trisha said. She looked down at her baby and pulled him away from her milk bag. Willie Jr. was full. Candace was happy to see that titty get put up.

"Go ahead and tell her," she said.

"Candace pregnant," Trisha said without pause. She wore a smug look of satisfaction.

Delia smiled. "You and Rilla having a baby?"

I sure hope so, Candace thought. "Yeah," she said. She brought her hand to her face and nibbled her thumbnail unconsciously.

Delia sneered a little. "Not me, girl. I'm not finna have my body all stretched out and *nasty.* CC knows he gets *no babies here.* He have to get some other bitch pregnant if he want a baby."

Candace didn't want to get anywhere near responding to that. Her palms were sweaty. The whole room was hot. Beads of sweat formed under her nose. She stood and stretched nonchalantly.

"I'ma go and get started on my homework," she said.

"Go ahead," Trisha said. "One of us need to do something with our lives."

"Uh, *excuse me,*" Delia said.

"Bitch, you ain't doing shit, and you know it," Trisha said.

CHAPTER 5
THE B SIDE

Rilla crept up behind Candace as she washed dishes. He kissed the side of her neck and wrapped his arms around her. He had to use a lot more of his arms to hug her nowadays. Four months had passed, and Candace looked like she had a basketball under her shirt.

"How my ladies doing today?" he asked.

Candace jerked her shoulder up and caught him under in the chin. "Leave me alone, Rilla."

He took a step back. "Damn, baby. It's like that?"

"What time did you get in last night?" she asked.

"I don't know. Two? Three?"

"Where were you?"

"On the cut, baby. Why?" He stepped forward again and palmed her booty with both hands. She kicked backwards and caught him on the shin this time.

"*Ouch!* Damn, girl, why you hitting me?"

She turned to face him. At nine o'clock in the morning, Rilla was already dressed and ready to go. He wore baggy jeans and a long T-shirt that hung to his knees.

Candace was dressed, too, but she hated her clothes. She had to get a new wardrobe to compensate for her changing figure, and all of the maternity outfits looked tacky to her; her pants were built funny, and her blouses were ugly and loose. She had classes until one o'clock today and another appointment with her doctor at one-thirty.

"Rilla, you said you were going to finish your CD."

"I'ma finish it this week."

"I've been with you a year, Raul. *A whole year.*"

"I know, baby. Why you trippin?"

She looked down at her stomach and then back to his face. "You don't see this?"

"Yeah, I see it, Candace."

"You said you were going to get your music straight," she nagged. "You said you weren't going to be selling drugs by the time she gets here."

"I'm trying, girl."

"How are you trying, Rilla? You don't have your CD ready. Nobody can look at it if you don't record it. *A whole year* and all you have is that same album—*Rilla Time.* Nobody's listening to that. You're not even doing concerts anymore."

"I'm trying."

"How are you trying, Rilla? Tell me *exactly* what you're doing to fix this. I really need to know."

"I don't have to explain myself to you," he said and turned to leave the room.

"*Yes you do!*" Candace followed after him, tears already welling in her eyes. She didn't know why, but she could cry at the drop of a hat nowadays. The sight of her anguish usually made Rilla wilt, but not today. He turned on her quickly—his arm poised for a vicious backhand.

Candace stopped short and threw her arms over her face.

"Get off my back!" Rilla barked. "I pay for everything around here! You don't want for shit, but yo ass can't never be happy!"

"That's 'cause you lied," Candace wailed. The tears streamed down her face. "You said you were going to—"

"*Bitch, quit telling me what I said!*" His hands were at his sides now, balled into fists for some reason. He'd never been physically violent with her, but Candace took the stance very seriously.

"So, what? You gonna hit me now?"

His face was a mask of frustration and pain.

"I'm not gon' hit you."

"If this is all you're going to do, you should've told me," Candace said. "You shouldn't have called me when I was in New York. I was happy. I had a good life."

"I didn't make you go with me!"

"*I trusted you.*"

"You coulda stayed over there! Ain't nobody put a gun to yo head."

"*You lied to me.*"

"I didn't lie to you!"

"*Stop yelling at me!*" she screamed. Her nose leaked in addition to her eyes now.

Rilla opened his mouth to say something but thought better of it. Instead he shook his head and grinned.

"You trippin', Candace. You jacked up in the head. Got them hormones, or whatever the hell is going on with you."

"It's not my hormones!"

"Well it *ain't me*."

"It is you, Rilla. I don't want to be with the *crack man*. You're either going to jail or the pen, or, God forbid, you get killed, but those are your choices. Everybody knows that. I don't know why you don't see it."

"Don't be wishing no bad luck on me," he said. He scooped his keys from the coffee table and headed for the door.

"You don't have to be a rapper," Candace conceded. "You can get a job at McDonald's, Rilla. I'll still stay with you."

"I ain't working at no goddamned McDonald's," he said on the way out.

Candace followed him onto the breezeway and appealed to him as he skipped down the stairs.

"Rilla, if this is all you're going to do, I'm not staying."

He stopped at the bottom step and looked up at her.

"Don't be threatening to leave," he said. "If you're gonna leave, then leave. But don't be threatening me. I do all I can for you. I don't see why you trippin'."

"I just want you to do what you said you would."

He sighed, a deep sneer forming on the left side of his face.

"Candace, it ain't that easy. You think every good rapper out here got a deal? Well, I can tell you for a fact they don't. For every fifty good rappers, one of them *might* get signed. It takes more than just being good. You have to be at the right place at the right time and all that."

"But you're not even trying," she countered. "It doesn't matter if you are at the right place and right time if you don't have your demo ready."

"I'm through talking," Rilla said. "I'ma do what I do. You don't like it, call yo bougie-ass mama."

With that, he was out of sight.

Candace went back inside and held the phone for a long time, but she couldn't dial the digits.

⌐⌐

Being *fully* pregnant at school was an interesting experience. In her College Algebra class, one of her peers gave up his seat at ground level so Candace wouldn't have to march the stairs to the upper level. Her religion professor stopped her after class and asked how her *condition* was going. He said he could allow extra time to finish her assignments if she needed it. Candace told him she was okay.

After Economics, a familiar face followed her out.

"Hey, Candace."

She turned and waited for Celestino to catch up.

"You sure move fast for a preg—*ooh*, I'd better not say that."

"Say what?"

"The last time I thought a girl was, *with child*, I made the mistake of asking how far along she was."

"And she wasn't pregnant?" Candace asked with a grin.

"No, she was just fat," he said. "And if that's what's going on with you, then let me apologize ahead of time."

She gave him a serious look. "Well, I hate to tell you this, but I'm not fat or pregnant. I've got a tumor. I have surgery scheduled this week."

He stared at her belly bulge, the smile slipping from his face. "For real?"

"No, goofy. I'm pregnant. You think I'd be at school with a tumor this big?"

"That's not funny," he said, that cute grin working its way back to his lips. "I used to know a guy who had a tumor that big."

"Really?"

"Well, I didn't really *know* him. I saw some pictures on the Internet. I read his blog."

Candace shook her head and continued the walk to her car. "Tino, you're crazy."

"You remember my name! That's awesome."

"You're the only friend I've made at this school," she said.

"*Friend?* Oh, hell no. Don't push me into that *platonic friend* category."

Candace was shocked. "Tino, are you still trying to hit on me?"

"Just because you're pregnant doesn't mean you're still with your boyfriend," he said. "Statistically speaking, one-third of all pregnant women in America are single."

"Where'd you hear that?"

"I made it up," he said. "It sounded good, though, didn't it? I've found that if you rattle off a *lie* with a statistic in it, most people will believe you. Especially if you put numbers or percentages in there."

Candace stopped and stared at him for a second. Today he wore a long-sleeved denim shirt with blue jeans. His white tennis shoes were a little scuffed. His hair was pulled back into a ponytail, held together with a black rubber band.

"I like you, Celestino," she said. "You're a good dude. You make me laugh."

He smiled and they started walking again. "*Sooo*, are you still with your boyfriend or not?" he asked.

"You're serious?"

"Yeah, I'm serious."

"Tino, I'm pregnant."

"So? I like babies."

"How old are you?" she asked.

"I'm seventeen."

"Are you a nerd?"

"A nerd? No. I don't wear glasses. My pants aren't high-water. I don't even like Star Trek."

"You're just a smart guy?"

"Just a smart guy," he agreed.

They were at her car now. Candace disabled the alarm and opened the door.

"You got time to talk for a minute?" she asked.

"Yeah."

"Get in on the other side."

Tino's eyes grew big. "Hell, yeah! This is definitely progress."

"Not really," she said.

She got in and closed the door. Tino plopped down in the passenger seat and did the same.

"Tino, if you're such a smart guy, why do you want me?" Candace asked. "There are plenty of girls here who're smart and pretty and *skinny*. Have you ever dated someone with a baby?"

"No," he said.

"Plus I'm still with my boyfriend. It's not going good. I might end up being one of your *fictitious statistics* pretty soon, but I'm not staying here if we break up."

"It's not going good?" he asked.

"No. Not really. Sometimes I think it will be over any day now."

"So I was right."

"No, Tino. You're not listening. If we *do* break up, I'm going back to New York."

"Why?"

"Cause my boyfriend is the only reason I'm down here. I don't know anyone in Texas. I don't have any family. I'm going to finish this semester, but I don't think I'll be back in the fall."

Tino looked seriously hurt by this news.

"You don't even know me," Candace said. "Why are you getting all depressed?"

"I don't know," he said. "I do this all the time. My brain just starts working things out on its own. I had all of these plans for us in my head. I saw us together this Christmas, at my grandma's house. My aunts make tamales from scratch. You would have liked them."

Candace was taken aback. "You saw all that?"

"It was just a daydream."

"If I break up with my boyfriend, I won't have anywhere to live," she explained. "I don't have a job. No money."

"You can get a job," he assured her. "Everybody's hiring in Overbrook Meadows."

Candace smiled. "Hey," she said. "Regardless of what happens, I want you to know you're the coolest guy I've met since I've been in Texas."

She leaned over and kissed him on the cheek. Tino's smile came back with full flair. He picked up the *Rilla Time* CD from the console and studied the Puerto Rican thug on the cover.

"You like this kind of music?"

"It's all right," Candace said.

"This guy's an idiot," Tino said. "He's from here. He had it all. Videos on TV, the money, the girls. But he ended up losing it. He's back now. On the south side, I think. A local celebrity, if you can call him that."

Candace couldn't help but laugh.

"What?"

"*That's* my boyfriend," she said.

Tino's jaw dropped. "Nuh-uhn."

"Seriously. That's Rilla. His real name is Raul Canales. That's the guy I live with."

Tino's eyes bugged and he studied the CD case again. "You're going with Rilla?"

"Unfortunately, yeah. I am."

"Oh, my God," Tino said. "You kissed me. He's not going to shoot me, is he?"

Candace giggled, but she saw that he was serious. "No, he's not going to shoot you."

"I never would have asked you out if I knew he was your boyfriend. I'm scared of rap guys. They got guns, knives, *grenades!*"

"They do not have grenades."

He looked around nervously and tugged at his collar. "But you're admitting they have guns and knives . . . It's hot in here. It's not hot to you?"

"No, it's not hot. Stop looking around like that. Are you seriously scared?"

"No. Not really. A little."

"I would never put you in harm's way," Candace promised.

"I'm sorry," he said. "I just never would have thought that. You don't seem like that type at all."

"I know," Candace said. "You're right. I'm not that type of girl. A year ago I was living in New York. I'd just graduated and I got accepted to Cornell and Columbia. I went to one of Rilla's concerts, and, I don't know what happened. He invited me on stage and I felt so special. He asked me if I wanted to see him later, and I couldn't believe it. He was this rich, famous guy. I was nobody. We hooked up later and he was a real gentleman. I was only seventeen. I fell in love with him and ran away to go on tour with him."

Tino stared in shock.

"Yeah. It's crazy," Candace said. "Now I'm pregnant, taking classes at a community college, and he's not trying to rap anymore. Every day I want to call my parents, but

I don't know what to say to them. I've made so many bad decisions, I don't think I could ever explain myself."

She waited for a while after she spoke, but Tino didn't respond. He just looked at her and breathed.

"You're going to have to say *something*," she prompted.

He thought about it a while longer. "Candace, all I want to say is this: I think you're a beautiful girl. A smart girl. You ran off with a rapper—yeah, that was bad, but what seventeen-year-old wouldn't want to tour with a rapper? Half of the girls at this school would drop everything if Eminem showed up and said he wanted to be with them.

"I think you should call your parents. I think they'll understand. But more than that, I still think you're pretty awesome. You're thousands of miles away from anyone telling you what to do, but you're still coming to school. Most girls would have left that dude after he got fired, but you stuck with him. And even though you're pregnant, you still didn't run home. You're trying to do everything on your own. I don't know if you can do it, but you're trying."

Tino's words made her feel really good. Candace smiled and checked her watch.

"Dang! It's already 1:30. I have a doctor's appointment."

"I'm late for my next class," Tino said.

"Thanks for talking with me," Candace said. "You made me feel a lot better."

"I'm a good listener," Tino said. "So long as you don't dump me in that platonic pile."

"Okay," she said.

He reached over and touched her hand.

Then he got out and went to class.

The prenatal assistance provided by the fair city of Overbrook Meadows could be described as no less than remarkable. The county hospital assigned Candace a caseworker named Kayla. Kayla not only set up appointments at an OB/GYN clinic free of charge, but she also instructed Candace on how to get diapers, milk, a car seat, *a stroller,* and even *cash money* through the many mother/baby services throughout the city.

After her doctor visit, Candace met with the social worker to discuss the baby's postpartum needs. There was no way she was going to cry again that day, but questions about her family life, financial standing, and overall knowledge of child-rearing had Candace on the verge of tears.

"I've been thinking about putting her up for adoption," she said out of the blue, as casually as if she were asking where the restroom was.

"Really?" Kayla said. She wore a gray skirt suit with a white blouse. Her hair was styled in baby dreadlocks. Candace's caseworker was slim and attractive.

"Yeah," she said. "Do you have the number for any agencies?"

Kayla cocked her head at her young client. "Why do you want to put your daughter up for adoption?"

"That's what I've decided."

"But why?" Kayla asked.

Candace immediately didn't like where this conversation was going. She didn't think she'd have to bare her soul this early in the game.

"What do you mean, '*why?*'?"

Kayla shrugged. "I think that's a very difficult decision, Candace. I'd like to know how you came about it."

"Are you trying to talk me out of it?"

The caseworker sat back in her seat and stared at her confused client. Candace was young and naïve. She was more educated than most of the girls who came to this office, but she was becoming more and more of an anomaly.

"I'm not trying to talk you out of it," Kayla said. "You don't have to get defensive."

Candace didn't think she had gotten defensive. "I think more experienced parents could take better care of her," she said. "I don't think I'm ready to have a baby."

"Those are perfect answers," Kayla said.

Candace thought so, too.

"What about the baby's father?" Kayla asked. "He wants to put her up for adoption, too?"

"No. He can't wait to have a daughter."

The caseworker chewed on the end of her pen. "Are you still with him?"

"Yes, but I'm leaving after I have the baby," Candace said. "I'm going back to New York."

"And you don't want to take the baby with you . . ."

Candace knew the woman was tying to judge her reactions, so she kept a straight face. "Right. I'm going to finish this semester at the community college, have the baby over summer break, and be back in New York by the fall. I'll have my credits here transferred to Columbia."

"Why don't you leave the baby with her father, rather than put her up for adoption?"

The color drained from Candace's face. "I don't want to give her to him. He's not a good father."

"How come?"

"He's a thug," Candace said. "He sells drugs. He won't treat her right, either."

"Do you think he might fight your decision?" Kayla asked.

"You mean, like in court?"

"It's his baby, too," Kayla said. "Just because you don't want her doesn't mean he can't have her. You might be right about him not being a good parent, but yes, the father could take you to court."

This was a worst-case scenario. Candace wished she had asked someone about it before. She felt like a fool.

"Listen," Kayla said. "I know you're scared. You're far away from home, and you're young, and you're pregnant. Giving your baby up may very well be the best thing for you, but the adoption process is not a simple thing—especially if you're fighting the father the whole way."

And, of course, the tears started then. Kayla offered Candace a box of Kleenex.

"I wanna go home," Candace whined. "I don't know if I can go if I keep the baby."

Kayla lifted an eyebrow. She was getting closer to the real source of the problem, but her client didn't want to divulge. Candace stood and gathered the papers in her lap.

"I gotta go."

"You don't want to talk more?"

"I got homework tonight," Candace lied and wiped her eyes with the back of her hand.

"Wait, Candace. Please sit down."

Candace did so out of obedience, but she never felt so uncomfortable. Her legs fidgeted. Her eyes leaked, and she felt perspiration sliding down her spine.

"Your parents still live in New York?" Kayla asked.

Candace nodded and sniffled.

"Do you have any family in Texas?"

"No."

"So you're in this big, new city with your bad-news boyfriend, and you've got a baby on the way," Kayla surmised. "You don't want to call your parents because they didn't want you to run off in the first place, and now you're pregnant and it's that much worse . . ."

Candace's eyes focused more clearly.

"And you're smart enough to know how bad your situation is," the social worker went on, "so to fix things, you decide to do the most selfless thing possible: give up the baby and run home, tell your parents how good you've been doing in school, and maybe they won't be so mad."

Candace was so shocked the tears stopped.

"Do you plan on telling them you left a baby in Texas or keep that a secret?" Kayla asked. "Do you think they might want to see their granddaughter? And what if you're not able to have another child? These are questions the adoption services will ask you."

Candace hadn't thought about any of that.

"I want to help you do the right thing for your baby," Kayla said. "The decision is ultimately yours. I'm just giving you things to consider. My advice, of course, would be to call your parents. You're a mature young lady, but you might want to get opinions from your family before you make a tough decision."

Candace knew there was knowledge in Kayla's words. And that was the best advice she was going to get from anyone else she queried. But it was still a hard pill to swallow. She told the lady she would think about it and left the hospital with her and her baby's future still undetermined.

CHAPTER 6
BAD BOYS

On the way home Candace stopped at the Evergreen Apartment complex on the south side of town. The compound was run-down and dangerous—not the place for a pregnant lady, or any type of *lady* for that matter, but Candace knew she was safe there; Rilla moved a lot of crack through the apartments, and he wouldn't let anything happen to her.

Candace rarely visited his dope spot, but the argument they had that morning left her depressed and contemplative. She knew it was wrong for her to threaten to leave while she carried Rilla's baby. Candace also regretted the way she was riding him about his music career. Getting dropped from his label had to be a hard blow. Maybe he was trying his best to get back in the studio. Maybe he was a little gun-shy. Either way, Candace didn't know if the timetable she put on her man was realistic.

She spotted Rilla's car as soon as she pulled in from the street. His Fleetwood squatted in a handicapped spot in front of the first building on the left. Candace parked next to the Cadillac and got out with the awkward wobble of a pregnant woman. She knew Rilla was upstairs in apartment 4F. Standing at the foot of the steps, she debated whether she should climb them or call Rilla on his cell phone and have him meet her outside. She wasn't worried about the thugs up there; it was the exercise that had her hesitant.

"What you doing here?"

Candace followed the voice, happy to see CC appear in the breezeway.

"I'm looking for Rilla."

"He up there," CC said, pointing a thumb the direction he just came from.

Candace looked up and saw her boyfriend milling around with a pack of undesirables. She called out to him, and Rilla's face registered surprise. He skipped gingerly down the stairs. CC walked away when he approached.

"What you doing here, girl?"

"I came to see you."

Rilla shook his head. "You need to get out of here. You shouldn't be coming around. Shit be going down all the time." He grabbed her shoulder and led her back to her car. Candace got in, and Rilla stood in her open door. "You all right?" he asked.

"Yeah."

"Didn't I tell you not to come around here?"

Candace nodded. "When are you coming home?"

"I just got here."

"Aren't you scared to work up there?"

"Don't worry about me," Rilla said. "These my peeps." As he said that, a huge crowd of hoodlums bounded down the steps. Candace wasn't one to judge, but they all looked like they should be in prison. Some loitered on the stairwell. Others headed for the parking lot.

She knew she wouldn't change his mind, so Candace started the car and turned down the radio when Alicia Keys started belting *No One*.

"What'd you come over here for, anyway?" Rilla asked again.

"I wanted to talk to you."

"About what?"

"I feel bad about what I said this morning—about how I was going to leave. I was nagging you about your CD."

He smiled. "You ain't doing nothing but keeping me on my toes, baby. I have been slacking on my music thang. I wasn't on the grind like I said I was. I need you to tell me when my shit ain't straight. I'm not mad at you."

His words made Candace feel substantially better. A weight lifted from her shoulders.

"You still love me?" he asked.

She nodded. "Yeah, Rilla. I do."

He ducked in and gave her a kiss. "You on your way home?"

"I'll probably go over Trisha's."

"All right. I'll give you a call later on."

"Are you going to be home for dinner?" Candace asked.

"I don' know. Why? What you got going on?"

"I just miss you," she said.

"I'll be home at six."

Candace left the apartment complex feeling better about her relationship. She was starting to think Rilla *couldn't* get signed, but hearing that he wasn't giving it his all left room for hope.

She idled at a red light at the intersection of Riverside Drive and Berry Street. She heard sirens long before she saw a police car flying in from her right. The old-school Caprice made a quick left in front of her and shot down Riverside—in the direction she had just come. Candace thought nothing of it until a second car sped by with its lights flashing, and then a third, all approaching from her right and all making a left on Riverside.

When a fourth, fifth, and sixth black-and-white repeated the pattern, a slight moan escaped Candace's lips. She looked in her rearview mirror to track the cops' progress, and what she saw made her heart sink. One by one, all of the police cars turned into the Evergreen Apartment complex. And they were coming from the other direction, too. Candace watched an eleventh, twelfth, and thirteenth squad car turn in. Then came two unmarked sedans and a dark-colored SUV.

She knew nothing about police or task forces, but Candace knew exactly what she was seeing. This was a raid, organized and premeditated. No 911 call would warrant such a show of force.

Candace cut her wheel all the way to the left and performed an ill-advised U-turn in the intersection. She flew down Riverside like she had sirens herself. Tears were already streaming down her face when she turned into the apartments. Flashing lights were everywhere. Police had their guns drawn in a hundred directions. Some thugs were running. Others were already on the ground with a knee in their backs. The air was filled with orders: *Stop or I'll shoot*, and *Hold it right there, asshole!*

Amid the chaos, Candace pulled in right behind the unmarked SUV and got out like she had important business there. She ignored orders to *remain in her vehicle* and *get on the ground*. She stepped towards Rilla's car in a daze. The sight reminded her of the D-Day scene in *Saving Private Ryan*. To her left a skinny Crip had his arm wrenched so far behind him she thought his shoulder would pop. He yelped like a frightened puppy. To her right another ruffian was putting up a good fight against three billy-club-swinging officers.

By the time someone grabbed her arm, Candace had reached the stairway. Eight people were on the ground being roughed up and cuffed. Candace scanned them and found the face she was looking for. Rilla lay flat on his stomach. He struggled profusely, but the deal was done; he was already shackled. A chunky officer squatted on him with a chubby knee on the back of his neck.

Candace tried to run towards him, but the guy holding her jerked her arm roughly.

"Do you hear me?" he screamed into her ear.

Candace turned and saw that she was being restrained by a large man with a long handlebar moustache. He wore a long-sleeved button-down with jeans rather than the black uniform of the Overbrook Meadows Police Department. He did have a badge clipped on his belt, though. He had a gun holstered there, too.

"*What the hell is wrong with you? Do you hear me?*"

He had his face close to hers now. They were nose to nose. Candace thought his breath smelled like peanut butter.

"Do you want to go to jail?" he bellowed, and the words startled Candace from her trance. She regarded him queerly, as if noticing him for the first time.

"*Get the hell out of here!*" he ordered. "*Get back in your vehicle and leave!*"

He turned her around and shoved her in the direction of her Sentra—shoved her a little hard, considering she was seven months pregnant. Candace stumbled but didn't lose her footing. She turned back towards Rilla, but the detective stood before her with his hands on his hips.

"*You got ten seconds to get the hell away from here!*" he barked. "*One! . . .*"

Candace got into her car and drove away.

She didn't know how she made it home, but Trisha found her in the parking lot thirty minutes later. Candace was sobbing uncontrollably, mumbling something about Rilla, the police, and a terrible place called the Evergreen Apartments.

⌒

After a day like this, you're apt to call your mama, no matter who you are. Candace got ten dollars in quarters from a Laundromat and made her call from a pay phone close to her apartment. Her mother answered after three rings.

"Hello?"

"Mama?"

"*Hello?*"

"Mama, it's me."

"*Candace?*"

"Yeah, Mama."

"Oh, my God, *baby*. Oh, my God. I can't beli—oh, baby. It's really you? Candace, we've miss—are you all right? We've missed you so much. *I can't believe it!*"

"I'm all right, Mama."

"Girl, you've given us such a fright. I haven't slept in a year. You should see me. I've got gray hairs everywhere! Where are you, baby? Are you ready to come home? Please tell me you're through with this nonsense."

Despite everything that was wrong in Candace's life, her mother's voice put a smile on her face. "Yeah," she said. "I want to come home."

"Oh, my God, did you say *yes*? Baby, did you say you want to come home?"

"Yes, Mama. I want to come back home."

"*Oh, Candace!* You don't know how happy I am to hear that. You should see me, I'm bouncing like a school-girl. Are you okay? Where are you? Everything's all right?"

"I'm fine, Mama. It's just . . . ."

There was a rustling on the other end of the phone. Candace heard her mother speaking excitedly to someone else: "It's Candace! She's on the phone. She says she wants to come back!"

There was more rustling, and then a man's voice came to the line. Candace dreaded this moment more than anything.

"Hello? Candace?"

"Hey, Dad. It's me."

"Where are you? Are you still in Texas?" He seemed a lot less enthused than her mother.

"Yeah," Candace said.

"So you're *finally* ready to come home?" he asked skeptically.

"Yes," she said. "If you're willing to take me back, I want to come home."

"You're always welcome," Gerald Hendricks said. Then, "What happened? Your boyfriend finally end up getting shot?"

"No," Candace said, a wave of uneasiness washing over her.

"Well, what happened then?" her step-father asked.

"He's in jail."

"Oh," he said. "So he gets locked up and now you wanna come home?"

In the background Candace heard her mother pleading, "Don't do that, Gerald."

"I was already thinking about going home," Candace said. "I didn't know how to tell him."

"But now he's in jail?" her father asked.

"Yes," Candace said.

"You missed a whole semester of school," he said. "You could have been halfway through your freshman year by now. It didn't do you a bit of good to graduate early if you were going to skip a year of college."

Candace didn't like the way this conversation was going at all. "I've been going to school," she said. "I took five classes at the community college."

"*Community college?*" Her father said it like it was a naughty word. In the background, Candace heard her mom again.

"Gerald, stop that."

"I'm pregnant," Candace blurted.

"She says he's in jail," her father said off line, then, "What?"

"I'm pregnant," she said again. "Seven months."

"I knew it!" There was more commotion on the other end. Candace heard her father speaking to her mother: "She's *pregnant*! And *he's* in jail! That's the only reason she wants to come back."

When he got back on the phone, Candace already had her finger poised to disconnect the line.

"So you're pregnant?" he asked. "You ran all the way over there and messed up your life—just like I said you would! Now everything's shot to hell and you wanna come back and be a burden to me and your mother? We stopped changing diapers a long time ago, Candace.

Don't think you're gonna come back and stick us with your baby!"

In the background her mother begged for leniency, but Gerald ignored her.

"You had it all," he ranted. "You could have gone to whatever school you wanted to! You could have had anything you wanted!"

"Daddy, please . . ."

"*Please?* Please what, Candace? You wanna call me for help, but you don't want to hear what I've got to say about it? We're disappointed in you, girl. You've *disgraced* this family. We've been lying to the neighbors. Your mother's been in counseling—"

There was more rustling. Candace knew her mother was trying to take the phone, but her father wouldn't give it up.

"Hold on, woman! She's going to hear what I have to say!"

But when he got back on the line this time, Candace had already hung up.

She sat in the phone booth and cried for an unprecedented *fourth* time in one day.

There would be no one to dry her tears on this night.

CHAPTER 7
THE FAME GAME

They say they know my name
They say they know my game
They say I'm guilty
Now they got my ass locked in these chains

Rilla
C Block

Candace slumped on Trisha's couch watching *The Simpsons* with the kids. It was ten p.m. Most families were getting ready for bed at that hour, but Trisha's apartment was still humming. In addition to the television, a radio blasted in one of the bedrooms. The apartment was filled with pleasant aromas from whatever Trisha was making in the kitchen. None of her children were in school yet, so they stayed up as late as 2 a.m. most nights.

Trisha emerged from the kitchen after a while looking like a Waffle House waitress. She toted two plates in one hand and had a third plate and a bottle in the other. She placed them on her dining table and called her children over for a late meal.

"You gonna eat over here or in front of the TV?" she asked Candace.

"I didn't know you were making anything for me."

"I didn't make this for you. I just had some left over. Do you want it or not?"

"What is it?" Candace asked.

"Hamburger Helper."'

"What kind?"

"What you mean what kind? They all the same, girl; noodles, meat, and seasoning. I don't know what kind it is."

Candace said she'd try it.

Trisha got her kids settled at the table and brought Candace's plate to the couch. She took Willie Jr. and sat down with him on the love seat. She bottle-fed him rather than pop out her boob this time, much to Candace's delight.

"Did they let you talk to him before they carried him off?" Trisha asked.

Candace munched on a mouthful of noodles before responding. It was pretty good stuff. "They wouldn't let me talk to him. I don't think he even saw me."

"You a bad bitch," Trisha said, "running up on them cops like that."

"I don't think it was *me* who did that," Candace said. "I was, like, in a daze. I never felt like that before."

"Cops don't care if you in a daze," Trisha informed. "They'll still crack yo head with they flashlight."

"They didn't give me any special treatment," Candace informed. "Look at my arm." She lifted her sleeve to show a purple, thumb-sized bruise on her bicep.

"Uhn-uhn. Girl, you should sue."

"Sue for what?"

"They not supposed to be putting they hands all on you."

"They're not supposed to sit on someone's neck, either, but they did that."

"They sat on Rilla's neck?"

"Yeah," Candace said and downed another mouthful. Trisha had a way with food. Hamburger Helper meals didn't call for paprika, but Candace tasted it. There was thyme in there, too. "It was a real fat cop, too. I tried to run up to him. I think I was gonna hit him or something."

Trisha chuckled. "That's *romantic*. I can see yo pregnant ass doing that shit, too."

"There was nothing romantic about my day," Candace said. "Watching Rilla on the ground like that . . ." She shivered. "I get chills every time I think about it."

Trisha nodded knowingly. She wiped her baby's nose and asked, "Them people still won't tell you what his bail is?"

Candace had made at least ten calls to the county jail since getting home.

"No. He's *still* not arraigned yet."

"That's messed up. Bet they don't be doing white people like that. They tell them what they charged with right then. They don't wait no eight hours to get arraigned."

Candace didn't know if that was true or not, but the longer they held Rilla with no charges, the longer she could hold out hope for a happy ending.

"They arrested my nephew for murder when I was pregnant with Peter," Trisha said. "They held him in the county jail for *two years*. When they couldn't build a case against him, they just turned him loose. They made him do two years for nothing."

Candace's whole face drooped. She brought a hand to her mouth and chewed on her longest fingernail.

"Did Rilla have dope on him?" Trisha asked.

"I don't know," Candace said. "I know he sells dope over there. That's the only reason he goes to those apartments." She scraped up her last spoonful of Hamburger Helper and almost licked the plate clean. She stood and took it to the kitchen instead.

"That was good. Thanks."

"It's cool. You can eat over here whenever you want to. And if you get lonely at your apartment, you can spend the night over here."

"Thanks," Candace said, realizing what a good friend Trisha was. "I really appreciate that."

"Maybe he didn't have nothing on him," Trisha said.

"They would have let him out by now if he didn't, wouldn't they?"

"Maybe," Trisha said. "When they do raids like that, they take everybody who's around there. If you don't have no drugs or a pistol, they'll take you for whatever tickets you got. Damn near every nigga in the hood got a warrant for something. Maybe they just holding him on tickets again."

That was Candace's secret prayer. "I hope so."

"What you gon' do if it *is* drugs?" Trisha asked.

Candace shook her head. She didn't want to cry again. She thought she had run out of tears, but her vision grew blurry anyway. "I don't know," she said, and tried to force the pain away.

"You thinking about calling your parents yet?"

Again, Candace's eyes twitched. She looked up at the ceiling this time to keep the moisture in. "I called them," she said. "I talked to them. They know what's going on."

"What'd they say?"

"It didn't go well," Candace said. She looked her friend in the eyes and allowed herself to weep. "They know I'm pregnant, but I'm not going home anytime soon. I don't want to talk about that anymore."

Trisha was usually unrelenting, but she let it go with that.

The front door swung open, and in stepped the only woman in the city who could make Candace feel ugly simply by walking into the room. Delia wore a sleeveless V-neck catsuit that evening. The material was dark blue and stretchy; it fit her like a rubber glove—except down past the knees, where it flared out into bell bottoms.

Delia had her hair down. It was jet black and shiny, straight and flowing. Candace wiped the tears from her face, all of a sudden aware of her fat stomach, swollen feet, and puffy cheeks.

"What's up, bitches!"

"Oh, God, it's Foxy Brown," Trisha said. "Girl, how you keep them titties from falling out?"

Candace wondered that, too.

"The same way Jennifer Lopez did when she wore that green Versace," Delia explained. She strutted like a model, bringing in the smell of Christian Dior perfume with her.

"Hell, I don't know how *she* did it, either," Trisha said.

"It's an industry secret," Delia informed her. "Don't hate." She walked right up to Candace and put a hand on her hip. Candace looked up at her and her heart stopped. The dreaded moment of truth had finally arrived. Candace steeled herself for the accusations:

Bitch, why you sleep with my man?

Speculations would follow:

I heard that ain't even Rilla's baby. Bitch, you got pregnant with CC?

Then would come the hair pulling and rolling around on the floor, the slaps and the scratches. In a way, Candace was ready to get it all over with. It would be a perfect way to end this awful day. Waiting for this confrontation was probably harder than the actual incident would be.

But Delia still didn't know about CC and Candace. She came to talk about something moderately worse.

"Why you ain't at the house?" she asked. "Rilla's been trying to call. CC's been calling, too."

"I have my cell phone with me," Candace said.

"Them jailhouse phones can't call to some cell phones," Delia said.

"Why not?"

"Hell, I don't know why, but they can't."

"How do you know Rilla called me?" Candace asked. "You talked to CC?"

Delia gave her a dumb look. "Girl, CC at the house. I just left from over there."

Candace's jaw dropped. "They let him out?"

"What are you talking about? He wasn't never arrested."

"He wasn't?"

"Naw, fool. Who told you CC was in jail?"

"I saw the police there," Candace said. "I saw Rilla. The police had *him* handcuffed."

"Bet you didn't see CC in no handcuffs," Delia said, and that was true.

"He got away?"

"The police can't never catch CC," Delia informed. "He got some long legs. He can jump a fence without climbing it."

"Yeah, I seen him do that before," Trisha agreed.

Candace felt like she couldn't get enough air in her lungs. The Hamburger Helper became a petrified log in her gut. How unfair was that? If not for CC, Rilla wouldn't have gotten wrapped up in the dope game again. He would have been more focused on his music, and would probably have his demo ready by now. Rilla had a girlfriend from out of state who depended on him. He had a baby on the way (*maybe*). Candace wouldn't wish jail on anyone, but CC deserved to be there much more than Rilla did.

"I can't believe he got away from all those police," she said.

"He just ate me an hour ago," Delia countered. "I'm pretty sure I know what I'm talking about."

That's messed up.

"He talked to Rilla," Delia said.

"When?"

"A little while ago. You could have talked to yo man, too, if yo ass was at home to answer the phone."

"What he say?" Candace asked. Her heart thumped so hard she felt it in her ears.

"Rilla said he had a *whole bunch* of dope in his pocket," Delia informed her. She dropped the bomb as casually as if she was giving directions. "They charged him with possession with the intent to distribute. He said they're already trying to railroad him. Because he's kind of famous, they set his bail at a hundred thousand dollars."

"*A hundred thousand?*" Trisha gasped.

Candace didn't know how to feel yet. "Is that a lot?"

"Hell, yeah, that's a lot," Trisha said. "A dope case ain't supposed to have nothing but a five, ten thousand dollar bail. *A hundred thousand—for dope?*" She wrinkled her face like she smelled something foul. "That's wrong. Your bail is only gonna be *fifty* thousand if you kill some-body."

"So what does that mean?" Candace asked. Her face was scrunched up, too. She couldn't stop her leg from shaking.

"It means he ain't getting out," Delia said.

And then it hit. Candace felt like a pipe bomb went off in her rib cage. The floodgates released in her eyes again, and she wanted her mama. More than anything in the world, she wanted to feel her mother's arms around her.

"They can't hold him *forever,* can they?"

Delia looked down at her like she was a mangy dog. "You don't know shit about jail, do you?"

Candace shook her head and dug for a napkin in her purse. Everything she pulled out was used and wadded. Trisha tossed her the baby's face towel, and Candace blew her nose into it loudly.

Delia sat next to her on the couch. "Here's how it works, youngster. Rilla's charged with something big. He's going to either say he did it, and take some time, or he can go to court and fight it. If he do that, he gotta get a lawyer. But *before* that, he gotta bail out of jail—if he can."

"He has to pay a hun-hundred thousand to bail out?" Candace's eyes were red and puffy. Her nose was pink. Her lips quavered.

"You have to get a *bail bondsman* to make your bail," Trisha said. "Like if your bail is five thousand, most people don't have that. But if you pay the bondsman ten percent he'll pay the rest for you."

"So Rilla can get out for ten thousand?" Candace asked. That was more money than she'd ever had in her entire life, but still, it sounded a lot better.

"Right," Trisha said.

"So unless you know somebody rich," Delia added, "Rilla has to stay in jail until he goes to court."

The only people Candace knew with that kind of loot were her parents, and they weren't even close to being an option.

"How, how long before he goes to court?" she asked.

"I told you about my nephew," Trisha reminded. "But it usually takes about three to six months."

Candace wondered what would happen to her in six months without Rilla. Or would it be only six months? Rilla got caught red-handed, and he was definitely guilty of his crime. Candace had to consider the fact that she might never see him again. She wondered if she still needed his signature for an adoption if he was in the penitentiary.

She leaned forward with her elbows on her knees. Her whole body was racked with sorrow. Delia sat right next to her, but she didn't put an arm around her or even a comforting hand on her shoulder. Candace rocked back and forth like an Alzheimer's patient.

"CC wanna know how much money y'all got stacked up," Delia said.

Candace looked at her like she was speaking Spanish. "*Money?* I don't have any *money*. Rilla was going in on something big with CC. All of his money is supposed to be with your boyfriend. He doesn't have it?"

"CC got some of it," Delia confirmed. "But he thought Rilla had some more at home."

"Rilla never told me about any money," Candace said. This was getting worse and worse. "I got about three hundred dollars over there, but that's for rent."

"You gonna put that with the bail money CC's putting together?" Delia asked.

"That's all the money I have," Candace said. "That's all I got."

Speaking that sentence brought it all home. Candace realized how screwed she really was. Somehow her life ended up like someone's tragic novel. "And that's still not enough!" she wailed, her lips pulled back, her braces glinting in the light. "I have to get two hundred more from somewhere."

Trisha got up then. She went to Candace and put a hand on her back. It was a big hand, nice and warm. She rubbed Candace's neck and hummed softly.

"Well, I don't know what to tell you," Delia said. "CC say he got some money, but not ten thousand. I don't know how Rilla's getting out if you not gon' help."

Candace couldn't believe what she was hearing. "How am *I* supposed to help?" A trail of mucus hung an inch off of her upper lip. She wiped it off, and Delia looked pretty grossed out.

"I don't know," Delia said. "But crying ain't gonna fix nothing. That's *yo* man. I'm just telling you what CC said."

Candace pushed herself from the seat. She almost fell back down, but Trisha braced her arm. "I got . . . I gotta go," she said. "I wanna talk to Rilla. Muh-maybe he's st-still calling."

"He can't call this late," Delia said. "They get locked down at ten. They can't use the phone again until breakfast."

"Wuh-what time is that?" Candace asked.

"It's early. At like six."

Candace looked at the wall clock mounted over Trisha's television. It was only eleven-thirty, but she wanted to leave anyway.

"I'm gonna go home and see if I can fuh-find any-thing. I think he would have tuh-told me, but I'll look anyway."

"Good luck, girl," Trisha said. "You can come back if you get lonely up there."

Candace looked into her friend's eyes, glad to see that she wasn't the only one upset about all of this. She thanked Trisha for the meal and thanked Delia for the bad news. She blubbered like an imbecile as she crossed the street, but she willed herself to stop before she got out of the car. Delia was an asshole, but she was right about one thing: Crying wasn't going to fix this problem.

When she got inside, the first thing Candace did was stumble around her desolate apartment looking for Rilla. She wondered if she was going crazy in addition to every-thing else.

CHAPTER 8
STANDING TALL

Candace didn't find any money under her mattress. She looked in the closet, but there were no hundred-dollar bills stuffed in the pockets of any of Rilla's clothes. The money wasn't in the bathroom, either, not taped to the inside of the toilet's tank and not under the sink. In the living room she pulled the cushions from the couch and love seat, checked for oddly placed books on the shelves, and even inspected the curtains.

Still no money.

She went to the kitchen and hesitated in the doorway, dreading the search she was about to embark on. But right about then, common sense kicked in. If Rilla had money hidden, he would have told her. In any event, she could simply ask him when he called in the morning. Candace was sure he'd call bright and early. According to the caller ID, she already had twelve missed calls from an UNKNOWN source. The last call was at 9:59 p.m.

She went to bed and slept by herself for the first time in more than a year. When she woke up, her eyes were so crusted with dried tears, it was hard to get them open. In a way, she hoped they would stay closed forever.

Rilla called at 6:30 a.m. Candace had been up for two hours already. When she picked up the phone, an automated recording began to play.

"Hello, you have a collect call from," another recording started, this one was short; Rilla barely had time to state his name, "an inmate in the Overbrook Meadows County Jail. To accept this call, press one. If you do not wish to accept—"

Candace pressed the button. A moment later her boyfriend was on the line.

"Hello?" The sound quality was poor and there was a slight echo, but hearing Rilla's voice made Candace giddy. She couldn't even sit down.

"Rilla? It's me."

"Hey, baby. Damn, it feels good to hear your voice. Where happened to you last night?"

"I was at Trisha's. I didn't know you can't call my cell phone."

"Yeah. Baby, you sound tired. You okay?"

"Not really," she said. "I feel like you've been gone for a month already."

"I ain't gonna be gone that long," he promised. "This some bullshit. They ain't gonna be able to hold me."

"I talked to Delia last night," Candace said. "She said your bail is *a hundred thousand dollars.*"

"I know," Rilla said. "Ain't that some mess? I'ma get that reduced for sure."

"Why is it so much?"

"Cause I'm a celebrity or something," Rilla said. "They're talking about how much money I got and how I'm a flight risk. They treating me like I still got videos on TV. I don't know why they're saying that."

"Who?"

"That bitch-ass judge. She did me bad, baby."

"What are you going to do?"

"Ain't nothing I can do, till I get me a lawyer. I can't pay that bond, and only a lawyer can get it reduced. I talked to CC. He's supposed to be getting some money together for me. You talked to him yet?"

"No, but I talked to Delia. They think I have some money over here."

"It's some money in that cookie jar," Rilla confirmed.

"There's only three hundred dollars in there. And the rent's due in two weeks. I don't have enough for that."

"I thought it was more than that."

"Rilla, where is all the money? I know you have money somewhere."

"Baby, I had to do something with it. Everything I got is wrapped up in something right now. But you straight. I got some shit in that duffle bag by the bed."

"I'm not selling drugs."

"I know. Give it to CC. See if he'll give you a couple hundred for it so you can pay the rent. That bag's worth at least a thousand."

"Rilla, I don't want to touch that stuff."

"All right. I'll tell CC to go by and get it."

Candace cringed at the thought of CC *stopping by to check on her* again.

"There's no more money in the house?" she asked.

"Naw, baby. Me and CC just went in on this *thang*. All my money's tied up in that. CC got my shit, though. Once he gets rid of that, he should have about twelve thousand for me."

Candace was glad for that, but she couldn't help asking, "What if he doesn't give me any? The rent's due in two weeks."

"Baby, you'll be all right. I'll talk to him today."

"I called my parents," Candace said.

There was a long pause. When Rilla spoke again, he sounded spooked. "You did?"

"Yeah."

"You still talking about going home?"

"I can't go," Candace said. "Not now, anyway."

"What happened?"

"My dad—he started getting really mad."

"Don't worry about them," Rilla said. "I'ma take care of you."

"I know, Rilla. But I'm scared. Once this money is gone, I don't have anything else. The phone bill is due. The electric is coming up next month." Candace's eyes glossed over and she cursed herself.

You gotta stop crying!

"I'm not gonna be locked up that long."

"But what if you can't get the bail reduced? What if you have to stay in there until you go to trial?"

"That's not gonna happen."

"But what if it does, Rilla? I don't know what to do. I don't know how to do all of this by myself. The baby's coming . . ."

89

"Listen: I'm not gonna be in jail when the baby gets here. I promise you that. I put that on my mama. I'll break out if I have to. I'm not missing that day."

That was encouraging, but who was he kidding. *The System* had him now. And as much as she hated The System at this moment, Candace had to admit it was working just fine in this case. Rilla sold drugs, he got arrested, and he was in jail. Everything was as it should be. If Rilla got out, he would have to *beat* The System. Could he do that with only twelve thousand dollars?

"You going to school today?" he asked.

"I don't know."

"Why not?"

"I don't feel like it."

"Candace, you need to go to school. That's a good thing you're doing. You started going by yourself, and you need to keep going. Don't let nothing stop you from doing right."

"I'm scared."

"Don't worry. I'ma make sure everything is all right."

It was hard to believe him, but what choice did she have? Either Rilla was going to make things right, or she was going to end up pregnant and homeless in a city with no relatives.

They talked for another thirty minutes. When they hung up, Candace sat on the couch and stared at the blank television screen for a long time. She never felt so alone; so stupid, lost, and *alone.*

↷

The first day without Rilla went okay. Candace went to school as normal and somehow maintained focus on her instructors' lessons. Finals were coming next week. If she could get through her first semester of college despite all of the drama in her life, Candace would consider herself a lucky person.

She didn't have any classes with Tino that day, but he always managed to find her.

"Hey, Candace!"

She was already at her car. She turned and saw him jogging to catch up. He usually had something to say that would make her feel better, but Candace wanted nothing to do with him right then. She cursed herself for stopping at the restroom after class. She could have been on the freeway by now.

"I've been looking for you," he said as he approached. Tino wore a short-sleeved Polo with sand-colored canvas shorts. He had black sandals that showed off his toes, and Candace noticed how cute they were. Today his hair was down, like Antonio Banderas in *Zorro*.

He stopped a few feet away and stared at her with a look of genuine concern. "You okay?"

Candace sighed and opened the car door. "I'm all right. I'm in a hurry, though, Tino. I don't have time to talk."

He nodded. He looked her up and down, his expression registering what Candace already knew: She looked like shit.

"I'm sorry about what happened," he said finally.

Candace tossed her backpack to the passenger seat. "What are you talking about?"

"About Rilla," he said. "I heard he got arrested yesterday."

Candace was shocked. Her *school world* and her *real world* were two separate entities. She hated for them to collide.

"Who told you that?"

"It was in the newspaper," Tino said.

That was even worse. Candace put a hand to her face and rubbed the tense spot between her eyes.

"It wasn't front page news or anything," he went on. "It was in the Metro section, tucked in towards the back: 'Rapper Arrested on Drug Charges.' I just wanted to tell you that I feel bad for you. I was thinking about what you said, about how he's the only reason you're down here. I didn't think you'd come today, actually."

"I've only got one more week till this semester's over," Candace said. "This is the only good thing I've done since I left New York. I'm not going to mess it up."

"What about your boyfriend? What's going to happen to him?"

"I don't think he's getting out," Candace admitted.

"You're going to stay here without him?"

"I'm going to finish this semester," she said again. "I don't know what's going to happen after that. I want to go home, but my dad's mad at me."

"You talked to him?"

"I called yesterday after Rilla got arrested."

"They said you can't go back?"

"No. I think they'll let me. He was just . . . so mad, my dad was. They're going to make me feel like shit if I go back. They'll never let me live this down. They think I've done irreconcilable damage to my future."

"You can stay," Tino offered. "If you get a job. The apartments I live in are real cheap. I pay for my school, all my food and clothes, and I still have enough for rent. You can do it, too, if you want to . . ." He trailed off because Candace was shaking her head.

"Look," she said, "you're a good guy, Tino. But I don't think we should talk anymore. I've got a lot going on right now. I don't think it's a good idea."

"I was just—"

"I know. You only want to help. I really like you, Tino, but I'm so screwed up right now. I don't want you involved with any of this."

"But—"

"Seriously," Candace said. As bad as she already felt, there was still room for heartbreak. Tino looked so pitiful. "You don't see how bad I am, so I have to do this for you. I'm messed up, Tino. And I don't want to talk to you anymore." A lone tear snaked down her cheek.

Tino stepped forward, as if to console her, but something in Candace's eyes made him change his mind. So he just stood there and watched as she got into her car and drove away. Candace checked the rearview mirror as she exited the parking lot, and Tino didn't move the whole time he was in sight.

The next day they had Economics together. Tino didn't look at her at all during class, and he didn't approach her afterwards. And although this was what Candace wanted, it still made her feel very lonely.

✑

Rilla called every morning, but this courtesy didn't get Candace any closer to solving her rent problem. He promised CC would show up with two hundred before the first of the month, but days went by with no word from Cordell. After a full week, Trisha came up with a solution that seemed viable.

"Girl, you need to pawn some shit. I know you got something up there worth two hundred."

Candace ran the idea by Rilla the very next morning.

"Do you still talk to CC every day?" she asked.

"Naw. Nobody answers the phone most of the time I call."

"Does he still have some of your money or what?" Candace asked. "It's been a week, Rilla. And he won't call or come by. I don't think he's going to give me anything."

"He will," Rilla promised. "I just need to get in touch with him."

"What about your lawyer money?"

"He says he got some saved, but not enough."

"Rilla, what if he's not doing that? You said he had a bunch of your . . . stuff. What if he's keeping the money for himself?"

"My nigga wouldn't do that. I been knowing him—"

"I know, Rilla, since middle school."

"Then why you think he'd do me dirty?"

"I don't know. All I know is he's not doing what you said about the rent. Today's the twenty-fifth. I got five days to get two hundred dollars."

"I'll get in touch with CC today," Rilla said.

"I think I'm going to pawn something to get the money," Candace said.

Rilla didn't respond for a while. "Something like what?"

"Well, we've got two TVs. I don't need the one in the bedroom. If that's not enough, I got some jewelry, too."

"I don't want you to pawn nothing *I* gave you."

"I don't want to get evicted, Rilla. I'm telling you, CC's not doing what you said. I have to do this by myself."

"I'll talk to him today," Rilla promised.

"Baby, do you really trust CC?" Candace asked.

"Don't ask me no stupid shit like that."

"I'm sorry, Rilla. I'm just saying, you're putting a lot of responsibilities on him. He's supposed to help me with the bills. He's supposed to get you a lawyer. If he doesn't do all of that, both of us are screwed. This is two lives he's responsible for. Three, really."

"He's going to take care of business."

"But he hasn't yet. The rent's due, and he's not doing anything."

"You need to quit whining," Rilla said.

Candace hung up on him and left the apartment when he tried to call back.

She didn't have anywhere to go, so she sat in her car and listened to the radio. She thought about how Tino said she could stay if she wanted. All she had to do was get a job and pay the bills like a regular person. She thought about when her caseworker said she wasn't as helpless as she was making herself out to be.

Candace made a decision right then to only depend on herself from then on. If CC came by, that would be cool. But if he didn't, then so be it. She wouldn't expect or request anything from him anymore. If Rilla wanted to put his fate in the hands of that lowlife, that was his business.

On the thirtieth, Candace took her last final and left the community college in a chipper mood. She'd just completed her first semester of college and was confident she made all A's. She was also seven and a half months pregnant with a stack of bills and no income, but that didn't spoil her day.

When she got home, Candace begged Trisha to carry her television to the car for her. In addition to the television, Candace took her biggest herringbone necklace, a pair of diamond earrings, and Rilla's DVD player to the pawn shop. She was glad for the excess. All together, she got only two hundred and fifty dollars, but that was fifty more than she needed. She got a money order and paid the rent one day early.

When CC showed up later that evening, Candace was poised to tell him his ill-gotten gains were not needed, but CC wanted to get a few things off his chest as well.

"Why the hell you tell Rilla I'm trying to take his money?"

He stood in her doorway wearing a black shirt with camouflage pants. His Afro was freshly braided down to his scalp. He'd grown out a full goatee by now. His face was a mask of unbridled animosity.

Candace took a cautionary step back into her apartment. "I didn't tell Rilla that."

"Bitch, quit lying." CC took a step towards her, but Candace held her ground. If he wanted in, he would have to go through her.

"You gonna let me in?" he asked.

"What do you want?" Candace wore jeans and a Fruit of the Loom sweater, but she still had the chills.

"You talking about you need some money," CC said. He reached into his pocket and produced a wad of twenties. "Here's the two hundred. Go get that duffle bag."

But Candace still didn't move. "I already paid the rent," she said defiantly. "I don't need your money."

A slight smile tweaked the corner of CC's mouth. The smile never reached his eyes. The two hundred disappeared back into his pocket. "Cool," he said. "Then go get that bag."

"Rilla said that bag was worth a thousand dollars."

"I'ma get it for him."

"Why don't you give me the money now?" Candace suggested. "Then you can keep whatever you make when you sell it."

CC's smile went away as quickly as it came. "Ho, I'm not finna give you no thousand dollars."

"Then I'm keeping the bag," Candace said. Her heart punched through her chest. She knew she was on the verge of tears again, but she also knew she had to take a stand. Sometime, *somehow,* she had take control of her life.

"What you gon' do with it?" CC asked. His face was set in a threatening scowl.

"I'm going to give it to Rilla."

"Didn't he tell you to give it to me?"

"Yeah, but he said you were going to give me some money, too. I waited a whole week and you never came. I took care of it myself."

"What you do? Sell some ass?"

Candace was the one with the scowl now. "I'm finna go lay down." She put her hand on the doorknob, but CC didn't step back to let her close it.

"Gimme that bag," he said. He looked like he was willing to do anything to get it, but Candace didn't think he'd go as far as attacking a pregnant woman.

"I'm gonna hold it for Rilla," she said. She gave him the sternest look she could muster, but she also felt her eyes watering up. CC must have seen it, too. His face softened. He smiled and nodded.

"You a stupid-ass bitch. He need that money to get out, so it's yo fault if he stay in there, you dumb ho."

Candace lost it. He face screwed up and the tears flowed anew.

Dammit! Am I ever going to stop crying?

"Why are you doing this?" she bawled. "Why are you talking to me like this?"

" 'Cause I can't stand you," CC said matter-of-factly. "You a ho. I hate that my nigga so sprung on yo ass."

"*I'm not*," Candace said.

"Yeah, you is. You think I forgot about that shit that happened?"

"That was *you*!" She shrieked. "You jumped on me!"

"Bitch, you wanted it!"

She shook her head. "No! I didn't! *You raped me!* That's why I'm pregnant now!"

"Bitch!" He swung quickly.

Candace had never been in a fight before, and her vision was blurred by the tears, but she saw *something*. Maybe it was in his eyes. Maybe his shoulder hitched a little. Whatever it was made her throw her hands over her face—just in the nick of time.

His punch landed on her forearm, but it was still powerful enough to send her falling backwards. Candace yelped like a child and landed hard on her butt. She kept her hands over her head in case there was more to come.

CC stepped in and stood over her with his fists balled. Candace's heart pounded. Her brain raced. She thought she might have peed her pants.

"*Stop*!" she screamed.

"You'd better not *ever* tell nobody about that shit!" CC shouted. "*That baby ain't got nothing to do with me!*"

Candace looked up at him through her parted fingers. He looked angrier than she had ever seen him. She trashed all of her preconceptions about the lanky thug. If he would steal from his friend and hit a pregnant girl, what else was CC capable of?

"Gimme that bag!" he bellowed. "I'm sick of playing with yo ass, bitch!"

"Get out of my house!" Candace shouted. Actually she screamed it at the top of her lungs. And it was loud. She didn't know she could get that much volume, but the adrenaline rush gave her the pipes of Pavarotti. *"Get out of my house!"*

The ruse might not have worked in her native New York, but Texas folk are a lot friendlier and nosier. Candace heard a door open outside of her apartment. She looked past CC's legs and saw the neighbor across from her standing in his doorway with a frightened expression.

"*Leave me alone!*" Candace shouted, this time more for her neighbor's benefit than for her attacker.

CC looked down at her with fire in his eyes and noticed Candace was looking elsewhere. He turned to check behind him.

"What the hell you looking at?" he shouted at the stranger.

Candace's neighbor was a sweet and docile man, but he was also huge. At six feet, three inches and two hundred and sixty pounds, he didn't really have to be the aggressive type—so long as he looked the part.

"What are you doing?" the neighbor asked.

"I'm minding my business, nigga. Why don't you try that shit?" CC played the tough role, but he wasn't stupid. Assault and battery on a woman with child would have him sharing breakfast with Rilla.

"I'm calling the police if you don't leave," Gentle Ben said.

CC wavered in indecision for a second but finally chose a more prudent course of action. "I'm finna go," he told the neighbor. He took a step back and Candace lowered her arms. CC stared down at her audaciously.

"This how you wanna play it, ho?"

"Just leave," Candace said.

CC nodded. "All right. Cool. You keep the bag. I got something for you."

With that, he turned and disappeared through the doorway. Candace got up a moment later and went to close her door. Her neighbor was still standing on the breezeway.

"You okay?" he asked.

"Yeah. Thanks a lot."

"You want me to call the police? In case he comes back?"

"He's not coming back," Candace said. "Thanks, though. Really. I really appreciate it."

The man nodded, but he didn't go back inside. Candace closed her own door and locked both of the dead bolts.

∽

Two hours later Candace finally felt safe enough to take a shower. She made an omelet and ate it in the living room, then stretched out on the sofa watching *The Tonight Show*. Her future was uncertain, but her spirits were surprisingly high. She stood up to a monster and knew he wasn't coming back. Even without Rilla, she felt good about her chances.

She had a car and an apartment for at least another month. She had a semester of college under her belt. She believed that if she could get a job within the next week or two, things might work out after all. It was going to be hard, but Candace believed she could do it.

The only thing that bothered her was CC's ominous departing words.

I got something for you.

For the life or her, Candace couldn't think of anything he could do to get her back.

She fell asleep on the couch at 1:00 a.m.

❧

When someone pounded on her door an hour and a half later, Candace lifted her head from the cushion, and then lowered it again, poised to ignore it. She had no idea who it could be. The obvious guess was CC, but he was afraid of her neighbor. He wouldn't bang that hard in the middle of the night.

Boom! Boom! Boom!

No way would he pound on my door like this.

That thought made Candace lift her head a second time. Whoever was at the door was really knocking *hard*. It was almost as if it was the—

"Police! Open the door!"

Candace woke up then. She sat up with a start and turned to her front door just in time to see it crash open—*literally*, the whole frame cracked. Splinters flew towards her like shrapnel.

Candace got a glimpse of a battering-ram-toting police officer, but only for a split second. His comrades rushed past him with guns drawn in every direction. They were all wearing black. Some of them had on dark masks and bulletproof vests. They spotted Candace right away. Flashlights and pistol barrels settled on her face and chest.

"Get down on the floor!"

"I'm pregnant!" she screamed.

"Get on the goddamned floor!"

I got something for you.

But he wouldn't do *this*? Would he?

CHAPTER 9
THE RAID

It was like one of those sick dreams when you know you're asleep, yet you're powerless to wake up, powerless to stop the parade of ignorance going on around you. For Candace it was a lot worse because she knew that she was, in fact, awake. Any doubts about this were vanquished when a man dressed like a ninja shoved the barrel of his MP5K between her eyes.

"*Let me see your hands!*"

Candace's arms flew up like a jack-in-the-box. "*I didn't do anything!*" she screamed.

"*Shut up!*"

Another cop swooped in from behind and grabbed the back of her neck with a big, rough hand. "*Get on the floor!*"

Candace was sitting on the couch wearing pajama bottoms and a T-shirt. The burly officer could have shoved her face into the soft cushions, but he yanked her sideways instead, pulling her off the sofa and sending her crashing to the floor.

Candace rolled her body at the last second, taking the brunt of the impact on her hip rather than falling to her belly.

"*I'm pregnant!*" she screamed, but no one seemed to care. The guy on top of her kept a rigid claw on the back of her neck. He pressed something cold and hard on the side of her head.

"*Don't move, lady,*" he warned.

"*I'm pregnant!*"

"*I said don't move!*"

But Candace had no intention of moving. She was petrified; she didn't think she could get up if she wanted to. Visions of Amadou Diallo flew past her eyes. All it took was for one guy to pull the trigger.

And Candace only thought she'd been crying before. That was nothing compared to the racket that emanated from her now. She sobbed uncontrollably. Her breaths were shallow and ragged.

From her position on the ground, Candace could only see feet, and they were running in every direction. Four, five, at least six people were in her apartment. They stomped loudly and screamed at people who weren't even there.

"Clear!" someone finally yelled.

"I'm clear this way!" another barked.

"Who's here with you?" the man standing over Candace asked.

"*Nobody! I'm by myself! Please get off of me! I'm pregnant.*"

"Hold on, toots. *We all clear?*" he yelled in another direction.

"*All clear!*"

"*We clear!*"

"*I'm clear!*"

"*All clear!*"

105

The frantic pace slowed considerably then. The cops started to trickle back into the living room one by one. Candace shivered frantically and watched their shoes. She focused on one set in particular as they ambled towards her. These feet were different than the rest of the tactical squad. They were clad in peach-colored Stacy Adams rather than dark tennis. Khaki slacks shot up from them instead of black trousers.

"Let her up."

The metal was removed from the side of Candace's head. She strained her neck to look up at the man in charge. He sported a long-sleeved white shirt that was tucked into his slacks. He wore a big, Texas-sized belt buckle. There was a badge clipped to his belt, but no gun. He was handsome and clean-shaven with short hair. Candace thought he looked a lot like Mark Wahlberg. She wondered if he would call her a nigger or punch one of her eyes out of its socket like Mark Wahlberg was known to do.

"Please. I'm pregnant," she breathed.

"She's pregnant. Let her up."

The guy in the white shirt seemed to be her savior, but Candace suspected this was only his *good cop* routine. The man standing over her reached down and helped Candace into a standing position. With a firm hand on her shoulder, he eased her down until she was sitting on the couch again.

She sat there in a state of suspended emotion. On one level she understood that she really was in the middle of a police raid. But from a logical standpoint, she knew this couldn't be. She looked around at all of the people in her apartment. It was surreal. Most of them still had on masks. They wore their badges on a dog chain hanging from their necks. They all toted weapons, enough to take out a whole camp of terrorists, it seemed.

And Candace was in the midst of them shivering like a wet kitten. Tears and fear marred her delicate features. These people had come to kill her baby. She knew that as well as she knew her first name.

"I'm Detective Judkins," white shirt said. He presented a small stack of papers Candace hadn't noticed he was holding. "This is a search warrant for your apartment." He held the documents in front of her face, but the legal jargon meant nothing to Candace. She didn't even really look at it.

"I didn't do anything," she whimpered.

"What's your name?" the detective asked.

"Cuh-Candace."

"What's your last name?"

"Hendricks."

"I'm gonna have to search you, Candace," Judkins said. "Is it all right if I get a female officer to search you?" He looked back to his minions. "TJ, can you search her for us?"

TJ wore the same dark attire as her comrades, but she didn't have on a mask. She had blue eyes, blonde hair, and a sharp nose. She walked up to Candace and holstered her weapon.

"Could you stand up, please, ma'am?"

Candace shook her head. "Please. Please don't do this."

"Could you stand up, please, ma'am?"

"Go ahead, Candace," Judkins said. "It'll be okay." He spoke with the patience of a preschool teacher.

Candace stood slowly, wringing her hands as if she were arthritic. She looked to the detective for respite. "I didn't do anything," she moaned.

"It's okay, Candace. TJ's just going to check you for any drugs or weapons you might have."

"I don't have anything."

"It'll be okay."

"Could you turn around, please?" the woman known as TJ instructed.

Candace turned slowly. Every eye was on her. She shook her head and looked to the ceiling rather than meet them. If there was a God, He would save her now. She was one of the innocent. She was being unlawfully persecuted.

"Do you have anything sharp in your pockets? Any needles?"

Candace didn't even have pockets. She looked back to the woman, hoping she would see the sincerity in her eyes. "No. But I didn't do anything. *Please listen to me.*"

"Could you raise your arms, please?"

Candace did as she was told. She stretched out her arms and looked up to the ceiling again. This was God's time to shine. She stood there, like Jesus on the cross. Tears snaked down her face like blood from a crown of thorns.

"Please . . ."

But the hands were on her then. They felt under her arms, slid down her sides. They patted her hips, went down her legs all the way to her ankles. The hands were between her legs, then around her stomach and under her breasts.

Candace didn't think she'd ever felt so violated, so insecure, so exposed. She cried. She cried like when she was five and her mother told her Daddy was going to live in heaven now. Her head fell and bobbed up and down with her jagged breaths.

She wanted to wipe her nose but was afraid the move might get her shot. Everything she thought of doing might get her shot, so she just stood there and took it. But it was over with fairly quickly. The female officer backed away and Candace turned to look at the detective.

"Sit down," he said. "You got any paper towels in the kitchen? TJ, can we get her something so she can wipe her face?"

The female officer walked off in the direction of the bathroom, and the detective took a seat on the couch next to Candace. He crossed his legs and turned his body towards her.

"Please tell me what's going on," Candace pleaded.

The detective looked through his papers as if he had no idea himself. "We're here because we believe there to be drugs in this apartment," he said bluntly.

Candace's thoughts immediately raced to Rilla's duffle bag. Her eyes might have flicked in that direction, too; she wasn't sure. But they couldn't pin that on her, could they? She'd never touched Rilla's bag. For a moment, Candace thought she might actually be okay. But there was more.

"An informant has identified this apartment as a location for drug activity."

Informant? Candace's mind raced. Rilla hardly ever sold drugs out of the house. Even if he did, Rilla was already in jail. Why were they just now coming to arrest him for it?

"Furthermore," Judkins went on, "the informant has identified you, 'a pregnant girl named Candace,' as the person he buys drugs from."

That's when the world fell from beneath her. Candace almost passed out. A timely kick from the baby was probably the only thing that saved her.

An informant?

I got something for you.

"Listen," the detective said. "Before we get into the whos, whys and whats, I need to let you know that you *are* under arrest for suspicion of drug trafficking. You have the right to remain silent. Anything . . ."

Candace stared at his mouth in abject horror. She saw his lips moving, knew he was saying something devastatingly important, but she didn't hear anything past *you are under arrest.* Not even in her most bizarre dream would she have imagined this. Not in her most convoluted nightmare.

"*I didn't sell any drugs!*" she cried.

"If you chose to speak without an attorney present, anything you say can be held against you in the court of law . . ."

"*I didn't do anything!*" Candace wailed. "*I never sold any drugs!* My boyfriend did, but he's in jail already." She felt like she was begging for her life. This was awesomely stupid. Insanely ridiculous. What informant were they talking about? And why would they take his word for it?

The female officer came back and handed Candace a small towel from her restroom. Candace wiped her face with it and blew her nose. It was a loud honk that sounded like a mother goose's mating call. She couldn't get her hands to stop shaking. Her teeth were actually chattering.

"Who's your boyfriend?" Detective Judkins wanted to know.

"His name is Raul. *He's a rapper. Rilla.* Everybody knows him. He just went to jail a couple weeks ago." Candace sang like a bird. The words flew past her lips so fast she didn't know what was coming next. She didn't know if what she was doing could be considered *snitching*, but she didn't give a damn either way. She wasn't going to jail for Rilla or anyone else. If she had to stand up in court and point him out and say, *That guy was selling drugs, your honor: Raul Canales*, she would do it in a heartbeat.

"So you never sold any drugs yourself?" Judkins asked her.

Candace stared at him like he asked if she was down with a threesome. "No. *Never! I swear to God*, I never even touched that stuff. I never sold drugs to anybody! Who told you that?"

"Are there any drugs in the house?" the detective asked.

Candace's eyes flicked again, and her heart didn't beat at all for a few seconds. Her hesitance wasn't lost on the Mr. Judkins.

"Does *Rilla* have any drugs still here?" he asked, and that was the out Candace was waiting for. She nodded, and then another wave of sobs wrecked her features. She lowered her head and moaned into the face towel.

"Candace."

She looked up and met the detective's eyes. They were gray and green, with crow's feet in the corners.

"We have a warrant to search this whole apartment," he said. "We can run through here and tear everything up like you see on TV, or you can be a good girl and tell me where Rilla's drugs are. Either way, we're not leaving without them."

"In the cl-closet," Candace said. "A bl-black duffle bag." She knew she was sealing Rilla's fate, but self-preservation had to come first. For her and her baby.

A few of the men left the living room. They came back quickly with the bag in question. It was unzipped. One of them set it on the coffee table and looked inside. He looked back to the detective and nodded.

"Well, *okay*," Judkins said. He stood and folded his search warrant. "You've been a lot of help," he said to Candace. Then he looked around for the woman who frisked her earlier. "TJ, can you get some cuffs on her? Put her in my car."

Candace didn't hear right. "Wh-what?"

Detective Judkins looked down at her with the traces of a smile in the corner of his mouth. "Candace, you're going to jail. You understand that, right?"

"Buh-but I gave it to you. It's not mine." She wore the expression of a very confused child.

"It's in your house, Candace. By your own admission, you knew it was there. Rilla's in jail, and my informant made a buy from you just a few hours ago. You're the only one here. As far as I'm concerned, that's *your* bag."

Another floodgate opened. This time it was in Candace's panties. She looked down at herself with more shame than the mother of a rapist. "I, I think I pee—"

"Her water broke!" Officer Teri Jacobs said knowingly. "Get an ambulance in route!"

CHAPTER 10
THE MERRY OLD LAND OF OZ

At some point many years from now, Candace will look back on the next few days of her life and wonder which event had the most profound effect. Being the target of her very own drug bust was certainly a top contender. The whole thing lasted less than ten minutes, but every second would forever be ingrained in her psyche. It was like the tragic climax of a thoroughly faltering life. But as bad as that was, it was nothing compared to having a premature baby at the county hospital.

In the ambulance Candace had to be mildly sedated. Every hand on her wanted to help, but she fought her caregivers off like a wounded puma. She couldn't shake the notion that all of these people wanted to kill her baby. The masked EMTs were just an extension of the police who assaulted her in her home. It was during this frantic ride that Candace decided she wanted to keep her child. The baby was all she had left. The baby was the only person in the world as divinely helpless as Candace herself.

At the hospital Candace was too distraught to fill out her admission paperwork, and she wouldn't provide a phone number for her next of kin. She couldn't say whether she wanted to deliver naturally or have an epidural. The only thing Candace understood about the whole process was that she should push when told to do so.

There was no comforting hand to hold, and no familiar faces around from which she could draw strength. There was no one pacing in the waiting room and no one praying for a safe delivery. There was only Candace, her doctor and nurses, and the uniformed police officer who sat outside her door reading a Donald Goines novel.

But Candace did fine all by herself. At 6:42 a.m. she delivered a tiny little girl who weighed only six pounds and nine ounces. Candace didn't have a name for her, but she came up with one as soon as they handed her the fresh bundle of joy: Leila Denise Hendricks.

❧

Next to the police raid and having a baby in a foreign land, holding Leila for the first time was another moment Candace would never forget. The police had her cuffed to the bed, and her nurse said CPS would take custody of the child, but nothing could take away from that treasured moment. Lying there with a brand new baby in her arms was a turning point in Candace's life.

But it was nothing like going to jail.

The police wanted Candace recovered and out of the hospital within forty-eight hours of her childbirth experience. The nurses allowed her to see the baby a lot during this time period, and every moment was precious to Candace. Leila was nearly bald, but she had a thick tuft of curls on the very top of her head. Leila's feet were extra tiny, no longer than Candace's middle finger. She was also very fair-skinned, but her knuckles were a few shades darker, providing a glimpse of what her actual skin tone would be.

And Leila liked to hold onto Candace's pinky finger when Mama fed her. Leila liked to hum when the bottle got really good to her. She had the most beautiful eyes in the world.

Candace savored each moment with Leila, but not with the dread other women in her situation might have felt. As fantastic as it was, Candace truly believed she would be exonerated of her charges. They could take her baby, but with all her heart, she knew she would have Leila back soon. The source of this faith was a simplistic and almost childish belief that at some point life had to treat her fairly.

Lying in that hospital bed, Candace realized she literally had nowhere else to go but up. So when the powers that be deemed she was well enough to go to jail just twenty-seven hours after the delivery, Candace handed over her baby with lighthearted tears in her eyes.

"*I'm gonna fix my life,*" she promised sweet Leila.

Candace figured this promise would be easy to keep because she had no choice.

The Overbrook Meadows County Jail is a magnificent structure made of steel and concrete, iron and fiberglass. Once there, you become property of the state. The guards will tell you when to eat, sleep, laugh, and cry. To make sure you understand this, they put you through the ringer immediately.

Upon entering, Candace was fingerprinted and photographed. This was her first mug shot, and she had to take it fresh out of the hospital. She wondered if it looked as bad as Nick Nolte's.

Candace wore a red T-shirt and blue jeans with white canvas shoes. They made her strip nude, wiggle her tongue, spread her toes, and bend over. They lifted her breasts, pawed through her hair, and sprayed her for lice. This was a terrible start to jail life, but luckily it was the most humiliating thing to happen to her at the facility.

They took Candace's shoestrings and ushered her to a holding cell where she waited two hours for her arraignment. It was cold in there, and it would be cold everywhere else for the remainder of her stay.

⌒

The judge set Candace's bail at twenty thousand dollars. From the courtroom, the guards took her to a small office and asked if she was homosexual or in a gang. They had a phone there, but Candace declined her free call. She'd already decided not to call her parents until she got out. The only other person who might care about her whereabouts was Trisha, but Trisha had no home phone.

They gave Candace a handful of toiletry essentials and a blanket and assigned her to a small room built for two. It was 7:35 on a Tuesday morning. When Candace got to her cell block, breakfast was long gone, and all of the cages were open. There were approximately thirty women on the unit. Most of them occupied a large bench ten feet away from the only television. Others read books or played cards. Some were still in their beds, huddled in their blankets like a cocoon. Candace felt a little sleepy herself.

She staggered through the multitude oblivious to the odd looks she attracted. One inmate in particular, a large woman with dark eyes and dark lips, watched with barefaced angst as Candace found her bed.

"Damn. Why I always end up with the crazy ones?" she muttered.

Candace climbed into her bunk and turned her back to the sounds of strangers in the common area. Her mattress was way too small and tragically thin, but she tried to pretend she was at home. She thought about New York and closed her mind to the sounds of calculated madness. And though it left her vulnerable, she closed her eyes and thought about her daughter. Every now and then a guard came over a loudspeaker with an important announcement, but pretty soon Candace didn't hear that, either.

She slept through lunch.

When the guards showed up with dinner, her cell mate woke her up with what would come to be a typical request.

"Say, if you don't want your dinner, will you get it and give it to me?"

Candace wondered why the woman didn't take the tray on her own.

"They won't give you nobody else's plate," her cell mate clarified. "You have to get it yourself if you want to give it away."

Candace rolled over to face the female who would be her closest companion for the weeks to come. The first thing she noticed was her short hair. It was *really short*. The sides were shaved lower than the top. Candace's cell mate sported a tan-colored jailhouse jumpsuit rather than street clothes, which made her look even more like a boy. The woman was also large, two hundred pounds at least, and she had a part in her left eyebrow. She was no older than twenty-five.

"I'm Neci." She had a raspy voice and large hands with pudgy fingers.

Candace almost laughed. This was perfect. A movie of her life couldn't have gone any better. Here she was, young, sweet, and innocent, adapting to her first day in jail. And what type of cell mate does she end up with? Not the scared little white girl. Not the anti-social older woman. No. In the Merry Old Land of Oz, Candace got the meanest bull dyke on the cell block. Of course she got Neci, pronounced *knee/see*. This was the woman who would jack her meals, steal her shoes, and take the most sacred prize of all one sweltering night when the guards were too far away to hear Candace's screams.

"I'm just saying," Neci went on. "If you not gonna eat it, you might as well give it to somebody else. They don't feed us enough in here. We always hungry."

For a second there, it sounded like Neci had no intentions of strong-arming the meal. Candace decided to call her bluff.

"No, I'm going to eat."

"All right," Neci said. The disappointment made her look like a woeful bulldog. "You'd better hurry up, then. Everybody's in line already."

Candace eased out of her top bunk on wet noodle legs and retrieved the rations provided to her by the state. Their dinner consisted of two breaded fish fillets, a roll, milk, corn, and a ladleful of mixed fruits. Candace stood with her tray and surveyed the eight metal benches. They were filling quickly, usually with people of the same race. Candace spotted her cell mate eating with two other black women.

What the hell, she thought, and took a seat across from the only person she knew there.

Neci was immediately talkative. "Hey, y'all. This my cellie."

"Sleeping beauty," one of the other girls remarked. This one was light-skinned and attractive, but there was something ugly about her. Candace couldn't place it.

"Was I asleep that long?" she asked, cutting into her fillet. The only utensil the inmates were trusted with was a plastic spork, but the meat was pretty tender.

"Not really," the fourth woman at the table said. "Fresh off the streets, everybody wants to go to sleep. I slept four days when I first got here." This girl was small, no more than ninety pounds. She was about thirty-five years old, and a foot shorter than Candace. Her eyes were too close together. Candace thought she looked like a bird.

"I'm Keisha," she said.

"I'm Candace."

"I'm Cheryl," the light-skinned girl offered. She was in her early twenties. She had large eyes and sunken jaws.

"And you already know my name," Neci said.

"You're my cell mate?" Candace asked.

"Yeah, and don't trip about the food. I can get some cookies later on."

"But you'd better eat as much as you can," Keisha advised. "We don't get nothing else to eat till six in the morning."

Twelve hours with no food. That would explain Neci's anxiety.

"I see you got you a dope case," Neci said to Candace.

Candace was taken aback. "How do you know that?"

"It's on your wristband." Neci pointed with her spork. "Whatever color it is, say what you're here for."

Candace looked around and saw that all four women at her table had different color wristbands. Hers was dark blue.

Neci pointed to Keisha. "Yellows are for tickets. Them bitches is probably going home soon. You can see it in their faces. They look happier than everybody else."

Keisha smiled as if to illustrate this point.

"Green is assault, or something violent," Neci said.

Cheryl was the one with the green wristband. Candace made a mental note to keep her distance.

"Mines is white," Neci said. "White bands are for fed cases. They trying to get me for cashing checks."

Candace had no idea what was wrong with cashing a check.

"Red is for murderers," Neci went on. "Ain't nobody in here with no red, but we had this one bitch a couple weeks ago."

Keisha shivered. "She was creepy."

"And you got blue," Neci said to Candace. "That means you got a dope case."

"I didn't do it," Candace said immediately.

Neci smiled. "Everybody in here is innocent, baby girl. You sound like one of us already."

◦——

After dinner the inmates settled into whatever activity they would spend their waking hours doing. Some selected a book from a small cart and stretched out in their bunks. Others wrote letters or washed their clothes in the sinks provided for personal hygiene. Next to the phones, the television was the most attractive venue. The women had to agree on one program to watch, but Candace didn't see any anger in any of the faces gathered there.

Keisha and Cheryl wandered off looking for a card game, leaving Candace and Neci at the table alone.

Candace had a million questions about doing her time there, and Neci had an answer for every one of them. Like most of the jailhouse documentaries Candace had seen, the code for survival all boiled down to one thing: Minding your own business. Neci assured her that every girl who got beat down on the unit deserved it. And since Neci had been in there four months already, Candace listened carefully to everything the big girl told her.

Neci also broke down the general layout of the unit, something Candace had been wondering about since lunchtime.

"Where do we take our showers?" she asked.

Neci gave her a foreboding look. "The showers are over there." She pointed to an area just barely out of view. "It's three showers in there, but nobody will go in there with you. You pretty much have it all to yourself."

"What about those cells?" Candace asked and pointed. "They can look right in."

"Yeah. If you have to go to the bathroom, you can see in there, too. That's why most people here don't take showers. They'll either wash up in the sink, or they won't bathe at all until they get out. If they only here for like, five days, they definitely won't take a shower. I wash up in the sink."

"I *have to* take a shower," Candace confided. "I just had a baby the day before yesterday."

Neci looked upset for a moment, but it washed over quickly. "Yeah?"

Candace nodded.

Neci shrugged. "It's like I said, people can see you in there. They won't really look. Ain't nobody supposed to look at you, but they can see if they want to."

That was weird, but Candace didn't have another option.

"Where do I get a towel?" she asked.

"They shoulda gave you one when you checked in."

"I didn't get one."

"You can get one from the guards," Neci said, pointing to a station at the front of the room. "It's somebody there all the time. Or you can use one of mine. I got an extra one."

Candace was leery of any *gifts* from this woman, no matter how insignificant.

"I'll get one from the guards. I need to have my own."

Neci shrugged. "Good thing you didn't come here pregnant."

"Why?"

"Cause if you got into it with somebody, you'd be worrying about your stomach."

"I'm not going to fight anyone," Candace assured.

"Sometimes you don't got no choice."

"They would fight me while I was pregnant?"

Neci chuckled. "They got a saying here for situations like that: *Yo face ain't pregnant!*"

Candace didn't think that could be true.

"You had a baby right before you came to jail?" Neci asked. But that was a conversation Candace wasn't going to have in the middle of the unit. Neci had to wait until they were locked down for the night to pry that information from her.

Next to the initial intake, taking a shower proved to be the second most embarrassing thing jail had to offer. But Candace did it that night, and every other night she was locked away in the facility. Afterwards she watched a little TV before finally selecting a novel from their scantily stocked cart. Of the twenty-two books available, eight were different copies of the Bible. Most of the rest were tawdry romance novels. Candace lucked out with a Jackie Collins mystery.

She was already on her cot when the guards instructed everyone to return to their cells for the night. Neci came in but didn't get right into bed. She brushed her teeth, washed a pair of socks and underwear, and hung them on the bunk to dry. Candace was glad she was already settled, because the cell wasn't big enough for both of them to move around down there.

The lights went off at ten-thirty, but *lights out* was only a relative term. The fluorescent bulbs in their cell only went to half power, and the main area where they ate their meals was still well lit. With Candace on the top bunk, she took the brunt of this unnatural illumination, but there was a bright side to everything: She could read anytime she wanted, all the way till breakfast if the nights found her sleepless.

Neci finally lay down at eleven p.m. Two minutes later she wanted to talk.

"You still 'wake, cellie?"

"Yeah."

"Was you still gonna tell me about your baby?"

"Might as well. I don't think I'm going to sleep."

Candace told her the whole sordid story, from Rilla to Leila. When she was done talking, Neci had a million questions. Candace only had trouble answering one of them.

"How can you sit in here without going crazy? I'd be on them phones every minute trying to get out."

"I didn't do it," Candace said. "They're going to let me out."

"But what if they don't?" Neci asked. "They done put cases on niggas with less evidence than that. Plus you said they found the dope."

"But I didn't do what they said I did."

"But they got the dope."

"*Based on a lie*," Candace said. "They're not going to be able to bring an informant to court. And if they got that search warrant based on a lie, then the warrant's no good."

"You been watching too much TV," Neci said.

"Maybe so, but I think they wanted to arrest a drug dealer. Once they find out that's not me, they'll let me go. I really believe that."

"You still need to let your people know where you are. You over here all by yourself. You need a lawyer."

"They're going to let me go."

"But what if they don't?"

"I feel it," Candace said. "It's just something I know, Neci. I'm going through all of this for a reason. I think it's 'cause I wanted to give up my baby. I'm being punished for that. And for running away."

"What if you're still here in a month?"

"If I'm still here in a month, I'll call my parents," Candace said.

"For real?"

"For real."

"So why you ain't crying? You not scared? You don't miss your baby?"

"I am scared," Candace said. "And I do miss my baby. She's all I think about."

"This is your first time getting locked up," Neci said. "Everybody cries."

"I can't," Candace said honestly. She shook her head and chuckled at the light fixture no more than two feet from her nose. "If you knew how much I've been crying in the last nine months . . . I'm through with that. I'm out of tears. Plus I feel like if I start crying again, I'll snap. I'll be stuck like that, depressed, crying for the rest of my life. They'll have to put me in a padded room."

"You think you're going to get your baby back?"

"I know I will."

"Then what are you going to do? Go home?"

"Maybe. I kinda want to see if I can do it myself."

"You crazy," Neci said.

"Just wore down," Candace corrected. "If you'd been through what I've been through, you might be a little crazy, too."

"I guess," Neci said, then asked, "What about your boyfriend? He's here, too, right? In this same jail?"

Candace wondered how far away Rilla was physically. "He's here," she said, "but I don't think about him. I'm not thinking about him. I'm never going to feel the same way about him."

"Even if both of y'all get out?"

"I'll never get back with him," Candace clarified. There was a break in the conversation, so she asked, "So why would they arrest you for *cashing checks*?"

Neci laughed. She explained how she not only cashed checks, but she wrote the checks herself with a fictitious bank, fictitious account number, and fictitious signee.

"You can do anything with a computer," Neci said.

"I'll say," Candace said.

∽

Neci did not come out of the closet that night or even bring up the possibility of gay women on their unit. Candace certainly didn't bring it up herself.

∽

An hour before breakfast Candace was awakened from a horrible dream. She sat up in her bunk not sure where she was for a second. It was odd waking up at night with so many lights on, *if it was still night*. There was no way of telling time in there. Candace was sweating, and her heart raced. The dream slipped from her consciousness quickly, and she was glad she couldn't remember it. She knew it was something bad, and her baby was involved in some way.

The noise that woke her up was still going on, even more loudly now.

"Get off—"

"Shut up!"

Whap!

"Sto—"

Whap! Whap!

"Bitch!"

"Ooh, they fighting!" Neci said. She hopped out of bed and rushed to the bars. She strained her neck in all directions. "Damn, I can't see them." Neci usually wore long shorts and a wifebeater to sleep. From behind, she looked like a full-grown man standing at the door.

"Who's fighting?" Candace asked.

"I think it's some Mexicans," Neci said. "I can't see them though. They're right next to us. Somebody getting they ass whooped."

The ruckus went on for a few minutes more before three guards charged the unit.

"Get off her! *Get off!*"

One of them had a radio. "I need cell four opened!"

Another had pepper spray on the ready. "Get off her or I'm spraying the whole cell! Get off her! Both of you lay flat on the floor!"

Candace was out of bed now, and she saw that all of the women on her unit were awake. Two pairs of eyes stared out of each cell. They might sleep through a meal, but no one missed the fights.

The guards got the door open and charged the cell like linebackers. They pulled out a wild-haired black girl and a bloodied Hispanic woman. Both women looked slightly deranged to Candace, but the Latin girl was worse for wear. Not only was she crying and bleeding, but she couldn't even tell the guards what happened; neither of them spoke Spanish.

"She was messing with *me*!" the black girl insisted, but everyone knew she was the aggressor. One of the guards wrenched her arm behind her back and led her off the unit with a tight grip on her hair. The Hispanic lady was led away, too, but without all the roughness.

"See, that's why you should stay in a cell with your own people," Neci said, but Candace didn't think that was right.

The days Candace spent in jail crept by one lowly minute at a time. She eventually got into a routine she could live with, but the time never flew by like she thought it would. There were a lot of things to complain about: the smells, the cold, the food, and the company, but Candace found that sheer boredom was the worst incarceration had to offer.

You could watch TV for a while, play with home-made cards and dominoes, and read every book on the cart, but sooner or later you were going to be locked in your cell. You got locked down for eight hours at night. After breakfast you were locked down another five hours until lunch.

With all of the time spent in your cell, you had no choice but to develop an emotionally intimate bond with your cell mate. Candace and Neci talked about everything imaginable. By the time Candace got out, she knew about every one of her friend's stays in jail, arrests, and traffic stops. Sometimes Neci would get animated in the retelling of her stories. She would stand up and act it out, and Candace would rest her head on the heels of her hands and watch from her bunk.

Neci was fun to be around. Sometimes in the wee hours of the morning, she would have to put the brakes on herself.

". . . Man, that was wild. But I better quit talking. I know my cellie don't get no sleep."

"I'm all right," Candace would say. "I get most of my sleep after breakfast."

⌒

The *freedom* they got after lunch and dinner was the best part of the day. You could associate with everyone then, a much-needed change after so much time with your cell mate's smells. There were two women on the unit who only spoke Spanish. The powers that be had them in separate cells, and they sought each other like sisters during mealtimes.

The only problem with this freedom was the catty squabbles women cramped in such close quarters were bound to have. Candace didn't make a lot of friends, and rumors were flying about her showers and her pudgy belly. She told them she wasn't pregnant, but no one wanted to leave it at that. Did she miscarry? Did she have a crack baby? Did CPS have her baby? Why does she take so many showers? Did she have the baby in the shower?

"They ask me about it all the time," Neci told her once. "I told them you didn't have a baby, but these bitches is nosey."

Candace only half believed her cell mate. Why would the other women know specifics, like the CPS involvement, unless Neci planted the suspicion?

Another issue Candace found harder and harder to contend with was the availability of outside contact. There were four pay phones mounted on the wall near the guard station. These phones did not take money. When you picked up the receiver an automated voice instructed you on how to place your collect call. The only call Candace knew to make was to her parents, but she refused to make that call from jail. Every time she called them her situation was worse.

So Candace watched the others. They talked to their lawyers and mothers and brothers. Mostly they talked to their husbands and boyfriends. Some of the roughest women you'd ever want to meet stood there with their back to the wall, one leg propped up. They would smile and gaze out into nothingness and twirl a finger in their hair like they were in high school.

Days turned into weeks.

After two of them, Neci dragged Candace into their cell for a little heart-to-heart. She directed Candace to sit on her bed, which was generally taboo. Neci sat down right next to her, which was equally uncomfortable.

"You still not ready to call your parents?"

"It hasn't been a month."

"What you're doing is stupid, Candace. You need to call them. They can get you a lawyer. If it happened like you say it did, you can probably beat it."

"I'm not calling them from here."

"You need to let go of that pride."

"It's not pride." Candace shook her head. "I'm not proud of anything I did."

"Whatever it is, it's *stupid.* You know they can help you."

"Neci, I'm going to get out. They're trying to put a case together, and when they do, it's going to fall apart."

"And you're just going sit in jail—like you don't care?"

"I do care. I hate it here, you know that."

"But you not taking it seriously." Neci's face was distorted in frustration.

"Neci, I'm going to get out. I still have two weeks. Isn't that what we agreed on?"

"You're waiting for the police to prove you innocent! That's not what they do. You got the stupidest plan in here, Candace. You need to quit acting like a baby."

Neci got up and marched into the dayroom.

∽

But stupid or not, it was Candace's life and her story to play out. And Neci didn't think it was so stupid when Candace got a visitor a few days later. As the guard led her out of the unit, Candace expected her court-appointed attorney or possibly even Trisha. But she wasn't surprised to see Detective Judkins waiting for her in an interrogation room. She sat across from him with her hands cuffed behind her back.

"How you doing, Candace?" he asked.

"I never sold drugs to anyone," she said.

"I know," he said, and Candace felt like she would float right out of her seat. "If you're willing to testify against Raul, I'll drop the charges against you."

"When can I get out?"

"In about two hours."

Again Candace swooned. "Where's my baby?"

"That's not my deal," the detective said. "I can give you the number to CPS, but you have to go through them to get your baby. I just want to put Raul in prison."

"But you're going to tell them I didn't do anything so they'll give her back, right?"

"I'll tell them we dropped the charges against you, Candace, but they know about the drugs we found in your apartment. I don't know what process you have to go through to get your baby back."

"All right," Candace said. She hadn't shed a tear since the first time she saw this drug-fighting cowboy, but she cried like a baby in that interrogation room.

It was a good cry.

⌒

Candace walked out of the front doors of the Overbrook Meadows County Jail at 9:34 on a bright Wednesday morning.

CHAPTER 11
FAMILY MATTERS

Candace stepped out into the bright sunlight wearing a shirt with two and a half weeks worth of funk and a pair of jeans that were visibly filthy. It was mid-June now, seasonably temperate in great cities like New York, but June in Texas is like something out of a hellish nightmare. Beads of sweat formed on her forehead within seconds. She couldn't wait to get under an air conditioner.

But that was the thing; Candace didn't think she had anywhere to go to. The last time she saw her apartment, it was filled with cops, and the front door was smashed in. The manager would have fixed it, but she might not let Candace back in. Especially if the police told her Candace was a big-time dope dealer.

There was an easy way to get answers to these questions. When she got arrested, the police let Candace grab her purse. They gave it back to her when she left jail, and it still contained the fifty dollars she had left over from pawning her valuables. This was all she had to her name. Candace was in a hurry to get home, but she knew a cab ride would take half that loot.

She spotted a bus stop across the street and headed that way.

❧

The Overbrook Meadows County Jail is located in the downtown area of the big city. This was extremely beneficial for Candace because the public transit system had a central hub downtown. She sat at a random bus stop and the number two pulled up after only ten minutes. The doors swung open, and she was very happy to see a man in uniform who couldn't tell her what to do.

"Where is this bus going?" she asked.

"I go to the Meadowbrook, Handley area."

"I need to get to Eastwood."

"You're going to want the number, uh, five," he said. He was a chubby guy. He reminded Candace of Comic View comedian Bruce Bruce. "You can catch that at the transit center."

"Where's the transit center?"

"It's on Eighth Street. The number five goes by every thirty minutes. Come on. That's where I'm headed."

Candace hopped on the bus with a big grin. She thanked the driver for the information and took a seat directly behind him. The bus took off, and she stared out of the huge side windows like a kid on vacation. She couldn't keep a smile off her face. Six months ago she would have scoffed at the idea of riding the *city bus*, but two weeks in jail changed all of that. She would ride in the back of a manure truck to get away from that place.

Jail had her feeling like she was on the *Amistad*. *Goddammit! Give us free!*

~2~

She arrived at the transit center five minutes after boarding the number two. She found the bus stop for the number five, and it was already there. Commuters were boarding, and some of them didn't look too much better than Candace. She wondered if they just got out of jail, too.

Everything was going so smoothly, Candace forgot she gave the first driver her last bit of change. When she pulled out her smallest currency, a ten, the driver for the number five sneered at her.

"I ain't got no change." This one was a woman, but it would be hard to determine that from a distance. She sported an asexual jheri curl, wore Stevie Wonder shades, and had a good bit of stubble on her chinny-chin-chin.

"Does anybody have change?" Candace asked the strange faces on the bus. Everyone shook their head.

"Where can I get change?" she asked the driver.

"There's a store in the station."

"Are you going to be here for a minute?"

"For a *minute*," the woman confirmed, but when Candace got back with the finances, the number five was gone. All of the busses were gone.

That was cool. She went back inside to get more quarters for the pay phone. If she had to sit there thirty minutes, she might as well do something constructive with her time.

Her mother answered after two rings.

"Hello?"

"Hey, Mama. It's me."

"*Candace?*"

"Yeah, Mama. How you doing?"

"My God! Oh, baby! Please don't hang up the phone."

"I'm not going to hang up, Mama. I'm not doing that anymore. That's why I called. I want to apologize for the way things have been going."

"*No!* No—baby, you don't have to apologize for anything. Oh, I can't *believe it. I can't believe it's you.* I answered this phone a million times hoping to hear your voice. Baby, where are you? Please come home."

"I can't come home right now."

"*Baby, please.*"

"Mama, don't do that. You're going to make me cry."

"We miss you so much. Everybody does. Gerald, too."

"I know, Mama. But listen: I can't come home right now, but I want it to be different between us. I miss you, Mama. I miss not talking to you."

"*Oh, baby.*"

"I was wrong, Mama. I thought I didn't need you, but I did. I do. I'm not going this long without talking to you anymore."

"Let me come get you."

"I can't come home right now. Mama, please respect that."

"Okay, Candace. Okay. Anything. Tell me what you want me to do."

Candace closed her eyes and smiled. A lone tear fell from her eye. "I don't need you to do anything, Mama. I just want you to know that it's not going to be like it was before. I can't come home, but I still want you and Dad in my life. I'm going to call more. Every week, if you want."

"*Why* can't you come home?"

Because I have to stay in town so I'll be available when my boyfriend goes to court. They want to give him some time in prison, and I might have to testify against him. I'd be the star witness. Detective Judkins said he'll put me back in jail if I skip out on him. Oh, yeah. Didn't I tell you I was in jail? Plus I don't have my baby back yet, Mama. I can't leave without her, and I haven't even talked to CPS to see what they want me to do.

"I just can't," Candace said.

"You're going to call, Candace? *Really?* Promise me you're going to call."

"Mama, I'm going to call. I promise."

"When?"

"Whenever you want me to. How often do you want me to call?"

"*Every day*, Candace. I worry about you *every single day.*"

"I can't call every day," Candace said. "But I can call once a week for sure. Maybe twice."

"*Twice.* Twice would be better."

"Where's Dad?"

"He went to get his oil changed. He's going to hate that he missed you. Can you call back later so he can talk to you? He's sorry about what happened last time. He talks about it every day."

"I'm sorry too," Candace said. "I shouldn't have hung up. He was right."

"No, no, he didn't have to talk to you like that."

"Mama, it's all right. I'm different now. He was right and I knew it. I just didn't want to hear it."

"So this boy you're living with, is he out of jail, or what happened with that?"

"No, he's not out of jail yet. I don't think he's getting out."

"So you're down there all by yourself? Baby, you should come home. You're going to have that baby, and you'll need help."

"I don't need help, Mama. I already had the baby. We're fine."

"*You had the baby?*"

"Yes."

"When?"

"On the thirtieth."

"*Candace!* That was two weeks ago! Why didn't you call?"

"I wasn't ready yet. I'm sorry."

"Oh, my. Baby, we should have been there for you. Is the baby healthy? Are you all right? You need to come home, Candace. Cut out this foolishness."

"Mama. I can't. Come home. Right now. If you can't respect that, I won't be able to call you every week." She hated putting this ultimatum on her mother, but could think of no other way to do it.

"No, Candace. It's fine. However you want to do it. Just, don't stop calling."

"We're all right, Mama. Don't worry so much."

"Are we never going to get to see the baby? Not that I'm asking you to come home, I'm just asking if we can see you guys. We miss you, Candace. Please don't get mad."

"I miss you, too," Candace said. "And I'm not mad, I just, I just messed up pretty bad down here. I know I can run back home, but I don't want to do that. I want to get myself straight. I want to see you guys, but I can't. Probably not for a few months. Is it all right if I just call until then?"

"Are you in trouble, Candace? Tell me the truth."

All right, Dad. I won't go to Rilla's concert. I promise.

"I'm fine, Mom. There's nothing at all to worry about."

"The baby," Mrs. Hendricks said. "Tell me about my grandbaby. Is it a boy or a girl?"

"It's a girl. And she's beautiful." Candace's eyes glossed over. "She's the most beautiful thing I've ever seen in my life."

She spoke with her mother for another ten minutes and made it back to her bus stop five minutes early.

∽

Back at her apartments Candace found everything the same, but everything was still different. The first problem was the absence of her car. She always parked in the same spot, and there weren't a lot of vehicles to sort through at twelve o'clock in the afternoon. There was

141

only one car parked in front of Candace's building, and it wasn't her Nissan Sentra.

She marched up the stairs knowing what she would find, but was still not prepared for her landlord's tactics. Her front door was fixed. Candace got closer and realized this one was brand new. The fresh paint had no scars or chips that she could see.

But there was something wrong with the new door. Rather than change the locks, the apartment manager affixed a device Candace had never seen before. It was like a metal doorknob *glove*. It fit perfectly and had a small keyhole Candace didn't have access to. She wrestled with the fixture, but it turned loosely in her hand, providing no traction on the actual doorknob.

Great, she thought and headed across the street. More than half of the residents at the neighboring apartments were at work this time of day, but Candace knew of at least one person who would be home. Trisha's door was open, so she walked right in.

"Hey," she called. Her friend's apartment was eerily quiet. There wasn't even a television on. Candace rounded the corner and found Trisha stretched out on her couch, fast asleep. Willie Jr. lay on top of her, nestled between her soft bosoms. Little Sammy dozed on the loveseat. Petey was nowhere to be found. Candace hoped he was napping in one of the back rooms and not exploring the apartment grounds.

She stood in the living room and grinned at the snoozing family. It felt good to be around normal people for a change.

"Must be nice," she said.

Trisha stirred from her sleep only moderately. "What you talking about?" she asked, her eyes still closed.

"I say it must be nice to be able to chill at home all day."

"You lazy, too. You don't do nothing but take a couple classes," Trisha mumbled, and then lifted her head from the cushions. She squinted at Candace and sat up quickly, almost sending Willie Jr. crashing to the floor.

"*Girl, where the hell you been?* I heard they took you to jail!"

"I have been in jail," Candace said. "Two weeks and three days. I just got out."

"No shit? *Damn, girl.* I can't believe they arrested you. That's messed up. You never did nothing to nobody." Trisha stood and bounced anxiously. "Gimme a hug, Candace. You all right? Nobody hurt you?"

"No. Nobody hurt me." Candace stepped between the big woman's arms and felt good in the embrace. She couldn't remember the last time a female wanted to hug her.

Trisha backed away with her nose twisted. "You need to take a shower."

"I know. I don't need you to tell me how bad I smell."

"Why they arrest you?" Trisha asked.

"Somebody said I was a drug dealer."

Trisha's face went slack. "Who said that?"

"I don't know. They never told me. But whoever it was said they bought drugs from me and everything."

"That's crazy."

143

"Who are you telling? I think I know who it was."

Trisha stepped in closer. "Who?"

"I can't tell you, Trish. You'll tell everybody."

Trisha stomped her foot. "C'mon, Candace, I won't tell nobody!"

"I'll tell you later."

"Uhn-uhn. Tell me now."

Candace hated herself for bringing it up. "CC."

Trisha threw a hand over her mouth. Her eyes were as big as silver dollars.

"That's just what I *think*," Candace said. "Don't tell anybody. If he finds out he'll start tripping."

"Why would he do that?"

"There's something up with him. For real."

"They said it was drugs up there," Trisha said.

"Yeah. Rilla had a duffle bag in the closet."

"The cops found it?"

"I told them where it was. I thought they'd leave me alone once they got it. I was so scared. I'd never been that scared in my whole life."

"Why would they believe CC over you?"

"I got an idea."

"Like what—" Trisha stepped back and stared at Candace again. Her jaw dropped. "Bitch, where's your baby?"

"I had her already." Candace giggled. "She's beautiful. You should see her."

"When did you have her? Not in jail."

"Right before. My water broke when I was up there with the cops."

"Where is she?" Trisha asked, but Candace's whole demeanor changed with that question.

"I don't know," she said. "The police said I have to call CPS to get her back."

Trisha looked like a doleful grandmother. "You'll get her back. You a good girl."

"I know."

"For real. Once they find out what kind of person—"

"I know," Candace said. She looked her friend in the eyes. "I'm getting my baby back."

Trisha wisely changed the subject. "Girl, they tore your apartment *up*. The manager was mad as hell. It was—*ooh*, you really do stink, Candace!"

"Uh, *yeah*. I've been wearing the same thing for two weeks."

"Why you didn't take a shower before you came over here?" Trisha asked with a hand over her face.

"I can't get in my apartment," Candace said. "They've got this thing on the doorknob."

"A metal cover?"

"Yeah."

"The manager put that on."

"They can't do that. The rent's not due yet."

"She must wanna talk to you before she let you back in."

"I don't want to talk to her."

"Well, if you want your stuff, you're going to have to. Girl, you look *bad*."

"Thanks," Candace said. "Listen, I don't want to trouble you too much, but do you think I could take a shower over here? And I don't have any clean clothes to put on, either. They're all in my apartment."

"Candace, you know you can take a shower here. I don't know about the clothes, though. You can't fit nothing I wear."

"I can wear the same pants till I get in my apartment if you have another shirt."

"No, Candace. You cannot wear those pants till *anything*. I'm surprised they not making you itch. I think I have some warm-ups in there. They big, but you can tie the string."

"That's perfect," Candace said. "You're a lifesaver, Trisha. I really appreciate it."

"Girl, I'd do anything to get you out of those clothes. You're going to have to throw them away, you know. That smell never comes out."

∽

Candace's shower was like an Herbal Essences commercial; she actually moaned aloud a couple of times. The water was hot, the steam was soothing, and no one at all could see her. It was funny, the things you appreciate after a couple weeks in jail.

CHAPTER 12
A DOLLAR AND A DREAM

Candace dressed in the sweatpants and T-shirt Trisha provided for her. The shirt was pretty close to her size. She combed and styled her hair with real-live cosmetics for the first time in half a month and stepped out of the bathroom looking like her former self. She found Trisha in the kitchen making another Hamburger Helper meal.

"Do you have any shoes?" Candace asked her.

Trisha turned and grinned at her. "You look good! Bet it feels good to have some clean clothes on."

"It does," Candace agreed. "Except these." She held up her badly soiled Keds.

"*Ewww.* I can't believe you're touching those. You need to throw them away, Candace. And wash your hands."

"These are the only shoes I have until I get in my apartment. I need to get my cell phone out of there."

"You going to talk to the manager?"

"Yeah."

"What size are those?"

"Seven," Candace said.

Trisha shook her head. "I wear a nine."

"Let me try them."

Trisha looked over her friend's outfit. Candace wore a plain blue T-shirt with the gray jogging pants.

"I got some white tennis in there, but they're too big, you'll see."

"It's better than nothing," Candace said. "Do you have any socks? I feel helpless, asking you for so much stuff."

"Don't trip, girl. I know how it goes sometimes. You can stay here for a while if they won't let you in your apartment."

For the second time, Candace was taken aback by her friend's generosity. "For real?"

"Why you looking so shocked? You act like nobody ever helped you out before."

"I don't think I ever needed help before," Candace admitted.

"Well, I got three bedrooms. Willie sleeps in there with me. Petey and Sammy don't need a room all to theyself."

"How can you afford a three-bedroom apartment?" Candace asked, but she already knew.

"Section 8, baby. I pay thirty dollars a month."

⌒

Candace clomped down the stairs in the too-big shoes, but at least she was clean. She smelled good and felt good. And she thought she looked pretty good, too. Now that she was out of jail, she could work on losing her baby weight. She tried while she was locked up, but you're in bed more than half the day in there.

The manager's office was at the very front of the complex. Candace cut through the buildings and was wiping sweat from her forehead by the time she got there. Why anyone would chose to live in such a sweltering city was beyond her. Temperatures like this belonged on oven dials.

She walked into the leasing office and was immediately hit with currents from a high-powered air conditioner, but the cool reception didn't last long. Candace walked up to the first desk she saw and greeted the woman sitting behind it.

"Hi. Can I speak with the manager?"

"I'm the manager," the woman said. She was a redhead with a fat nose and flabby jowls. She wore a black blouse with white pearls.

"Hi. I'm Candace. I tried to get into my apartment today, and there's this thing on the doorknob. I can't open it."

"That's because you didn't pay your rent," the manager said. She began to shuffle through a pile of files on her desk.

"I did pay my rent."

The woman gave her an angry look. "What apartment are you in?"

Candace almost didn't want to say. "Apartment 3216."

The lady's eyes narrowed. "You the one with the drug bust? You're with Canales?"

"Yes," Candace said. "But I didn't sell any drugs. I—"

"Your door's locked because the police broke it down and I had to replace it." The woman stuck a pudgy finger in Candace's face. "You can't go back in there until you pay me for my door. And you have to be out of here by the first."

"Why do I have to be out by the first?"

"Because we don't rent to drug dealers."

"I told you: I'm *not* a drug dealer."

"Why are you just now coming to see about this?"

"What?"

"Why haven't you come to see me before? That locks been on your door since the first."

Candace lowered her head. "I was in jail."

"Mmm-hmm."

She met her eyes then. "But I didn't do anything. They let me go."

"Listen, I don't care about that. If you beat your case or whatever happened with you and the police, that's your problem. All I can tell you is Forest Crest Apartments does not lease to drug dealers."

"I'm—"

"And we don't rent to people who get their doors kicked in, either."

"Fine," Candace said. "Can I at least get some stuff out of there?"

"No. That lock stays on until you pay for the door."

"I just want my cell phone."

"Then pay for the door!"

Candace huffed and puffed but couldn't blow this bitch down. "Whatever. How much is the door?" After the bus ride and the call home, Candace had forty-two dollars and seventy-five cents left.

"Five hundred and eighty-four dollars—"

"*Five hundred?*"

"*And* eighty-four dollars and sixty-five cents. But if you get five eighty-four, I'll let you go with the change."

"All right," Candace pouted. "So where's my car?"

"I don't know. We don't have anything to do with your car."

"Well, it's not where I left it."

"Maybe it's stolen."

Maybe it's stolen? Candace wanted to slap the smug sense of satisfaction off her face.

"Who would have stolen it?"

"Have you called the police?" the lady asked, and that didn't seem like such a bad idea.

"No. I haven't. May I use your phone?"

"You can use the one in the lobby."

"Do you have a phone book?"

The manager rolled her eyes, but she produced the directory. Candace took it to the foyer and found the number for the local law enforcement. Butterflies danced in her stomach when the police told her they did have her car. And it wasn't stolen. Detective Judkins towed it downtown to search it for drugs, but they were done with it now. Candace got directions and called a cab rather than wait for a bus this time. She knew she could get some money when she got her car back.

Her Nissan was at one of the police substations close to her apartment rather than at the actual jail. There was no charge for picking up her vehicle. They rolled the car out to her with no muss and no fuss, and Candace was as happy as the day Rilla bought it for her. She got behind the wheel and knew everything was finally coming together. There was even half a tank of gas.

Instead of heading home, Candace drove to the south side of town and found the tire shop where Rilla purchased her flashy rims. She watched him pay $1,900 for the wheels less than a year ago, but the owner of the shop only offered Candace $1,000 to buy them back. She agreed to it, under the condition he put four normal wheels on in place of the rims. The grateful shopkeeper took normal to mean *ugly*, but Candace was in a rush to get back so she didn't haggle.

She took her ten crisp $100 bills and hit the streets a new lady.

Who said I can't do it on my own? I'm going to show them.

When she got back to the apartments, Candace parked in front of the leasing office and sauntered in like a woman with money in her purse. She stomped up to the manager and dropped six greenbacks on her desk.

"Can you open my apartment now, please?"

The woman's eyes lit up. "Um, we don't accept cash."

But Candace saw the drool. "Lady, you're making me pay for a door I didn't even break. And you're kicking me out for something I didn't do. I've had a real long day. I'm not leaving to get you a money order. Either take the money or you can keep the apartment. I don't care anymore."

The landlord scooped the bills up like it was a dice game. "You still have to be out by the first."

"You still owe me sixteen dollars," Candace said and smiled. It felt good to be in control.

ᔋ

We can run through here and tear everything up like you see on TV.

Or you can be a good girl and tell me where Rilla's drugs are.

"Why'd he even ask if he was going to do this anyway?" Candace spoke aloud as she surveyed the tragedy that once was her apartment. Detective Judkins seemed friendly enough, but it was clear he never believed a word Candace had to say. They didn't break every electronic, but every nook and cranny had clearly been explored, and turned upside down, and thrown on the floor, and stepped on.

Her couch was dismantled. The cushions weren't shredded, but they were all unzipped and vacated of their contents. Candace stepped into her living room and looked around in dismay. She moaned when she peered into the kitchen. All of her cupboards were open and most of their contents were strewn about on the floor.

Candace shook her head in awe and walked through every room with a hand over her mouth. It would take her days to get things back like it was. The more she saw, the more eager she was to get started, but there was something more important she had to do first.

Candace dug through her purse and found the card Detective Judkins gave her at the jail. It was a business card for a woman named Gabriella Sands. She was a caseworker for Child Protective Services, the woman Candace had to speak with to get her baby back.

Candace went back to the kitchen bar where their home phone normally sat, but it was missing. She found it on the floor, but she couldn't use it because someone yanked the cord from wall. Colorful wires jutted from the jack.

Why would they do this, she wondered, but Candace would ask that question many times while she cleaned up.

A hole in the microwave door.

Why?

Pine-Sol and Comet dumped on the bathroom floor.

Why?

A big hole punched or *kicked* in one of the bedroom walls.

Why would they do any of this?

Police are evil people, Candace told herself, but deep down she knew that wasn't true.

The only house phone was out of commission, so Candace went back to the living room to look for her cellular. Or was it in the bedroom? It was hard to guess, but she knew she'd find it somewhere in the mess.

The work looked overwhelming, but there was no way around it. Candace shook her head and sighed. She grabbed two trash bags and got down on her knees to begin the exhaustive task. It was already after two. She had to find her phone within the next three hours if she wanted to catch the caseworker in the office.

By 2:30, she was pretty sure the phone wasn't in the living room.

At 3:15, she was done in the front room but still hadn't found her phone.

At 3:30 she had to stop work in the bedroom to answer the front door. It was Trisha.

"Hey," Candace said, wiping her forehead with the back of her arm.

"Damn, girl. What the hell you doing in here?"

"I'm cleaning up. The police threw stuff everywhere. Look at this floor." She stepped aside to let her see.

"What's that?" Trisha asked.

"That's Comet. They tracked it all the way in here from the bathroom."

"Why you didn't tell me you were back? I didn't know if you got in here or not."

"I'm sorry," Candace said. "I've been so busy. I sold the rims off my car to get the money for the landlord, and now I'm looking for my cell phone. They broke my house phone."

Trisha came in and did a quick 360. "Damn, girl. They went crazy in here. You should've came and got me. I got a phone cord you can use."

"I thought you didn't have a phone."

"I don't have phone *service*, but I got a phone. Who don't have a phone in they house? Girl, you're gonna have to learn how to ask for help."

"I didn't think anyone would want to help."

"I'ma go get that cord," Trisha said. "I'll see if Miss Flora can watch the boys. Put some music on. You can't clean up without music."

Candace smiled and let out a grateful sigh of relief when she was gone.

$$\backsim\!\!\!-$$

When Trisha came back with · the cord, Candace's apartment was rocking to the tunes of Kanye West.

"Where you want me to get started?" Trisha asked.

"Take your pick," Candace said. "I'ma go call that CPS lady right quick, all right?"

"Go ahead."

Candace took the house phone to her bedroom so she could make the call in private. As badly as she wanted Leila back, this was a call she dreaded. She knew she would have to explain her whole life to a stranger who already had negative thoughts about her.

She plugged in the new cord, and sat on the side of the bed nibbling her thumbnail. She wondered what she should tell them. Her fingers trembled as she dialed the number. Inwardly she hoped to get a voice mail, but someone answered halfway through the second ring.

"Hi, this is Gabriella."

"Hi," Candace said. "This is . . . Gabriella Sands?"

"Yes. Speaking."

"Uh, hello. Hi. My name is Candace. Candace Hendricks. I got your number, I mean your card, from the police. I had a baby while I was in jail. I mean, I was

156

going to jail. I just got arrested." Candace sighed. "I'm sorry. I'm nervous."

"It's okay," Gabriella said. "Did you say you had a baby?"

"Yes. I got arrested two weeks ago. I didn't do anything, though. They let me go today. When, when I got arrested I had my baby. They said I have to talk to you about getting her back." Candace took the phone away from her face and exhaled loudly. She felt like a fool. Her palms were slick.

"What did you say your name was?"

"Candace Hendricks. My baby's name is Leila. Leila Denise Hendricks."

"Hold on for a second."

Candace waited and listened to fast typing. She knew what was coming. The woman was going to tell her that she couldn't have her baby back. Leila had been adopted by a well-to-do family, and she was better off where she was. If Candace wanted her baby back, she should have retrieved her within the first forty-eight hours. After that, Leila became a ward of the state.

"I do have your file here, Miss Hendricks."

Candace held her breath.

"It looks like you delivered on the thirtieth and went to jail on the second."

"That's right. Where's my baby?"

"She's fine. She's been placed in foster care."

"What does that mean?"

"That means a foster family is looking after her. She lives with them."

"Where? Can I go get her?"

"You want to—no. *No*, Candace. You can't just *go get your baby*. It doesn't work like that."

"When can I get her?"

"Well, Candace, this is the first time I've talked to you. You're going to have to come down here and fill out some paperwork. I have to meet with you."

"But when can I get my baby?"

"It's not going to be an overnight thing. You understand that, right?"

"No," Candace said. She lowered her head and rubbed her face with her free hand. She felt tears welling in the corner of her eyes, but they weren't going to fall. She wasn't a crybaby anymore. That part of her life was over. Whatever she needed to do, she would do it as a woman.

"CPS does not want to keep your child," Gabriella said. "We believe that the best place for any child is with his mother or father or both."

Candace was glad to hear that. She exhaled hot fumes from her nostrils.

"Is this your first child?"

"Yes," Candace said.

"Well, this is your first experience with CPS, and I'm sure you have a lot of questions. Would you like to set up an appointment so we can meet? I can explain the process to you."

"I just want to know when I can have my baby back. I didn't do anything wrong."

"There's no set schedule on that," Gabriella said. "All I know about you is what I read in your police report."

"I'm not a drug dealer. I already cleared that up. It was a mistake."

"Well, obviously that's something we're not going to take your word for. We have a process, Candace. It takes time."

"Well, can I at least see her?"

"Yes. She's your baby. I can arrange for visitations with the foster family."

"When?"

"Candace, listen. You're going to have to slow down. Before you get anywhere near your daughter, you're going to have to meet with me. The very soonest you'll be able to see your daughter is, hmmm, let's see, today's Wednesday . . . Monday's the absolute soonest."

Candace felt like she got punched in the stomach.

"Why don't you come see me tomorrow," Gabriella offered.

Candace relented. She got directions to the CPS office and scheduled an appointment for the very next morning. When she got back in the living room, Trisha read her expression and didn't ask too many questions.

"Is it gonna be all right?"

"I have to meet with the caseworker tomorrow," Candace told her.

"It'll be all right," Trisha promised. "Once she meets you and sees what kind of person you are, you'll be fine. Most of them bitches going up there be smelling like smoke, tracks and shit on they arms. They got teeth missing."

Candace smiled halfheartedly.

"What you gon' tell Rilla about those rims?" Trisha asked.

"I don't have to tell him anything," Candace said. "He's not getting out after I testify against him." Trisha's mouth fell open, and Candace laughed. "Let's talk about it after we get done."

CHAPTER 13
CPS

Trisha found Candace's cell phone in the kitchen sink, of all places. She plugged it into the charger, and they took a break from cleaning at 7:00 p.m. The mess wasn't as bad as it looked. Trisha restocked all of the groceries that weren't damaged, and Candace got all of the clothes picked up in the bedroom. The bathroom turned out to be the worst, but Candace got it spic-and-span in only thirty minutes. She ordered a pizza and took the garbage out while they waited.

By the time food arrived, they were both exhausted. They lounged in the living room watching the tail end of Jim Carey in *The Mask*. That was an old movie, but still a good one.

"The police never said who the informant was?" Trisha asked.

"No. They didn't even say if it's a guy or a girl."

"You really think CC would do that?"

"He was mad, Trish. *Real mad*. He told me, '*Don't you ever say nothing about that baby being mine.*' And before he left, he said, '*I got something for you.*' I'll never forget the way he said it, like he knew he had me. The next thing I know, the police were banging on the door. I can't think of anybody else who would lie on me."

"Why would CC lie?"

"I think he hates me that much. He said he can't stand that I was with Rilla. You should have seen him, Trisha. I thought he was going to shoot me or something."

"You tripping."

"No. I'm not. I'm really scared of him."

"Are you going to tell Rilla?"

"I don't even want to talk to Rilla anymore. I hope he *never* gets out."

"You don't care about him at all now?"

Candace sighed. "I guess I do. But it's hard for me not to hate him, Trish. Everything that happened to me is his fault. Rilla knew he had responsibilities. He knew me and the baby depended on him. He could have got a regular job. I never asked him to do anything spectacular. But he wanted the quick money. You shouldn't do that when people are depending on you."

"So you're going to testify against him?"

"What choice do I have? I'm not going back to jail for his drugs."

"I don't know," Trisha said. "Some people might think that's kind of shady."

"What do *you* think?"

"I don't know."

"You wouldn't do it?"

"No, I wouldn't, but you gotta do what's right for you. I guess."

"Trisha, it's either him or me."

"I know."

"I would still be in jail if I didn't agree to testify."

"Yeah, you told me."

"I might have lost my baby."

Trisha nodded.

"But you still don't think I should do it?"

"Candace, I'm just saying I wouldn't do it. But you and me is different. You got dreams and shit you want to do. I'm just saying, me, I couldn't do it."

Candace frowned, wondering if she made the right decision. Trisha put a hand on her knee.

"Don't trip, girl. Most women would do what you did. It's only a small percentage that are *down-ass bitches* like me."

Candace grinned. "When I find the right man, I'll be a down-ass bitch, too. But if I have to go to jail for somebody, it had better be over some multi-million-dollar investment scam. The only way I'll do six months is if I got a couple million waiting in the bank."

Trisha laughed. "All right, Martha Stewart."

Candace laughed, too.

"So what are you going to do on the first?" Trisha asked.

"I don't know. If I don't have my baby by then, I'll have to stay here. I have to move, though."

"You got some place in mind?"

"The complex next door is pretty cheap."

"What about the rent?"

"I guess I have to get a job."

"You'd better hurry up," Trisha advised. "It usually takes three weeks to get your first check."

Candace frowned. She didn't like that timetable at all.

⌒

At nine o'clock Candace put a hand to her face for an extended yawn. Trisha caught the move and took the cue to leave. Candace thanked her for the help and was glad to be alone when she was gone. She couldn't wait to sleep in a house all by herself, another thing people take for granted unless they've been in jail.

She picked out an outfit for her meeting with the social worker tomorrow. She thought of Leila as she ironed, and that reminded her to call her parents back. It was already after ten in New York, but Candace knew they would still be awake. She made the call from her cell phone, knowing they couldn't trace it back to an address.

Her father answered after four rings. "Hello?" He sounded a little gruff.

"Hi, Dad. It's me, Candace. Did I wake you up?"

"No, I wasn't asleep. Your mom said you called earlier. I was waiting up for you. Honestly, I didn't think you'd call back."

"I know," Candace said. "I told Mom I was going to be different now. I'm going to call more often. You don't have to worry about that anymore."

"Yeah. She said you sounded more mature."

Candace grinned. "I had no choice but to grow up."

"Are you going to give us a number we can call back? We should be able to get in touch with you, too, Candace. There might be an emergency."

"I can give you this number," Candace said. "I always have my cell phone with me."

"Okay. I got a pen."

Candace rattled off the number. "I'd still rather call you," she said.

"All right. I won't call you unless your mother dies," her father kidded.

"No one's going to die."

"Probably not. But I hear there's a new life over on your end."

Candace grinned. "Yeah. I had my baby. Her name's Leila Denise."

"Hendricks, right?"

"Yeah, Dad. She's a Hendricks."

"Good. How's she doing?"

"She's fine. She eats a lot. Just like you." Candace frowned and chewed on her lower lip. It was always hard to lie to this man, but it was a little easier over the phone.

"Who does she look like, you or your mom?" Gerald asked.

Candace tried to remember. "I think she looks like *me*," she said.

"Then she must be beautiful."

"Thanks, Dad. She is."

"Your mom says you still don't want to see us."

"I do want to see you," Candace said. "I just want to work things out in my own life first."

"Where's that boy?"

"Raul? He's still in jail."

"Good. That's where he should be. You're living by yourself now?"

"I am."

"Why do you want to do that?"

"I have to learn how to take care of myself," Candace said. "I know I made some mistakes, and I'm going to have to live with them. I'm going to show you I can do well for myself."

"You don't have to show me anything."

"Well, I'm going to show myself. I need to know I can do it."

"And you're not in any trouble?"

"No, Dad. I'm fine."

"Do you have a job?"

"Not yet."

"How are you paying the bills?"

"I'm going to get a job this week."

"I'm going to send you some money."

"No, Dad. I don't—"

"Candace, I'm not taking no for an answer. You've got my grandbaby over there. You're going to need diapers and milk and clothes for her. You might not be able to find a job that pays for all of that."

"I'll be all right."

"Do you want me to come down there? I know what city you live in. Don't think I can't find you."

Candace's heart froze. "No. Don't do that."

"Then let me send you some money. A thousand dollars, just to get you by till you get a job."

"Alright," Candace said. *Just don't come to Texas. Please.*

She got a phone book and found a Western Union store he could wire the money to. *A thousand dollars.* She never thought her father would give up that kind of money. She figured it was the baby who loosened his bank account. With the matter settled, he asked about something that had been on his mind for months.

"So, how did you do in school?"

Candace beamed. "I did great. I'm pretty sure I made straight A's."

"How many classes did you take?"

"Five. Just like you said I should."

"You're still studying physical therapy, right?"

"Yes. Nothing's changed."

"Are these credits going to transfer up here, or do you plan to stay in Texas till you're done?"

"No, Dad. I'm coming back to New York. I'm just doing one more semester down here. Do you know how hot it is in Texas?"

He laughed, and that was something Candace hadn't heard from him in more than a year. They talked for another fifteen minutes, and then Candace spoke with her mom briefly before hanging up. She promised to call every Monday at 8:00 a.m. sharp.

When she hung up, Candace felt good about herself and about her chances.

❧

But ten hours later, she felt like a lost little girl again. The CPS people wanted to know *everything* about her.

167

Candace had had pap smears that were less intrusive. She sat across from Gabriella Sands wearing the only interview-type outfit she had in her closet: A green skirt that went to her knees and a long-sleeved white blouse with a green vest over it.

Candace wore her shoulder-length hair down in a flip. Her lip gloss glistened, her braces sparkled, and her eyes twinkled. She thought they would take one look at her and see she wasn't an unfit parent, but the caseworker kept asking questions Candace didn't have an answer to. Every time she opened her mouth, she felt more and more inept.

"So your boyfriend, Raul, you're saying he's the one who was selling drugs?"

"Yes, ma'am," Candace said. "But he's not my boyfriend anymore."

"But he sold drugs out of the apartment you live in now?"

"Every now and then. Mostly he took it with him."

"But there were still drugs there when the police came. That's why you got arrested, right?"

"Yes, ma'am."

The caseworker looked over her papers again. She was an attractive Spanish woman, about forty-five years old. She wore a blue blouse with gray slacks and gray pumps. She had long, curly hair, and was a little chubby, but not to the point where it looked bad. It was just the two of them in the office, but Candace felt like the whole world was judging her.

"So why didn't you throw the drugs out?"

"I thought Rilla, I mean, Raul, was going to get out. I didn't want him to get mad at me."

Gabriella nodded. "So, this apartment that got raided. You still live there now?"

"Yes."

"And this is the place you want to take the baby to?"

That questioned sounded loaded. "No. I'm going to move on the first."

"Where to?"

"Another apartment. Probably right next door."

The caseworker entered something in the computer. "Where are you working, Candace? I don't think we have that in our files yet."

"I don't have a job."

"Well, who's paying your bills?"

"I have some money. I'm going to get a job this week. Plus my parents give me money." She was glad she had that bit of truth to throw in there.

The woman sat back in her seat. "Have you made *any* plans for this baby? Do you have her room ready? A crib? Any provisions?"

"Not yet," Candace admitted. "I'm going to get that stuff."

"You don't think you should get these things before you get your baby?"

"No. I want her now."

"Why?"

" 'Cause she's mine." Candace's eyes watered up so she closed them and took a deep breath. When she opened them, the caseworker regarded her oddly.

" 'Cause she's mine and I want her at home with me," Candace said. "I don't want somebody else taking care of my baby."

"It's going to be all right," Gabriella said. "The family taking care of Leila is doing a great job."

"When can I see her?"

"You're going to get a visit tomorrow."

Candace beamed like she won the lottery. "Really?"

"Yes. It'll be supervised."

Candace nodded. "That's fine. How do I set it up?"

"This is the first meeting, so I'll make the arrangements," Gabriella said. "They'll bring the baby here. After that we'll set up a weekly visitation schedule, and you might be able to go to their house for the rest of the visits. It depends on what they're comfortable with."

Weekly schedule?

Candace's smile went away. "How long is all of this going to take?"

"Do you know what a Service Plan is?"

Candace shook her head.

"A Service Plan consists of the things CPS requires of you before you get your baby back. This is a plan I'm going to write up based on the information I have about your case. I haven't finalized anything yet, but I can tell you what your plan is going to include."

Candace waited.

"The first thing I need to do is make sure you aren't a drug dealer."

Candace didn't think that would be too hard.

"You say you're moving on the first, so I have to see your new place and make sure it meets our basic standards. You're going to need somewhere for the baby to sleep, clothes and food for her, and a car seat."

"I'll get all of that," Candace promised.

"There weren't any drugs in your system when you had your baby, so I don't think we need you in a treatment program. But I am going to require that you take a parenting class. These classes meet once a week for two months."

That sounded like an enormous amount of time, but Candace tried not to let it get her down. "Is that it?" she asked.

The woman studied her computer for a few seconds. "Yeah, Candace. I think that will be it. We're here to help you. I'm not going to put you through the ringer."

Candace smiled. Two months was a long time, but at least it was a number she could look at. "When can I start the class?"

The caseworker played with her computer. "The next one doesn't start until July 1. They have a class that meets in the morning, and the other is at night."

"I have school, so I need a night class."

"All right. I can enroll you. I'll have the information ready when I give you a copy of your Service Plan tomorrow."

"When that class is over," Candace asked, "on September 1, I can have my baby back?"

The caseworker smiled. "If everything else checks out, you could have your baby the very next day."

Candace couldn't have been happier. She reached to shake the older woman's hand. "Thank you, ma'am. I won't let you down. You'll see."

Gabriella was surprised. "Well, I don't usually get that type of response, but you're welcome, Candace. I wish the best for you. I'll call you later on today to let you know what time your visit is tomorrow."

"Okay," Candace said and stood to leave.

"You don't have any more questions?" the caseworker asked.

Candace shook her head. "No. I can't think of anything."

Gabriella opened one of the lower drawers on her desk. "Great. Can you do me one quick favor before you go?" She came up with a clear plastic cup with a lid on it. "If you don't mind . . ."

Candace took it and eyed the woman queerly. "I thought you said you didn't think I was on drugs."

"I know," Gabriella said and smiled. "But it never hurts to be sure. If you don't mind . . ."

Candace smiled back at her. "No, I don't mind at all."

CHAPTER 14
A FAMILIAR FACE

Candace left the CPS office in good spirits. She thought her caseworker was going to be some cruel, inconsolable, inconvincible witch, but Gabriella's terms were reasonable. Candace knew she would benefit from a parenting class, and she had a whole two months to get her new apartment ready for the baby. The only problem was the lies she would have to continue telling her parents, but she only had to do that until September. If everything worked out, they would be none the wiser.

On the way home, she stopped by a Kroger's a few miles from her home. She went to the service center, and, sure enough, her thousand dollars was waiting. The clerk counted out ten $100 bills, and Candace added them to the four she already had in her purse.

She felt rich. She sashayed out of the store like a diva and walked to a Frost Bank in the same shopping center. Even without her parents there to nag her, Candace knew not to walk around with that kind of money. She was a little worried about opening her first account, but the customer service there was exceptional. Ten minutes later she walked out with a checkbook, a debit card, and a chest full of confidence.

On the way out of the bank, Candace stopped at a newsstand and bought the daily *Star Telegram*. She never read the newspaper, and wasn't about to start now. She discarded everything but the Careers section. She went home and embarked on a search for her very first job.

⌒

At ten the next morning, Candace walked into her caseworker's office again. When she saw a white couple sitting across from Gabriella, Candace thought she was too early, but something about the baby they cradled was all too familiar.

Seeing Leila again was an intimidating experience. Candace fought for air like she was in the grip of an anaconda. She swayed indecisively in the doorway.

Today she wore a gray skirt with a long-sleeved white blouse. She hoped the outfit would impress her caseworker, but Candace was actually dressed for a job interview she had in a few hours. She never thought of being a waitress, but an ad for Pappadeaux restaurant caught her eye in yesterday's paper.

"Come on in, Candace," Gabriella said. "This is Mr. and Mrs. Whitley. They're the family taking care of Leila until we get things settled."

The man and woman smiled brightly. In her peripheral vision, Candace noticed the man was going bald and the woman was a brunette. She saw that Gabriella wore blue today. Candace thought the man might have stuck his hand out for her to shake, but these observations were all lost to her, as if in a fog.

From the moment she walked into the room, Candace couldn't take her eyes off the brown bundle of joy nestled in the woman's arms. Leila's eyes were closed. Her tiny nose twitched a little as she took in new smells. Her eyebrows were thin and barely visible against her walnut-colored skin. She was wrapped up tightly, like a papoose.

Candace's feet moved on their own. When she stopped, she stood before the woman holding her child. Mrs. Whitley was in her late forties. Her shoulder-length hair was straight, dark brown with streaks of gray throughout. She had a warm smile and nice teeth. Crow's feet added maturity, but not age, to her features.

"Hi. I'm Martha Whitley."

"Oh, I'm sorry. My name is Candace. That's my little girl. I haven't seen her for a while. She's so beautiful."

"She is," Martha agreed.

"And I'm Doug Whitley," her husband said.

"Hi."

"Would you like to hold her?" his wife asked.

Candace could barely respond. She reached with trembling hands. Her face felt hot. Her eyes filled, and tears flowed like oil.

"Oh, it's all right," Martha Whitley said. She stood with the baby cradled in one arm like a football. She looked so natural. Candace didn't think she would ever feel that comfortable with Leila. She reached for her baby, and the handoff was slow and clumsy.

175

"No, you have to—just hold your arm naturally," the older woman instructed. "Let her head rest, there, and you can support her bottom with your other hand. There. You got it."

Candace finally got her arms right, and Mrs. Whitley backed away. Candace wavered with the little girl in her arms, and then took a seat in the third chair Gabriella had in her office. She wiped the tears from her face and stared down at the life she created. Leila's face was so cute. Her scent was familiar. Her body was so tiny.

Candace looked up and saw that everyone was watching her. They all smiled eagerly. Candace wondered if she was expected to do something.

The caseworker introduced the Whitleys again, and she may have said what they did for a living, Candace wasn't sure. There was some talk about the family's foster care history, and Gabriella told them a little about Candace's case. Most of what was said never fully registered.

Candace had her baby back, and that was all that mattered. That was a feeling she could compare to nothing she'd ever experienced. She studied every line in her baby's face. She held her nose close to Leila's head and took in the scent of her hair. She kissed her so many times she was sure someone would say something, but no one did.

Candace wanted to unwrap the blankets so she could see Leila's whole body, but she didn't know if that was inappropriate. She definitely didn't want to drop her baby, so she kept her movements to a minimum.

But it was all over so soon.

A whole hour passed like five minutes, and Candace's first visitation came to an end. Leila never woke up, and Candace never got to see her daughter's eyes. She didn't think to take a picture with her cell phone.

And though Candace hadn't spoken much, not at all to her recollection, the Whitleys decided they liked this young girl from New York. The rest of her weekly visits could take place at their residence, and these would last up to three hours.

The hardest part of the encounter was giving the baby back, but Candace was prepared for this. She handed Leila over graciously, and didn't cry too much. Mrs. Whitley said it would get easier as time went by, but that turned out to be a goddamned lie.

After the foster family left, Candace got her Service Plan from Gabriella. Everything was typed up and official. Candace was appreciative, but she did not shake the caseworker's hand when she left this time. She was starting to see Gabriella and the office she represented as a source of pain, much like the other parents who had dealings with CPS.

Next on the agenda was a trip to Pappadeaux. Candace arrived thirty minutes early to her first job interview, and this greatly impressed the hiring manager, Jesse Fuentes. He was a tall man, wearing black slacks with a white shirt. Candace looked around the restaurant and saw that all of the staff sported this color scheme.

Pappadeaux was a huge establishment, not the hole in the wall Candace expected. It looked like they could seat hundreds. Jesse led her through the restaurant, walking and talking at the same time.

"Basically, you want to be friendly," he was saying. "You want them to like you the moment you start talking." He had a thick accent. It was exotic, and kind of sexy. He looked back at her and smiled. "But you're a pretty girl. You're not going to have a problem with that."

Candace cocked an eyebrow.

"I'm just being honest about the business," Jesse said. "Ugly waitresses don't get as much as pretty ones. That's just the way it is. No one wants some ugly person bringing their food."

Candace never thought she'd make money with her looks, but wasn't opposed to the idea.

Jesse walked into a door marked "Staff Only" and Candace followed, finding herself in the largest kitchen she'd ever seen.

"This is Candace, everybody," he said, still moving.

Most of the chefs looked up and waved. Candace waved back. "Hey."

Jesse exited the kitchen through a second door, still talking and pointing things out as he went. Back in the main restaurant, he zigged and zagged until they reached an area occupied by six people, all wearing black and white like he was.

"Hey guys, this is Candace. She's going to be our new addition to the B shift."

That was news to Candace.

"Hey," the bulk of them said.

"Hi, Candace," another offered.

They greeted her with the same perky smiles that generated their big tips.

Candace said, "Hi" to them, too, but she was a little less bubbly.

Jesse led her to an office and gave her a study menu. "The main thing you need to worry about at first is memorizing the menu. When someone asks you what's in the Pasta Mardi Gras, you have to be quick: '*Linguine tossed with crawfish, andouille sausage and crimini mushrooms in a marinara cream sauce topped with jumbo grilled shrimp.*'" He sounded like a radio commercial.

"You have to say it like it's the best-tasting thing in the world," he went on. "Which, in most cases, it is!"

Candace had to pump the brakes. "Wait. So, I got the job?"

"Yes, Candace. I didn't tell you that?"

"No."

"I'm sorry." He turned to face her. "I would like to hire you. Would you like to work for us?"

"Yes." She glowed like a china doll. "What's the B shift?"

"That's six to close. On weeknights we close at ten. We stay open till midnight on Friday and Saturday. Sunday we stay open till eleven."

"I can't work Thursdays," Candace said, remembering her parenting classes.

"Okay. Are there any other days you can't work?"

"No. Just Thursdays. How much does this pay?"

"We pay two-fifty an hour."

Candace's face fell. "That's not even minimum wage."

Jesse laughed. "You've never worked as a waitress, have you?"

"This is my first job ever."

"Well, congratulations! You couldn't have picked a better place to work. All waitresses, all over the country, get paid two-something an hour. Your real pay comes from your tips. You'll make at least two-fifty on a Saturday night."

Candace tried to keep her eyes from bugging. "That's fine."

"Great!" Jesse handed her the study menu. "Get started learning your appetizers and I'll pair you up with someone on your first day. Is Monday okay with you?"

Candace couldn't believe her fortunes. "Monday's fine."

"Okay," Jesse said. He stuck out a soft hand for her to shake. "Be here at . . ." He paused to see if she had the answer.

"Six o'clock." Candace said.

"No, it's a trick question. Be here at five because you're training." He smiled and Candace smiled back at him.

⌣

She left the restaurant with her head in the clouds. When she got back to the car, she looked over the paperwork her caseworker gave her. Her Service Plan was self-explanatory. Candace had only five requirements for getting her daughter back.

- Complete parenting class from July 1 through September 1.
- Attain gainful employment.
- Obtain a place of residence and provide sleeping quarters, clothes, food, and other necessities for the baby.
- Maintain a drug-free lifestyle. Possession, use, and distribution of any narcotic is prohibited.
- Comply with visitation schedule set up by caseworker.

∽

None of that sounded too taxing. Candace was somewhat offended they put number five on there as a requirement. What kind of low-life had to be forced to visit their child?

∽

When she got back to her apartments, a car Candace recognized was in her parking spot. It was Rilla's Fleetwood. The sight of it made her heart shoot up in her throat. The color drained from her face.

No way was he out. She hadn't testified against him yet. Detective Judkins would have told her if there was a change in plans.

Maybe he bailed out.

But how? CC said he didn't have that kind of money.

Candace parked behind the car, wondering if she should even get out. She didn't want to be with Rilla anymore, and he might have a hard time accepting it. What if he interfered with the CPS investigation? Even worse, what if he found out about Candace testifying against him? What if he came to shut her up, for good?

All of these *what if's* fell into a dark pit of panic when Rilla's car door opened. But it was CC who stepped out of the Cadillac, not her ex-boyfriend. Candace didn't want to see this thug, either, but dealing with him was a much better alternative to Rilla. Besides, it was broad daylight. What could CC possibly do?

Candace got out, and CC stepped around the car to meet her. He wore a black T-shirt with blue jeans. His Afro was puffed out, and his face was clean-shaven again.

"*Looka here, looka here!* Candace! Is it really is you? They done let you out the pen!"

She narrowed her eyes. "What do you want, Cordell? I don't want to see you anymore."

He grinned. "Damn, baby. It's like that?"

"Yeah, it's like that. You hit me. I don't want anything to do with you."

He shook his head. "I didn't hit you, girl. I just pushed you a little bit. It wasn't on purpose, though. My bad."

Candace leaned against her car rather than head for her apartment and risk him following. It was a lot more wide-open in the parking lot.

"CC, I don't want you over here."

His eyes bugged. He looked her up and down and put a hand to his mouth.

"What the—you had yo baby?"

Candace just stared at him.

"Damn! You looking good, girl. Stomach all flat. I see you done got your figure back. I see ya!"

"What do you want?"

"Does Rilla know you had the baby?"

"I don't know what he knows."

CC lowered his eyes, but the smile never left his lips. "All right, girl. I was just coming by to check on my homeboy's baby mama. I don't think Rilla knows you're out."

"I'm not with Rilla anymore," Candace said. "I don't care if he knows or not."

"What you mean?"

"I mean he's not my boyfriend. We're through. I'm moving in a couple weeks, and I don't want to see either one of you again."

CC shook his head. "That's wrong, girl. My nigga took care of you. You gonna burn out on him while he's locked up? He needs you now more than ever."

"Whatever."

"Where you going? Back to New York? You can't take Rilla's baby out of state."

Candace was pretty sure she could take her baby, but didn't feel like arguing.

"I'm not going to New York. I'm getting my own apartment here."

"You screwing some other nigga?"

"Why do you always say something like that? You don't think a woman can do anything without a man? I'm moving out by myself, and I'm going to live by myself. Just me and my baby. I don't need help from anybody."

"I know you're not taking any of my homeboy's stuff out of that apartment when you leave."

Candace was stupefied. "I was with Rilla when we moved in here. I picked out most of that stuff myself."

"You didn't pay for it."

"Well, I'm taking it," Candace said.

CC nodded. "All right, girl. You a little feisty, ain't you?"

"I'm through with the bullshit," Candace confirmed. "And I'm not with Rilla anymore, so I don't need you checking on me. You can tell him I said so."

"That's how you want to play it?"

"Yeah," Candace said. "Just like that."

"Cool." CC turned and walked away, but Candace wasn't moving until she saw him drive off.

He opened the door but didn't get in the Fleetwood. Instead he watched her with that same shit-eating grin.

"How you get out of jail so quick?" he asked.

"I shouldn't have been in there in the first place. How'd you get away from that bust at those apartments?"

CC shrugged. "Maybe I got away the same way you did."

Candace knew she was in murky waters, but couldn't stop fishing.

"When you said you had something for me, I didn't think I'd get arrested."

But CC didn't respond to that. He winked at her and got into Rilla's car. A moment later he took off with a Tupac beat exploding from the Cadillac's trunk.

        ⌒

The next couple of months went by with no further interactions with CC. Candace disabled her home phone, so she wouldn't have to take any calls from the county jail, either. She knew Rilla would be on the phones twenty times a day once CC told him what she said. On one level Candace felt like she should talk to Rilla herself, but she just wanted to be through with him. Whatever he and CC had going on with the drugs and the police was much too messy for her.

In the meantime Candace had a few more visits with the Whitley family, and her interactions with Leila got better and better. When she was awake, the infant was very talkative, or very noisy, depending on whom you asked. Candace learned how to bottle-feed her daughter, and Mrs. Whitley showed her how to burp her and change Leila's diaper.

Candace originally resented this stand-in mother, but she gradually learned to respect and even appreciate what the Whitleys were doing for her. In turn, the Whitleys came to love and respect Candace also. They knew surprisingly little about her case, and neither could understand how a girl as sweet as her could lose their child to CPS.

Candace's waitress job went well from the very start. Always an apt pupil, she wowed the manager with her memorization skills. Candace had the entire appetizer menu down by her first day, and she picked up the rest of the menu with uncanny speed. Training normally lasted a full week, but Jesse cut her loose after only three days. Candace made $210 on her first Friday night and $240 the following Saturday. Jesse certified her a natural.

She called her parents every Monday as promised and had more good news for them each time. She sent them pictures of her and Leila taken at the Whitley's house. They thought their grandchild was beautiful and agreed she looked like her mother.

On June 25 Candace filled out an application for the apartment complex next door. She thought her rental history would be marred by the drug raid, but she got a call back from the manager the next day. Her application was approved and she could move in as early as the twenty-seventh.

Candace got all of the utilities put in her name, and Trisha's two burly brothers helped with the move. The whole relocation took only four hours, and on June 28, Candace had her very own apartment all to herself. She immediately began to fill it with things for her baby.

On the first of July she started her parenting classes. Some of the information the instructors provided was invaluable, but for the most part, Candace thought they should rename the class *Parenting for Dummies*. Not only did they teach her how to change a diaper, but they also taught her how to dispose of one.

They taught her that when baby is crying, that means she's unhappy about something. When baby is green, she's most likely sick. And when baby is blue and can't make any sounds, she's probably choking. Candace actually took notes before she realized her teacher was an idiot.

⁓

Midway through August Candace received a letter from the Overbrook Meadows Community College. It was time to register for her fall classes. She met with her counselor on a cool Wednesday morning and signed up for five core courses.

On the way back to her car, Candace spotted a familiar face heading in the opposite direction. She walked quickly to catch up with him and followed behind for a few paces before speaking.

"Wow, is that Johnny Depp?"

Tino stopped and turned to see who was teasing him. His face lit up when he saw Candace. Her face lit up, too. Tino looked a lot different from the last time she saw him. He had a thin moustache and a little hair on his chin, too. He wore black Dickey shorts with a white T-shirt. Candace wished her hair was as luscious as his. Celestino could star in a Pantene commercial.

"Candace! You're still here?"

"Yeah. What happened to you? You look like a *cholo* now," she said.

"I know you didn't call me a *cholo!*" Tino smiled and his jaw dropped. "You had your baby!"

Today Candace wore a pair of very short shorts with a small T-shirt that fit her close. Most of her baby weight was gone, but her hips and butt were still fuller than before she got pregnant. Her chest was bigger, too.

"Yep. I had her June 30."

Tino ogled her unabashedly. "Dang, you look good. I didn't know you had it like that."

Candace giggled. "You're the one who kept trying to talk to me. Following me around, looking at my butt."

"Yeah, but you were kinda fat then."

"Thanks a lot."

"No. I'm just kidding. But seriously, you look really good."

"Thanks," Candace said and blushed. The last time a man made her feel like that, it was Rilla. That was so long ago.

"So, are you here registering? I thought you were going back to New York."

"Not yet," she said. "I'm going to do one more semester here."

"Rilla got out of jail?"

"No. I'm here by myself. I have my own apartment. I got a job, too, just like you said."

Tino's smile grew wider. Candace thought his lips were cute. His dimples made her melt.

"You live by yourself, just you and your baby?"

"My baby's visiting with my parents," Candace said. The lie came easy, but she hated it as soon as it was out. "It's just me right now, for a couple more weeks."

September 1. Just two more weeks and no more lies.

Tino was pleased with this information. "So you're talking to your parents again?"

"Yeah. I talk to them all the time. After I broke up with Rilla, I decided I didn't want to keep them in the dark anymore. I love them. They really missed me. I missed them, too."

"Where do you work?" he asked.

"Pappadeaux."

"That's a big restaurant. I love it there, but I can't afford it."

"Why don't you let me take you sometime," Candace offered. "I can get us a discount."

Tino grinned. "You're asking me out?"

"You've got a girlfriend?" Candace guessed.

"No. But if I did, I would break up with her. I'd put her out with the trash."

Candace laughed.

"I didn't think you would ever go out with me," he said.

"I never said I didn't want to. I told you I couldn't."

"You're serious, though? We're really going to go out?"

"Yes, Tino. You know I like you."

"I like you, too," he said, and there was a comfortable silence between them.

"So, you're going to give me your phone number?" he asked.

Candace scribbled it on the corner of her registrar paper and tore it off.

Tino took it and stuffed it in his front pocket. "All right. Cool. This is great." He shook his head and grinned. "I knew karma was going to work out in my favor sooner or later."

"You been helping old ladies across the street?" Candace asked.

"I've been saving them from burning buildings," Tino teased. "Their cats, too!"

Candace giggled.

"We're not going to your restaurant on our first date, though," he said. "I don't want you to take me out."

"What are you, a chauvinist?"

"No. I'm a gentleman."

"So you're never going to let me pay for a meal?"

"Not the first time," Tino said. "After that you can pay every time if you want."

"Not happening." Candace chuckled. "Well, I'm on my way home. I guess I'll be waiting for your call. Don't wait a week, either. That's rude."

"What? Are you kidding? I'm calling today!"

Candace smiled. "All right, Tino." She turned to leave, but he grabbed her hand.

"Thanks," he said when she turned back to him.

"For what?"

"For giving me a chance. There's a lot of guys here who like you, but you chose me."

"You still won't tell me who those other guys are."

"If you really want to know, I'll tell you," Tino said sincerely.

Candace shook her head. "No. That's all right."

"Good," Tino said. He bent and kissed the back of her hand with those pretty pink lips. Candace felt electricity all the way up her arm.

He gave her one last smile before continuing on his way. Candace drove home thinking about a man who wasn't Rilla for the first time in a year and a half.

CHAPTER 15
CELESTIAL

"Some Mexican dude?" Trisha asked.

"He's not just some Mexican dude," Candace said. "He's my age. He's smart. He's cute. He makes me laugh."

"Ain't nothing special about him?"

"Like what?"

"I don't know. It just seems that if you go from a Puerto Rican to a Mexican, it must be something about them."

Candace shook her head. "Look, Trish, I go out with whoever I like. I don't discriminate. It's just a coincidence."

"Oh, okay. I didn't want to think you had something against the brothers . . ."

"Not at all."

They were in Candace's apartment. Trisha had all three boys with her. She cradled Willie Jr. in one arm and he sucked at her breast complacently. The other two monsters ran around the new apartment like they were on a playground. Candace never noticed how *bad* Trisha's kids were. The behavior was no doubt always there, but she didn't really see it until it was her house in danger of demolition.

"You wanna check on them?" Candace suggested.

"Y'all quit running around in here!" Trisha yelled without looking back.

"You don't think I should go out with a Mexican?" Candace asked. She sat on one end of her sofa with Trisha on the other side. Trisha wore a large, shapeless dress. One shoulder strap was down, providing an escape for Willie's meal.

"What about Rilla?" Trisha asked.

"We're through."

"You talked to him?"

Candace shook her head.

"You just gon' move on with your life without him?"

"To the best of my abilities."

Trisha laughed. "You a cold bitch. Okay, tell me about Celestial."

Now Candace laughed. "It's Celestino. He goes by Tino. But I think you're right. It does have something to do with heaven and the stars."

"That's why he's got your head all up in the clouds?" Trisha joked.

"I just think he's cool," Candace said. "He's a good guy. He cared about me when I didn't really know him. He always wanted to help. When I was with Rilla, he would come and talk to me to see how I was doing. He knew I had problems."

"Did you tell him about your baby?"

"No," Candace said, and the guilt changed her demeanor. "I can't. I don't want him to know I went to jail."

"If it's meant to be, he'll—"

193

"Yeah, I know," Candace snapped. "He'll accept me no matter what. You sound like a TV show."

"There's some truth to that," Trisha said, slightly offended.

"I know," Candace said. She sighed. "The whole situation is real stressful. I'm lying to my parents. Now I'm lying to Tino."

"Maybe it's time to give it up," Trisha suggested.

Candace shook her head. "I've made it too far, Trisha. Today's the eighteenth. I get my baby back on the first. No sense telling them now."

"So you gonna stay down here for another semester?"

"Yeah. I want to prove I can do it."

"And you'll get to see Celestial, too, huh?"

"Yeah," Candace said with unconcealed affection. "I'll get to see Celestial, too."

"It won't be that hard," Trisha said. "I can watch your baby whenever you need."

"Girl, I already had you booked."

There was a knock at the door.

Candace couldn't think of one person who would have cause to visit her. She looked over at her friend. "You didn't tell CC where I live, did you?"

"You know me better than that."

"Delia, either?"

"No. I didn't tell her."

Candace stood and squinted through the peephole. Of all people, it was Gabriella Sands on her welcome mat. Candace looked back to Trisha in a panic. "It's my caseworker!" she hissed.

"Who?" Trisha whispered.

"The CPS lady! She's here!"

"So what?" Trisha said. She didn't see a problem with it. But as if on cue, Willie Jr. unlatched from her nipple and took in a deep breath for a powerful wail.

"*WAAAAAHHHH*!"

The noise brought Little Sammy and Petey on the run. The younger boy toted Candace's bathroom plunger for some reason.

There was another knock. "Hello? Candace?" The caseworker knew someone was inside.

"Boy, go put that up!" Trisha yelled at Sammy. She threw Willie over her shoulder and tried to coerce a burp from him. He continued to scream mightily.

Candace watched the whole scene in horror and knew she had to open the door.

"Put your tittie up!" she told Trisha.

Trisha rolled her eyes at her but complied. Sammy ran off again in the direction of the bathroom and Petey followed. Candace put on her best "Welcome to Pappadeaux" face and summoned the will to open the door. Gabriella looked like she didn't like to be kept waiting.

"Hi." Candace smiled brightly. "How are you, Ms. Sands?"

"Hello, Candace." The caseworker wore a blue pantsuit today. Her hair was curled.

Candace looked back into her apartment and then at her visitor. "Hi," she said again.

Gabriella cradled a ledger to her chest and rocked on her heels. "Um, can I come in?"

"Sure," Candace said and stepped out of the way. "Come on in."

⁓

Contrary to Candace's dread, the visit with her case-worker didn't go badly at all. Gabriella was not shocked to see a house full of kids, not even kids as bad as Trisha's. Candace introduced the two women, emphasizing the fact that Trisha was her neighbor of more than a year. Trisha knew Rilla and she knew the truth about Candace's arrest.

But the caseworker didn't want to talk about drugs. She sat on the sofa and asked Trisha what kind of person Candace was. Candace was sure her friend wouldn't bash her while she sat right there, but Trisha was brutally honest.

"She's young. She is immature about some things."

Gabriella nodded. Candace wore the look of Caesar. *Et tu, Brutus?*

"But she's real confident, too," Trisha went on. "She thinks she can do everything by herself. And she can, too. Everything she has, she got it by herself. She's going to be a great mother. She's the only girl I know who really wants to do something with her life."

Candace took Gabriella to her bedroom, where every-thing was nice and neat. She had a crib for Leila right next to her bed and two dresser drawers filled with clothes for the baby. Candace had diapers in the closet and a stockpile of Enfamil in the pantry. Gabriella seemed to like Trisha, and she even picked up Little Sammy when he started his antics.

On the way out, the caseworker gave Candace a smile and a nod, and it was clear everything went well.

⌒

Candace drove Trisha across the street after the five o'clock news went off.

Tino called at seven. Candace was about to watch *For the Love of Gina*, but Regina Smith's love life came second to her own.

"Hello?"

"Hi. Is this Candace? May I speak to Candace?"

"Who do you think might be answering my phone, Tino?"

"I don't know. You're so beautiful, I thought you might have some evil stepsisters."

"Oh, man. You're laying it on thick," Candace said.

"Do you want me to stop?"

"You'd better not."

"So, what you got going on over there?" he asked.

"Nothing. Just watching TV."

"Don't tell me, *For the Love of Gina*, right?"

Candace smiled. "How'd you know?"

"Everybody's watching that show."

"You don't like it?"

"Oh, I like it, but she's giving women a bad name. She makes me think all y'all care about is big muscles, a big mouth, and big-time learning disabilities."

"You don't have any of those things," Candace said with a giggle.

"I know. That's why I never sent them my audition tape. The only good show was Flavor Flav's. After that, it all went to hell."

"You like Flavor Flav?"

"Hell, yeah," Tino said. "When I was in high school, I was friends with this guy named Marcus. I used to go to his house a lot after school. His brother was older. He graduated ten years before us. But he was cool. He would take us with him when he went out. We were too young to do *everything*, but he would still give up his night for us."

"So, where's Flavor Flav?" Candace asked.

"I'm giving you background information," Tino said. "I'm trying to create a mood for my story."

"Oh, carry on."

He chuckled. "Anyway, Marcus' brother, his name is Harold, by the way, he loves music. All kinds of music. Back then, he mostly listened to old stuff. Stuff that was popular when he was in high school. He listened to one particular group all the time. One day I was walking by his room, and I heard: 'Elvis was a hero to most, but he never meant shit to me.' Sorry about my language."

"You're fine. That was Public Enemy, right?"

"Yeah," Tino said. "I went in there and listened to that song, and it was like nothing I ever heard on the radio—the things they were saying. Harold had all of their CDs. He let me take some home, and I listened to every one. For a minute, I hated white people."

Candace laughed.

"But mostly," Tino said, "I started thinking about black entertainment differently. Those guys on TV, with the gold and the teeth, and—"

"Like Rilla?" Candace asked.

Tino snickered. "Yeah, like him. Those guys don't speak about the black experience and what y'all went through. All they talk about is drug dealing. Big cars with big rims. I started listening to Chuck D and the X-Clan, and the next thing I knew I was reading about Huey Newton and Fred Hampton. Those guys were deep."

"Wow," Candace said. "From Flavor Flav to Fred Hampton. You've thoroughly impressed me, Tino. You probably know more about the Black Panthers than I do."

"My mom's a history teacher," he said. "She loves when I read. Whenever she saw I was interested in something, she'd bring home lots of books about it and make me write a report."

"She made it a chore?"

"Yeah. But I liked it. She's a good lady. I can't wait for you to meet her."

"You want me to meet your mom?"

"Man, I can't believe I said that," Tino said. "I told you I do that sometimes. My mind starts to go way overboard. I think too much."

"That's something I like about you," Candace said. "I like the way you think, the way you talk."

"Good," Tino said. "You'd be surprised how many girls don't want to hear about Huey P. Newton."

Candace laughed. "Don't tell me you talk about him on your dates."

"Not anymore," Tino said. "I learned my lesson!"

"Tino, you should be a comedian!"

She made him hang up so she could call him back on her home phone. Her cellular minutes were a source of stress as of late, especially since she talked to her parents so often.

She chatted with Tino for another thirty minutes. Towards the end he said he wanted to take her to the famed Overbrook Meadows stockyards for their date. He said there would be action and excitement and promised the smell of bull poop wouldn't be overwhelming. Candace was happy to hear that.

When they got off the phone, she made herself a spaghetti dinner. Trisha thought she couldn't cook, but who couldn't make spaghetti? Maybe if you made your own sauce from scratch the meal might get a little difficult, but Prego already had a winning recipe. Candace wasn't about to compete with them.

CHAPTER 16
RIDE 'EM, COWBOY!

On Friday morning Candace had another visit with the Whitleys. This was the next to last one, and tensions were at an all-time high. Leila, as always, was at the center of the struggle. Today she didn't want to stop crying unless her foster mother held her. This made Candace's blood boil. The hair stood on the back of her neck.

"Give her to me," she said. They stood in the Whitleys' kitchen waiting for Leila's bottle to be ready in the microwave. Their kitchen was almost as big as Candace's whole apartment.

"Let me get her calmed down," the older woman said. She bounced with Leila's head on her shoulder. The baby continued to fuss, but she wasn't screaming like when Candace had her.

"There, there," Mrs. Whitley cooed in Leila's ear. "It's almost ready."

Candace couldn't stand the way the woman held her baby—like Leila belonged to *her* or something. Candace didn't like the way she leaned her head against Leila's, and Candace didn't like the way Mrs. Whitley kissed Leila on the side of the face. She didn't like how Mrs. Whitley made those cutesy sounds that weren't even words when she played with Leila. What kind of language was she teaching the girl?

"Give her to me. I can hold her." Candace had her arms outstretched. Mrs. Whitley saw them but turned towards the microwave instead.

"Okay, just a moment. Let me get the bottle and you can feed her."

Candace stared at her baby's face over the woman's shoulder. Leila nuzzled the woman's neck and had almost stopped crying.

"I don't just want to feed her," Candace said. "I want to hold her when she's upset. I don't like how you take her from me when she's fussy."

"I don't mean to offend," Mrs. Whitley said. "I was only trying to help."

"Then let me hold her," Candace demanded. "This is my visitation. You keep her all the time."

The microwave dinged.

Mrs. Whitley turned around, with a bit of an attitude, Candace thought, and handed the baby over. Leila immediately began to wail.

"See, now you've upset her again," Mrs. Whitley said and turned back to the counter.

"I didn't upset her," Candace said. "She's just used to your scent. She doesn't even know who her mother is."

"Well, she wouldn't be in this situation if—" Mrs. Whitley caught herself. She turned back with the bottle and screwed the nipple on. "I was only trying to help."

Candace took the bottle and went into the Whitleys' living room. Her visits were technically still supposed to be monitored, but Martha didn't follow her. Candace sat on the love seat and positioned her baby for feeding. Leila didn't stop crying until she had the bottle.

Candace's traitorous eyes were determined to cry, but she was equally determined not to let them. She could cry on the way home. She didn't want her daughter to see her as this woeful woman who came to feed her sometimes.

"*I'm* your mother," she whispered to the infant. "I am. I'm your mother."

Leila looked into her mama's big brown eyes and seemed to comprehend, but Candace knew there was no way she could.

⁓

Tino rang Candace's doorbell at 7:00 p.m. sharp. His face lit up when she answered it.

"Oh, man." He put a hand over his mouth and looked her up and down. "You really look nice."

For her date that night, Candace wore denim capris that looked pretty tight, but the stretchy material made them comfortable. Up top she had on a white halter top that tied up behind her neck. Her sandals were dark brown. Her hair was down and flawless.

Tino wore a white button-down and heavily starched jeans. Candace thought he had on maroon-colored Polo boots, but she looked closer and saw they were real cowboy boots. He had a shiny belt buckle, too.

Yippee ki yay!

His hair was down, jet black and as luscious as ever. His face was clean-shaven. His eyes were dark, his smile invigorating. He wore a sweet scent Candace couldn't place.

"You look good, too," she said. "You look handsome. You're wearing boots?"

"Yeah." He clicked his heels together. "You can't mosey too good if you don't have your boots on, I reckon."

Candace laughed. "We're going to mosey?"

"Everybody moseys at the stockyards," Tino said. "If you think I'm something, wait till we get down there. Those *charros* wear big hats, spurs, and everything."

"*Charros?*"

"Mexican cowboys."

"Real live cowboys?" Candace asked.

"Yep. They've got guns and everything."

"They do not have guns."

"All right, if they have guns, you have to kiss me," Tino said. "Right then. No matter where we are."

"Alright," Candace said. "If they have guns I'll kiss you."

Tino smiled brightly. Candace would kiss those soft lips right now if he wanted.

"What do I get if there are no guns?" she asked.

"If they don't have guns, I'll have to kiss you."

Candace smiled. "So you get a kiss either way?"

"Not just me. You get something out of it, too."

Candace giggled. "Okay. I'm ready. Let me get my purse."

She stepped inside, and Tino waited on the porch. When she got back with her purse, he took her hand and stared into her eyes.

"Hey," he said. "I want you to know that I think you're beautiful. I know a lot of guys will see you, and they'll want to be with you based on your looks. But I know you're a beautiful person on the inside, too. That said, you really look good tonight. No woman we see will be as attractive as you."

Candace blushed and looked away. "Tino, you're crazy." When she met his eyes again, he seemed to be staring into her very soul.

"I'm serious."

"Those *charros* really have guns?" she asked.

"Yeah," he said. "I think they shoot blanks, but the guns are real."

"Then I'll concede my bet," Candace said.

"Great," Tino said. "You owe me a kiss."

"Okay," she said and waited expectantly.

"You mean now?" Tino smiled nervously. "At the beginning of the date? This is weird. This is unnatural. Statistically speaking—"

"Shut up and kiss me," Candace said, and he did. He put his hands on her waist and pulled her close to him. His fragrance was stronger now. It was pleasant. Candace tilted her head and closed her eyes, and when their lips touched, she felt tingles down her spine. Tino's lips were moist and warm. His breath was minty. He pecked her lightly, and then kissed her bottom lip more intimately. Candace backed away with his smell still in her nose.

She looked up at him and smiled. He smiled, too, his lips glistening.

"You got lip gloss on," she said.

He wiped it away and then wiped his forehead. "Whew. I've never done that before."

"Me, neither," Candace said. "It took some of the edge off, though. Didn't it? Don't you feel more comfortable?"

"Yeah," Tino said. "Except for the heart attack."

Candace laughed. Tino grabbed her hand again and led her down the stairs.

"You know something," he said halfway down. "I do feel more comfortable now. I think all dates should start with the kiss."

"All dates with *me*," Candace said. "If you try that with somebody else, you'll probably get slapped."

"I'm not going out with anyone but you," Tino said, and then caught himself getting sentimental again. "Hey, there's something I've been meaning to ask you," he said when they got to the parking lot.

"What?"

"What the hell happened to your car?"

Candace didn't know what he was talking about until they rounded the corner of her building. Her Nissan looked pretty plain without the big wheels.

"I'm a simple girl," she said. "I don't need all that stuff."

"I am so glad you said that," Tino said. "Cause there aren't too many cars out there uglier than mine."

He walked her to a two-toned Honda Prelude that was manufactured sometime in the early nineties.

"Yeah," Candace said with a hand over her mouth. "You're right about that, Tino."

⌒

He drove her to the north side of town, where stagecoaches and cattle runs once barreled right down Main Street. Candace didn't think very much of the Old West had been preserved, but as they got closer, the paved streets gave way to brick and eventually cobblestone.

The buildings changed, too. One minute they were downtown in the brightly lit metropolis, looking up at office buildings that poked the clouds. The next thing Candace knew, they were driving down a road straight from a Wyatt Earp tale.

There were old-timey saloons, wooden sidewalks that creaked, and, yes, horses. The equines were in the middle of the street and on the sidewalks—and none of them were being ridden by police officers. Candace stared out of the window like a child seeing her first snow.

"This is unbelievable," she gasped.

"This is the best part of the city," Tino said. "You see all those people?"

Candace did. There were a lot of Hispanics, but most of the cowboys decked out in their best duds were white.

"Most of them are tourists," Tino said. "People come from all over the world to see this place, but people who live in this city don't even care about it."

He found a nice parking spot and came around to open Candace's door for her. They crossed the cobblestoned street hand in hand. Candace spotted a stage-coach, and immediately dragged Tino to it. She couldn't remember the last time she saw a horse close up.

Tino offered to pay for a ride, but Candace declined. The driver let her pet the animal, and that was all she wanted. She ran her fingers through the beast's thick mane and jumped when the horse sneezed suddenly. Tino laughed.

"That's not funny," she said, but she was giggling, too.

"Come on," Tino said. He grabbed her hand and led her away.

"Where are we going?"

"To the rodeo. I want to show you some real horses."

"That wasn't a real horse?"

"Naw," Tino said. "The stallions in here will put that lazy thing to shame."

And he wasn't kidding. They went into a large audi-torium where the night's festivities were already underway. Candace and Tino found their seat three rows up from ground level. The center ring was huge, about the size of a football field. A string of fifty horses galloped around, making difficult patterns that reminded Candace of a college band performance.

Their riders were dressed to the nines in big hats, floppy chaps, and shiny spurs. They looked like extras from a *Bonanza* rerun. They waved flags, whooped and hollered, and even swung lassos in the air.

Candace watched it all in wide-eyed amazement. "What's going on?" she asked.

"They're introducing the riding clubs," Tino said. "They come from all over the state. Oklahoma, too."

"They're beautiful."

"Check out that guy over there." Tino pointed out one cowboy who had his mighty steed up on its hind legs. The horse held the stance for a long time, while the cowboy yelled and twirled a big lasso over his head.

"Aww, I should have brought my camera," Candace said.

"I'll bring you back if you want," Tino said. "They do this every Friday."

Candace grinned. "I'd like that." She studied the buckaroos a little more closely. "Hey, they don't have guns!"

Tino grinned sheepishly. "You think I would lie to you just to get a kiss? Those are *gringos*. I told you the *charros* had guns."

"So where are the charros?" Candace asked.

"I don't know. I hope we didn't miss them."

Candace smiled at him skeptically.

"Hey," Tino said. "If I wanted a kiss, I would just say so."

"All right," Candace teased. "We'll wait."

And they did.

And once again, Tino was right.

Towards the end of the opening acts, everything went eerily quiet. Candace looked at Tino for an explanation, but he just grinned. The silence was broken by a high-pitched scream evocative of the Latin culture. A lone rider galloped into the ring with a huge Mexican flag held high. His skin was dark like a Mayan warrior. His hair was long like a Cherokee. He wore all black, even his chaps. And, as Tino said, he had a pistol holstered on each hip.

The *vaquero* stopped in the center of the ring and let out a call Candace couldn't duplicate if she practiced for years. Ten more Mexican riders rushed out, one after another. They waved their flags and shrieked loudly like the first one, and then they whipped out their firearms.

Candace flinched when the first shot went off. Tino put an arm around her shoulder. She leaned into him and felt quite cozy as the chaos erupted beneath them.

Yeee hah!
Aiiiee!
POP! POP! POP!
Yah! Yah!
POP!
POP!
Eeeee Hyaah!
POP!
POP! POP!

After the riding teams, things got serious when they got down to the actual rodeo. First came the bareback riding, followed by barrel racing and bull riding. Candace cringed every time a cowboy got tossed, and stood to cheer whenever one made it past the eight-second mark. At one point during the events, she got a little jealous as she eyed the other patrons.

"Why didn't you tell me to wear something western?" she asked Tino.

"Why?" he said. "You look great just like you are."

"But I want to look like a cowgirl," Candace pouted.

"Hold on," Tino said. He stood and scanned the crowd looking for one of the rodeo's many vendors. He called one of them over and purchased a souvenir cowboy hat for ten dollars.

He gave it to Candace, and it was a pretty good fit. She beamed like a schoolgirl. "How do I look?"

"You already know what I think," Tino said.

"Do I look like a cowgirl?"

"The prettiest one in the building."

They stayed for a while longer, but Candace found the events harder to enjoy once steer wrestling and calf-roping got underway. She wondered where the PETA people were.

"*Ewww*, I can't watch this," she said finally.

"I don't like this part, either," Tino said. "Let's go."

~

Once outside, Candace thought the date was over, but Tino didn't head to his car. Instead he led her through the perfectly refurbished western town. Candace started to feel like she was on a Hollywood movie set. Everything was perfect, the smells, the sights, and the sounds.

They stopped for a minute to listen to a mariachi band posted up on the corner, and then Tino took her to Billy Bob's, "The World's Largest Honkytonk," according to a billboard posted outside. Candace had never seen anything like it. The place was huge. There was a stage for live performances, a ring for bull riding, and dinner tables filled with the city's most prestigious rednecks.

Billy Bob's best attraction, in Candace's opinion, was the mechanical bull. Outside of television, she'd never seen one in real life. She grabbed Tino's arm and dragged him to the contraption. As they arrived a pasty blonde was unceremoniously bucked off the robot.

"You've got to get on that," Candace told Tino. She wore her hat and thought she fit in perfectly now.

Tino shook his head. "I'm not getting on that thing." His smile was contagious. Candace didn't think she'd ever been so happy.

She tugged his arm. "C'mon."

"No, I don't want to get hurt."

"That girl didn't get hurt."

"Uh-uhn!"

He pulled her in the other direction. But Candace didn't budge. She dug in her heels and put on her best puppy dog eyes.

"Please."

Tino stared at her lips and then her eyes. "*Aww*, don't do that."

Candace gave him a sexy look then. "Please."

"Hell, I'll ride a real bull for you!" he said and promptly got in line.

When it was his turn, Candace waved her hat and cheered, but Tino's ride only lasted four seconds. He picked himself up and dusted hay from his britches, looking around to see who was watching. His bashful smile melted Candace's heart. She could see his dimples from ten feet away. She rushed to greet him when he exited the ring.

"My hero!" she exclaimed, and threw her arms around his neck.

Tino put his arms around her waist and kissed her unexpectedly, more passionately than at her apartment. He slid his hands up her back, and Candace felt a sliver of lightning shoot from her chest. It quivered in her belly and settled between her legs.

"Let's go eat," he said, and Candace followed him, unable to speak for a few seconds.

They both ordered burgers, fries, and lemonade. It was a simple meal, but the atmosphere made everything very special. They made goo-goo eyes over their plates. Candace thought nothing at all could go wrong on that night, but Tino's conversation eventually drifted into putrid waters.

"Don't you miss your daughter?" he asked.

"I do," Candace said, and genuine misery changed her expression.

"You all right?" he asked.

"I'm okay," she said. "I just miss her. I really miss her a lot."

"Why'd you let your parents take her so soon?" he asked. "Why didn't you wait till she was older?"

Candace hated lying to him. Tino had done nothing but treat her good the whole time she knew him.

213

"It's a difficult situation," she said, and, surprisingly, he let her leave it at that.

⌒

They ended their date in very good spirits. Tino wouldn't get back on the metal bull despite Candace's urgings, but they stayed for a while and watched other cocky cowboys get bucked. That was just as much fun.

While they stood there, Tino got as close as he would on this night: he stood behind Candace with his arms wrapped around her front. His body pressed close to hers. He rested his chin on her shoulder and kissed the side of her neck *two* times. Candace knew it was exactly twice, because his warm breaths tickled and her heartbeat increased on both occasions.

When they got back to Candace's apartment, Tino walked her to the door like a proper gentleman. His touches were starting to stimulate urges, so Candace was glad when he didn't linger at her doorway. He kissed her once on the cheek, and then pecked her gently on the lips. He took her hand and kissed it slowly, staring at her with those dark eyes the whole time. It was all Candace could do to keep from squirming.

She waited thirty minutes, then called to make sure he made it home okay. They chatted for a little while, but it was late in the evening. Candace began to yawn, and Tino said he was tired, too.

Before they got off the phone, Tino wanted to make a confession.

"I know you may not believe this," he said, "but I've been in love with you for a long time. And I know I'm not supposed to say that on a first date, but I do what I want to do. I don't care what people think."

Candace was speechless, but always the gentleman, Tino let her off the hook. "I don't want you to say anything," he said. "I just wanted to you to know how I feel."

He hung up abruptly.

Candace called him right back.

"Why'd you hang up on me?"

"I didn't want to put you on the spot," he said. "I didn't want you to feel like you had to say something back."

"But I want to say something back."

"Okay."

"Tino, you're a great guy. You're the coolest guy I've ever gone out with. You show me so many things." She paused. "I can't say I love you right now, but I am definitely falling for you."

"Then fall," he urged.

"Okay," Candace said. "I will."

And she did.

CHAPTER 17
I'M YOUR MOTHER

On Saturday, August 25, Candace and Tino had their second date. After the loot he dished out at the stockyards, Candace insisted she pay. She took him to Pappadeaux, much to the chagrin of the waiters there who thought they might have a chance with their coworker from New York.

Tino had fried shrimp and fried catfish fillets. Candace had chicken breast with mashed potatoes and broccoli. For dessert, her manager brought them a complimentary turtle fudge brownie with vanilla ice cream. They ate it with one spoon. Tino fed her a couple of times.

On Tuesday, August 28, they started their second semester at Overbrook Meadows Community College. They had no classes together this time.

On Saturday, September 1, Candace went to the CPS office for her final visit with Gabriella Sands. The caseworker went over the Service Plan point by point, certifying her a success in all areas. Best of all, the Whitleys were at this meeting. Being done with all of this was a reward in itself, but Martha Whitley sat across from Gabriella with the most prized gift of all in her arms.

Leila was wrapped snugly in a yellow blanket. She was awake. Her eyes darted here and there but didn't register any recognition when they fell upon Candace. The baby grinned gleefully at her foster mother.

Leila's real mother sat in the third chair in Gabriella's office. Candace checked her watch again, wondering what the hell was taking so long. This was supposed to be a quick meeting, a simple transferal of the merchandise. But they had been in there for thirty minutes already because Gabriella was an anal bitch. She wanted to make sure she had all her P's and Q's lined up.

Candace waited and gritted her teeth. She knew this meeting had to end at some point, and when it did, Mrs. Whitley would never lay her crusty hands on Leila again. *Never.* If the couple was crazy enough to ask Candace for a few visits, they had a rude awakening coming.

Gabriella eventually finished her spiel. She applauded the Whitleys for always being there when her office needed them, and she said Candace went above and beyond in proving herself worthy of these new responsibilities.

"Candace, your case is closed." Gabriella smiled and gestured towards Mrs. Whitley. "You can take your baby home."

Candace stood quickly and was immediately overcome by a wave of dizziness. She fought through it and forced her eyes to remain focused. She reached for her baby, but Martha Whitley didn't immediately rise to her feet. Instead she held Leila up at eye level with her hands in the child's armpits. She stared into the infant's face longingly.

217

"I'm gonna miss you," she said. Her eyes filled with moisture, and a tear rolled down her cheek. Leila clucked and kicked out with her chubby legs. Mrs. Whitley brought her in for one last kiss and one more hug. She handed her off to Candace with what looked like obvious reluctance.

"She's a good girl," she said. "As sweet as jellybeans."

Yeah, jellybeans. I get it. Gimme!

Candace accepted her daughter like she was receiving the bouquet at a Miss America pageant. A warm flood of euphoria washed over her. She felt weak and over-whelmed and energized at the same time. The whole world was right again. Her baby felt good, so soft, so *precious*. Candace took a deep breath and exhaled slowly.

It was done. It never should have happened in the first place, but now it was done. She felt like they returned a missing piece of her heart. A piece of her very soul.

She tried to put her baby in the car seat she brought with her, but the straps weren't as self-explanatory as they looked. Mrs. Whitley knelt to help, but Candace shot her a look that made her back away. Candace figured it out by herself and stood with a new burden she was happy, if not proud, to bear.

"Is it over?" she asked her caseworker. "I can go now?"

Gabriella nodded. "Yes, Candace. It's over. Good luck!"

Candace's smile magnified. She thanked everybody one last time and stepped out of the office a new woman. Walking through that door was like walking into a totally new world.

Mrs. Whitley called after her, offering tips on what she could do when the baby does *this* or *that*, but Candace didn't pause or even look back. She wanted no part of that woman's techniques.

Later she would regret not taking these last-minute instructions.

∽

She was in such a good mood, Candace called her parents on the way home.

"Hello?"

"Hey, Mom! How's it going?"

"Candace? Oh, hi, baby! What's going on? I don't expect to hear from you on a Saturday."

"I know, Mom. I was just . . . I'm having a good day. I thought I'd call to say hi."

"You know you can call me anytime. Why are you so happy? What's the good news?"

"There's no news, Mom. I just . . . I feel good."

"Oh, okay. How's the baby?"

Candace smiled so big she could have had her braces removed without a bite block. "She's great, Mom. She's chilling. She's so beautiful."

"I know she is, Candace. Listen, we've been real patient about this. I'd like to think me and your dad have been understanding."

"You have, Mama. I love y'all so much."

"We love you, too, baby. But tell me, how long are you going to make us wait to see our grandbaby? I'm glad you're calling more, but it's been two months. She'll be walking and talking by the time we set eyes on her."

"Mama, school started last week. I won't have time off until Christmas. I can come visit you then."

"That's great, Candace. Your dad will be glad to hear that, but that's a long time away. Why can't we come see you? You say nothing's wrong, but the longer you keep us away, the harder that is to believe."

"Okay," Candace said, still beaming.

"Okay what?"

"Okay, you can come see me if you want."

"Candace, please tell me you're serious. Gerald will be on a plane tomorrow if I tell him you said that."

"I'm serious. I was planning to come up for Christmas, but if you want to see me before then, it's okay now. I want to see you, too."

"Candace, I'm standing here shaking. I've been through so many ups and downs with this. Do you mean it, baby? Can we really come see you?"

"Yes, Mom. I'll give you my address now, if you want."

Her mother breathed deeply into the phone.

"Mama, what's wrong?"

"Oh, it's nothing, baby. Nothing's wrong."

"Are you crying?"

Katherine Hendricks sniffled. "It's okay, Candace. Lord knows this is a good cry. It's okay, baby. This, it's just fine."

Candace called Tino after she got off the phone with her mom. She wasn't prepared for the multitude of deceit she'd have to dispense.

"Hello?"

"Hey, what's going on?" she asked.

"Nothing. Thinking about you."

"You say that every time I call."

"You don't think it's possible?"

"Not twenty-four hours."

"How come?"

"'Cause you'd be a blubbering idiot," she teased. "Or a psychopath. And I wouldn't go out with either."

"Touché," he said.

"You busy?"

"I'm playing Madden with *mi tio.*"

"*Uncle?*"

"Yeah, that's right. *Ugh!* I'm getting my ass kicked over here. He gets a first down every time. What's going on with you? Did you go to the airport yet?"

"Yeah. I'm on my way back," Candace said. "I got my little girl."

"That's great! I can't wait to see her. Hold on, dude," he said off-line. "Are your parents staying for a while?"

"No. They're on their way back already. And it was just my mom. She came by herself."

"She flew all the way from New York and she's flying right back? She's not staying overnight?"

All of Candace's lies were pretty far-fetched, but now they were getting ridiculous.

"Yeah. But she flies all the time. That's nothing to her."

"Still . . ."

Candace bit her lip. She knew her story was dumb. And now she had to tell him the truth, which was going to sound even dumber.

"My mom and dad are both coming down next week," she said. "Probably Monday or Tuesday. They'll stay a little while then."

"They're coming *back*?" Tino exclaimed.

"They didn't get a chance to visit this time."

"I know, but . . . Listen, don't get me wrong. I'm not dissing your parents or anything, but why didn't they both come today? Why would they waste a ticket if they're coming next week anyway?"

What a tangled web we weave.

Candace thought fast. "I guess I'm spoiled, Tino. I told them I wanted Leila back. My mom told me to wait till they come next week, but I told her I wanted my baby *today*. So she brought her."

"Just like that?"

"Yeah."

"And they're still coming next week?" Tino asked.

"Yeah."

"*Damn*," he said. "Your parents must have a shitload of money! If I asked my mom to do something like that, she would laugh in my face."

Mine would, too, Candace thought, hating that she suddenly felt like shit on such a wonderful day.

She couldn't call her friend to tell her the good news, so Candace stopped by Trisha's on the way home. Leila had been so quiet during the drive, Candace thought she was asleep, but when she opened the back door, the infant stared up at her curiously.

"Hi there," Candace said. "You doing okay?" She spoke cheerily as she undid the straps on the car seat. Everything was going fine until Candace reached in and actually *touched* her baby. When she did that, Leila's features molded into an unmistakable frown of displeasure.

It was one of those *who the hell are you* looks.

Undaunted, Candace lifted her baby from the car seat. Leila immediately began to scream, *loudly*, as if she were in pain. In her eighteen years on earth, Candace had loved and lost and even had her heart broken a few times. But no pain she ever felt could compare to being rejected by her own baby. She put Leila on her shoulder and tried to comfort her in the parking lot.

"Shhh," she cooed. "It's okay, baby. *I'm your mother.*"

But Leila didn't care to hear that. She didn't want this strange woman holding her, and she didn't want Candace talking to her, either.

"Come on, baby." She rubbed Leila's back and the baby stopped crying for a second. Candace let out a sigh of relief, but it had only been a ploy. Leila was simply taking a breath. With fresh lungs, she belted out a prolonged shriek that nearly split Candace's eardrum.

"Oh, don't do this," Candace pleaded. She bounced her daughter up and down. She rocked side to side. She even twisted right and left, but Leila didn't respond to anything. Candace grabbed the diaper bag and quickly climbed the steps to her friend's apartment. Leila screamed like a banshee the whole time. Candace busted through her friend's door with sweat and tears streaming down her face. Instead of the beautiful baby she promised, Candace looked like she found a wounded animal outside and wasn't sure what to do with it.

"*Whoa!* What the—" Trisha sat up in the couch, spilling a bag of Cheetos from her stomach. "Candace! You got your baby! Girl, what's wrong with her?"

"I don't know," Candace moaned. She dropped the diaper bag and wiped her face roughly.

"Is she wet?"

"Huh?"

"*Is she wet?*" Trisha almost had to yell over Leila's racket.

Candace felt the bottom of her child's diaper and shook her head.

"Is she hungry?" Trisha came closer so she could see the baby's face. "Let me hold her, Candace."

Candace reluctantly gave the baby up. She planned to snatch her back if Leila stopped crying in Trisha's arms, but that didn't happen. Even this well-seasoned mother couldn't get the baby to stop fussing.

Candace stayed there twenty minutes. Leila didn't scream the whole time, but she never stopped crying. She never stopped frowning or looking like the saddest baby in the world. They tried to feed her, sing to her, and entertain her with shiny toys, but nothing worked.

"What should I do?" Candace asked. She managed to stop her own tears from falling, but was still close to panic. Maybe her baby was hurting somewhere. Maybe she swallowed something while riding in the back. Candace wondered if one of Mrs. Whitley's last-minute instructions might pertain to this.

"I don't know what her problem is," Trisha said after a while. She handed the infant back to her befuddled friend. "Take her home and hold her for a while. She can't keep this up. She'll tire herself out sooner or later."

Sooner or later?

"That's it?" Candace asked. "Let her tire herself out?" That seemed grossly inadequate. Maybe even dangerous.

"She needs to get used to you," Trisha said.

"But can't you—"

"She needs to get used to *you*," Trisha said. "That's what your problem is now. She doesn't know who her mama is. You keep letting other people take care of her, and she ain't never gon' get it right."

Candace knew her friend had a point because she felt the same way a couple of weeks ago. "I have to work tonight," she said. "Are you still going to watch her?"

"Yeah," Trisha said. "Whenever you need. But right now . . ." she looked at the wall clock, ". . . it's eleven o'clock. That gives you seven hours to bond with your baby. So take her home. I'll see you later." Trisha yawned and rubbed her eyes.

"You're kicking me out?" Candace asked.

"Naw, girl. I wouldn't kick you out." But Trisha walked to the door and opened it as she spoke.

225

Candace followed. "What if she doesn't stop?"

"She will," Trisha said. "She can't keep that up much longer."

⌒

When Candace put Leila back in her car seat, the baby stopped crying almost immediately. Candace bit her nails and drove across the street as slowly as possible. She thought the ugly episode was over, but Leila started up again when Candace took her out of the car a second time. The baby continued to cry when they got in the apartment.

Candace tried everything she learned in her parenting classes, but her baby wasn't hot or cold. Leila wasn't hungry or full or sick. There was nothing in her child-rearing books about what to do when your baby doesn't know you, and that sour fact was enough to make Candace start crying again, too. So she sat on the couch with the baby in her arms and they cried together, just two little kids who didn't know what the hell was going on in the world.

Leila stopped first. Out of sheer exhaustion, her yells eventually slowed to sobs and finally soft pants. When Candace looked down and saw that she was finally asleep, she didn't take her to the crib as she originally planned. Instead Candace unbuttoned her shirt and positioned the baby's head between her breasts. She hoped her scent would trigger something in the infant's memory.

"*I'm* your mother," she whispered. "*I'm* your mother."

Candace's cell phone rang at two o'clock. She didn't realize she'd fallen asleep. Leila was still on her chest, snoring lightly. Candace carefully placed the baby on the couch next to her, but the gentle move was enough to wake her. Candace rushed to the love seat, where her phone called out from her purse.

"Hello?"

"Hey, Candace. What's going on?" It was Tino.

"I must've fallen asleep," she said. "I gotta—I need to feed the baby." She dug for a bottle in the diaper bag Mrs. Whitley gave her. She really didn't want to keep or use anything from those people's house, but Candace didn't think she'd have time to mix her own formula.

"That's just like parents," Tino said. "Borrow your baby and don't fill it up when they bring it back."

Candace laughed. She took the bottle to the kitchen and yanked the nipple off. In the living room Leila had gone from fussing to crying already. Candace threw the bottle in the microwave and rushed back to the front room. She scooped her baby from the couch, and Leila actually quieted down. Candace crooked the phone on her shoulder and headed back to the kitchen.

"Hey, let me call you back," she told Tino.

"All right. I just wanted to let you know I was coming by later."

"Tino, I work tonight."

"I thought you were off."

"Sorry."

"Oh, I see how it is," he said.

"What?"

"You got your *other* baby back now, so I get put on the back burner."

"You're kidding, right?"

"Yeah. But still . . . I told you I wanted to see her today. I got her a gift and everything."

"Really?"

"Really."

"Tino, you never even got *me* a gift."

"See, there you go running your mouth. I got you something, too."

"Seriously?"

"Yeah. What kind of crappy boyfriend do you think I am?"

The microwave dinged. Candace put the nipple back on the bottle and positioned the baby for feeding. Leila took the milk easily and enthusiastically. Candace smiled, happy to be right about what she wanted for a change.

"That's sweet," Candace said. "But you're going to have to wait until tomorrow."

"Why didn't you call me when you got home?" Tino asked. "I could've went at lunchtime."

"I fell asleep. I'm sorry."

"It's the *bebita*," he said. "Already you don't have time for me."

"I'll make it up to you."

"Oh, yeah?"

Candace smiled. "You sound like you like that."

"I think I do," he said.

"You got something in mind?"

Tino giggled. "We can talk about it tomorrow."

"All right," Candace said. "And don't forget my gift!" She hung up before he could respond.

৽

Her stepfather called at five to make sure his wife wasn't crazy and they could indeed catch a plane to Texas. Candace told him it was true. She told also told him about the classes she was taking for her second semester of college. Gerald said he was proud.

৽

At 5:30 Candace dropped her daughter off at Trisha's house on her way to work. She made it to the restaurant at 6:02, late for the very first time, and she had the most stressful night ever. By the end of her shift, she decided she would either have to get a new babysitter or talk Trisha into getting a home phone.

Candace didn't make it home until 12:30 a.m. She heard screaming as she mounted Trisha's stairs, and it got louder when she approached her friend's door. She hoped it was Willie acting up in there, but of course it was Leila again. Candace rushed in apologizing. Trisha looked the most frazzled, but Petey and Little Sammy looked pissed off as well.

Trisha handed over the fussy baby as soon as Candace was within reach, and much to everyone's surprise, Leila stopped crying immediately. She grabbed a fistful of Candace's work shirt and buried her face in her mother's chest. She whimpered softly like a frightened puppy.

"Ain't this a bitch," Trisha said.

Candace laughed. "Trust me, I'm as surprised as you. Was she crying all night?"

"No. She was earlier, after you left, but I finally got her settled down. She was cool till she woke up at twelve. She's been going since then."

"I'm sorry," Candace said.

"It's all right," Trisha said, "but we need to redefine our babysitting arrangements. This might get to be too much to do for free."

Candace frowned. "I never wanted you to do it for free, Trisha. I thought I told you I would pay."

"No, I don't remember that," Trisha said, but she was clearly interested in the idea. "How much did we talk about?"

"I guess we didn't," Candace said. "How much do you want?"

"Can you afford twenty dollars a night?"

Candace made that at one table. "That's all you want?"

"Yeah, girl. What you work, four, five nights a week?"

"Usually four."

"That's eighty dollars," Trisha said.

"That's fine."

"Oh." Trisha smiled. "I guess we ain't got no problem then! How was your night at work?"

Candace grinned. She sat on Trisha's couch and stared into her baby's eyes. Leila stared back at her. And she looked comforted rather than afraid of her new mom now.

❧

But the next morning Leila was inconsolable again. Candace changed her, fed her, and held her for hours, it seemed. She found that if she stood, Leila would quiet down long enough to fall asleep. But if Candace sat down, and Lord forbid she put Leila down, the baby would kick up a racket loud enough to wake the dead.

But when Leila woke up after her afternoon nap, everything was fine. She loved her mama. It was as if the earlier episode never occurred. Candace wanted to call the Whitleys and ask if Leila was always like this in the mornings, but she forced herself not to make that call. Whatever the baby was going through was essentially her mother's fault, so Candace bore the brunt and the guilt.

But it wasn't an ongoing thing. Leila only had two more bouts of *who are you and where am I?* It only happened in the mornings, and it didn't last very long. After the third day, Leila knew exactly who her mother was at all times.

CHAPTER 18
FIRST IMPRESSIONS

Tino came on Sunday bearing the gifts he promised. For Leila, he had the Laugh and Learn Puppy. This adorable stuffed animal sang ten different songs and boasted it could teach baby her ABC's, 123's, colors, and body parts. The doll had a huge head and big floppy ears and eight different areas you could squeeze to begin a lesson. The puppy was as big as Leila.

For his girlfriend Tino bought a silver keepsake plate, spoon, and cup set. Candace initially opened the box in confusion, wondering why he would give her dishes. But as she studied the set, Candace knew it was something she would keep forever. There was a monogram in the center of the plate. It read:

Leila Denise Hendricks
June 30th, 2010

Candace looked up in surprise. "When'd you get this?"

"I had it for two weeks already."

"Tino, this is great. I never would have expected anything like this. Maybe from my parents, but not you."

"I give good gifts."

"You do. How'd you know her middle name?" Candace asked.

"You told me. I don't remember when."

"I don't use her full name every time I talk about her, do I?"

"No, you've only said it once or twice."

"And you remembered?"

"I remember the first thing you ever said to me," he said.

Candace called his bluff. "What was it?"

Tino smiled. "I ran up to you after class and said, 'Hey, your name's Candace, right?' And you said, 'Yeah. How—'"

"'How do you know my name?'" Candace said. "I remember now."

"I remember what you were wearing," Tino said.

Candace cocked an eyebrow. "What?"

"Naw, I'm just kidding," he said. "But do I still get a kiss?"

"Certainly. I'm never throwing this plate away." She leaned in and pecked him softly on the lips. Tino grinned like he made it to third base. Candace never met a man who was so easy to please.

～

On Wednesday Candace went to the Dallas/Overbrook Meadows Airport for real this time. Her parents' flight came in at noon. Nothing could compare to the joy

233

they felt upon seeing their daughter and new grandbaby waiting at the terminal.

Her father was a tall, confident man. At six feet, four inches, Gerald Hendricks was the tallest person Candace knew personally. He was fair-skinned, the color of butter cookies, and always clean-shaven. He had a strong jaw line and stern eyes. After thirty years in the Navy, dressing neatly was as much a part of his life as breathing.

Today he wore khaki Dockers with a short-sleeved golf shirt. His shirt was tucked in, his belt was braided, and his loafers were without scuffs. His hair was as short and as neat as the day he entered boot camp. Mr. Hendricks had perfect teeth, much like he expected for his daughter, considering all the money he put into her mouth.

Candace's mom was much shorter than Gerald, but average height for a woman. Katherine Hendricks's skin was the color of well-aged brandy. At forty-one she was a few years younger than Gerald, but she didn't look over the hill. Her skin was still as smooth as it was in her twenties. The only thing that gave her away was a few crow's feet in the corners of her eyes, but they were only visible when she laughed.

Candace's mom wore a cardigan and dress styled by Dolce & Gabbana. The dress was black, knee length, and form-fitting. The cardigan was black also, and long, about an inch longer than the dress. Katherine Hendricks had dark eyes and full lips. Like Candace, she rarely wore makeup.

Candace ducked behind a pillar and managed to sneak up on her parents as they scanned the terminal for her. She tapped her father on the shoulder.

"Excuse me, sir, you'll have to wait for your daughter somewhere else," she said in her snootiest airport security voice.

Gerald turned, ready to raise hell, and his face lit up like a Christmas tree.

"Oh, my goodness! Candace!" He threw his arms around her in an embrace that threatened to crush the baby she cradled in her arms. He smelled like Old Spice, the only cologne worth wearing, in his opinion.

"My baby! It's Candace!" her mother screamed, as if she had no idea who was picking her up. She pushed her husband aside and grabbed her daughter for another bone-crushing hug.

"I missed you, baby," Katherine said. "I missed you—*I missed you—I missed you!* Don't you ever go this long without seeing us! You hear? Don't you *ever* go this long!"

"I won't, Mama. I promise."

"Let me see that baby!" Gerald said. He plucked Leila from Candace's arms and held her into the air. "Look at her," he said to his wife. "Look at those chubby cheeks. Who'd she get those from?"

"That's *Candace*," Katherine said.

"I don't have big cheeks," Candace said.

"You did," her dad assured her. "You must have forgotten your baby pictures. She's a spitting image."

"She is," Katherine agreed.

Everyone smiled at the child, and Leila liked being the center of attention. She grinned brightly, showing off a mouth full of gums.

Gerald held the baby close to his chest. Leila was almost swallowed up in his big arms.

"Come down here, let me see." His wife bounced with anticipation.

Candace heard her daughter giggling from inside the huddle.

⌒

Candace thought she would ride back into town with both parents, but her stepfather was insistent that they not become a burden during their stay. He rented a car at the airport and said they would get a motel room once they got to Overbrook Meadows. Candace offered to make space for them in her apartment, but her parents were staying until Sunday. Gerald knew all four of them wouldn't be comfortable in a one-bedroom for that long.

So Candace drove back with Leila and her mother. Her father followed behind in a brand new Lincoln Navigator. Even fifteen hundred miles away from home, Candace's parents were used to a certain level of luxury.

The ride back took forty-five minutes, during which Candace told her mother everything she wanted to know about her new life. Candace told her about the city and the few friends she made since moving down there. They talked about school and her job at Pappadeaux. The conversation eventually made its way to her love life, and Candace couldn't keep a smile off her face when she talked about Tino. Katherine could tell she was seriously smitten.

"But don't tell Dad," Candace tacked on at the end.

"Why?"

"Mama, you know how he is."

"Girl, Gerald never had a problem with anyone you went with until you messed up with that *rapper*."

"I know," Candace said. "But after Rilla, I don't want him to know I'm going out with someone else. He's going to think '*Okay, here we go again.*' "

"Not if you talk to him," Mrs. Hendricks said. "This new boy sounds like a totally different person. He's in school. He's your age."

"He is, Mom. He's special, a real good dude. But I don't want Dad to worry about me. I'll tell him when y'all get back to New York."

"Candace."

"Seriously. Don't tell him. Please."

"Haven't you had enough secrets?" her mom asked. "*Please.*"

"All right, Candace," Mrs. Hendricks said, but she didn't sound convincing at all.

∽

They went straight to Candace's apartment, where she wowed her parents with her homemaking skills. Not only was her apartment exceptionally clean, but Candace had baby supplies in abundance. Her father went through everything. He even investigated the refrigerator and cupboards.

"When'd you start eating brussels sprouts?" he asked as he pawed through the freezer. "And baby corn?"

"What do you mean?" Candace asked.

237

"You didn't eat this stuff in New York."

"I had a nutritionist when I was pregnant," Candace said. "He gave me a diet plan so I could eat healthy for Leila. After she was born, I guess I kept eating like that."

He turned and stared at her oddly. "Who the hell are you? And where's my daughter?"

Candace laughed. "So does this mean you're proud of me?" She stared up at him like a much younger child.

"Yeah, baby," he said and kissed her on the forehead. "I'm very proud of you."

⁓

After checking out her apartment, Candace's parents left to get their own sleeping quarters situated. Candace wanted to go with them so they wouldn't get lost, but her dad got a map with the rental car. Plus the Navigator had a GPS tracking system. He figured that was all he needed.

"If I can find the Panama Canal by submarine, I can damned sure find the Great Western off Lancaster."

Mrs. Hendricks rolled her eyes. "We'll call you if we get lost, honey. Keep your phone on."

"All right," Candace said. She walked them outside with Leila on her hip. Back in the apartment, she fed the baby, bathed her, and put her to sleep in the crib, but her parents still weren't back when she got done. She called Tino to keep from worrying.

"Hey."

"Hey! What's up, Candace. Are your parents here yet?"

"Yeah. I just got them from the airport."

"Great!" he said. "When do you want me to come over?"

"Come *where*?"

"To meet your family. You do want me to meet them, right?"

"Tino, you can't come over here. I haven't told my dad about you."

"Oh. Okay. When are you telling him?"

"I don't know," Candace said. "I don't want to tell him until they go back to New York."

"What am I, the hunchback you keep in the basement?"

"Don't be like that."

"You really don't want me to meet your family?" The news was obviously a shock to him.

"Tino, it's nothing against you. It's *me*. I don't want to tell my dad I have a new boyfriend because he'll think it's gonna be like it was with Rilla."

"I'm nothing like him."

"I know, but everything is good right now. Everybody's happy."

"And you don't want me around to mess it up?"

"Don't say stuff like that."

"What is it for real? He doesn't like Mexicans?"

"My dad's not racist. Why would you say that?"

"It hurts my feelings that you don't want me to meet your parents," Tino said. "I know I'm a guy and I'm not supposed to talk about my *feelings*, but I do what I want."

"Tino, I'm sorry."

"It's cool," he said. "You don't get to meet my mama now."

"You're not serious."

"I don't know, Candace. I'm starting to think you don't like me like I like you."

"That's not true."

"Am I supposed to believe what you *tell me* or what you *show me*?"

"What does that mean?"

"It means—"

But someone knocked at Candace's door. She knew it was her parents. "Hey, I gotta go, Tino. I'll call you back."

"Yeah, exactly," he said.

"Don't do that, please."

"Bye, Candace."

"Tino, are you mad at me?"

"Just hang up. Go do what you have to do."

"All right. I'll call you back on my way to work."

"Whatever," he said and disconnected.

Candace rushed to the front door and was surprised by the stern look her father greeted her with. She thought it was because she took too long to answer, but that wasn't the problem.

"So," he said. "I understand you have a new boyfriend."

Candace looked to her mother and Katherine Hendricks shrugged like, *Yeah I told him. And? What about it?*

"Um, yeah. I do have a boyfriend," Candace said.

"We're not leaving until we meet him," Gerald said as he entered. In the living room he turned to face her with his arms crossed over his chest.

"Okay," Candace said. "That's fine."

"When?" he asked.

"I'm off tomorrow."

"Tomorrow's perfect." With the matter settled, his cheery grin came back. "All right, where's my grandbaby?"

~

Candace's parents wanted to keep the baby while she was at work. They said they would stay at Candace's apartment rather than take Leila to their hotel room. Candace didn't have anything in there she was worried about them finding, so this arrangement was fine with her. It felt good not to be hiding anything from them anymore.

She left at five-thirty and had to stop by Trisha's house because her babysitter still didn't have a home phone. Trisha was cool with getting the night off, so Candace didn't feel bad about the late notice. She left her friend's apartment in a great mood and called Tino on her way to work.

"Hello?"

"*Hey, baby,*" she said.

"Hey, baby? What's that about?"

"C'mon, Tino. Don't stay mad at me. I have good news."

"What? You're going back to New York?"

241

"That would be good news to you?"

"No, but maybe it would be for you."

"All right, Tino. I'm sorry. I should have told my parents about you. I am not ashamed of you at all. I think you're the perfect guy. And I'm not going to hide you from them. I told my dad about you, and he wants to meet you tomorrow."

"You told your dad?"

"Well, actually my mom told my dad, but I told my mom. Let's not split hairs."

"He wants to meet me?"

"Yes. Tomorrow. Is that cool?"

"Yeah, but now *I'm* kinda scared. He was in the army, right? You said he's real big?"

"It was the navy, and I know you're not tripping after the way you acted."

"I'm just saying. It's one thing for me to want to meet him, but now I feel nervous. He's going to have all of these expectations. Ask all these questions."

"And you're going to speak intelligently and smile, and once he sees what a great guy you are, he's going to fall in love with you just like I did."

"You fell in love with me?"

Candace felt like her whole car got a little warmer. "Yeah, Tino. I did."

"Interesting," he said.

"So? You're in love with me, too," she said. "You were in love with me a long time ago."

"I was, and I am. But you didn't tell me you felt that way."

"I was going to."

"Cool," he said.

"Cool," she said.

⤳

Candace had a good day at work. When she got home, she found her father lying on his stomach on the living room floor. Leila was on her stomach facing him.

"C'mon," he urged. "C'mon, girl."

"What's he doing?" Candace asked her mom.

"He's trying to get her to crawl," Katherine informed her.

Candace tossed her purse on the couch and rushed to the bedroom. She came back with a camera and got a quick shot of the peculiar scene. Since she had the camera out, her parents posed for a multitude of pictures with their grandbaby. Katherine got behind the camera and took pictures of Candace and her father, and then Gerald took pictures of Candace and her mom.

Candace promised to send duplicates of all the photos, but Gerald said there was a Walmart close to their hotel. He said he would develop them in the morning and have duplicates for Candace when they came tomorrow. She said that would be fine.

When her parents left for the night, Candace was glad to be alone with her baby. But Leila fell asleep shortly afterwards. Candace called Tino, who was always up for a chat. They stayed on the phone until the late *late* show went off.

Candace had classes on Thursday, so her parents couldn't visit until after one. When they got there, Gerald had the pictures he promised, and he had a few of them framed already. The chosen three were Candace with her father, Candace and her mother with the baby, and the two grandparents with the baby. Candace set the frames up decoratively in her living room. They were the first display photos in her home.

The elder Hendrickses took their daughter and grandchild to lunch, and afterwards Candace showed them a few sights in the big city. By the time they got home, it was time to get ready for their dinner with Tino. Candace called her boyfriend and arranged for him to come to her apartment at six so they could all ride together. Her parents went back to their hotel to change, and Candace was left alone in her apartment for a little more than an hour. That was plenty of time to take a shower, get dressed, and ponder all of the things that could go wrong on this evening.

At six o'clock sharp someone knocked on her door.

"It's me," Tino called from outside.

Candace sighed. "I shouldn't have told so many lies, huh?" she asked Leila.

No, you shouldn't have, Leila said. She didn't actually say it, but Candace knew what she was thinking.

For his date with Candace and her parents, Tino wore a long-sleeved white button-down with black slacks and black loafers. And he had on a tie. It was black and wide and knotted perfectly. He was as strikingly handsome as ever. His hair was tied back, his face clean-shaven, and his dimples aglow.

And while all of this black and white played well with his dark hair and fair skin tone, Candace thought he might be a little over the top.

"A *tie*, Tino?" Candace wore slim blue jeans with a blue blouse and black sandals.

He looked around nervously. "Are they here?"

"No. They went back to the hotel to change."

He put a hand on his chest and sighed. He looked seriously spooked. "Man, this is stressful."

Candace shook her head. "Tino, you're the one who wanted to meet them so bad."

He sat hesitantly on the couch. "I know, but I've been thinking. Maybe you were right about not telling them about me until they went back to New York."

Candace rolled her eyes and grinned. "What are you worried about?"

He looked up at her frightfully. "You know I'm going to take a lot of heat because of Rilla."

Candace did know that. "You're nothing like him. You said so yourself."

"Yeah, but it's always harder for the next guy. Your father's going to put me through the ringer."

"No," Candace said. "Once he sees your tie, you're home free."

Tino smiled sheepishly. "You don't like my tie?"

She chuckled. "I'm just kidding. You know you look handsome."

He rubbed his temples like his brain was about to explode. "He's big, right? A lot of muscles?"

Candace shook her head. "Give me a kiss," she said. "This is still a date for us too, you know."

"Oh." Tino shot to his feet and stood before her. He put a hand on her waist and smiled pleasantly. "You look gorgeous tonight."

"Why, thank you," Candace said. She batted her big brown eyes. Tino seemed to get lost in them.

"Oh, *man*," he said. "You make me feel weird."

"What do you mean *weird?*"

"I don't know. It's hard to explain. Just the way you look at me sometimes. I get a feeling. And when you touch me . . ."

Candace knew exactly what that felt like.

Tino leaned in for their pre-date kiss, but someone rang Candace's doorbell. Tino's eyes were getting low and sexy, but they flashed open like an alarm clock went off.

"That's them!" he hissed.

"So hurry up and kiss me," Candace said.

He did, but it wasn't a sultry one like she wanted.

⌒

Tino's tie turned out to be a good idea. Gerald Hendricks showed up wearing a tan suit, and Katherine looked equally dressed for church. Candace was the one left feeling inadequate, but she had the home-field advantage; her parents didn't care what she looked like. They walked into her apartment and stared at Tino like he was an art exhibit. Instead of greeting him head-on, Gerald put his hands on his hips and began to circle the boy. Tino didn't know whether he should follow with his eyes or remain sculpture-still, so he froze up.

Candace felt so bad for him, she rushed in for the rescue. She put her arm around Tino's waist and turned him so they could remain face to face with her circling father.

"Um, Dad, this is Tino."

Gerald stopped, stared him down, and then began to circle the other way. "I see 'em."

Candace went the other way with Tino, too. It was turning to a bizarre dance.

"Gerald! What are you doing?" Katherine called from the doorway.

"I'm getting a good look at the boy," Mr. Hendricks said. He stopped again, and Candace positioned Tino for another face-off. Tino was very rigid by then. It was like trying to maneuver the Tin Man.

Gerald finally stuck out his large, strong hand. "I'm Gerald Hendricks."

Tino didn't do anything, so Candace bumped him with her hip.

"I'm—I'm Tino. Celestino DeLeon." His hand shot out and was swallowed up in the handshake. His face was as white as a cotton ball. "Hel-hello. Hello, Mr. Hendricks."

Their arms pumped once, twice, but no one let go. Candace knew her boyfriend was trapped.

"Dad, you're scaring him!"

"*Stop that*, Gerald!" her mom called. She rushed forward and pulled them apart. She then cradled Tino's hand in her far more delicate grip.

"Hi. I'm Katherine, Candace's mom."

"Nice to meet you," Tino said. He met Katherine's eyes for a second, but his gaze kept floating back to her taller, more frightening husband.

"Dad, stop looking at him like that," Candace said. "Here, hold her." She thrust Leila into his arms, and Gerald reluctantly accepted the baby.

"What, wait, Candace. Hold on." But once he had her, the magic started to work. Gerald looked down at his granddaughter, and his stern expression slipped into a doting smile. He looked back to Tino and tried to bring the animosity back, but it was too late.

Katherine ogled her grandchild, too, and Tino took that moment of distraction to remove Candace's arm from his waist. He took a healthy two steps away from her as well.

By the time Gerald looked down at Tino again, his venom was gone. But he found it quickly. "Here," he said, passing Leila off to her grandmother. "Let's get a move on, everybody." He stepped forward and put a hand on Tino's shoulder. "You ride up front with me."

And that set the tone for the rest of the evening.

Candace was worried Tino would be the one with the hard questions like *Why did you take Leila away so soon,* and *Why did you fly down here twice in one week*, but Tino scarcely asked any questions at all; he stayed on the defensive the whole time.

On the way to the restaurant, Gerald drilled him thoroughly.

"Where are you from, Celestino?"

"I'm from here, Overbrook Meadows. I've lived here all my life."

"In this city?"

"Yessir."

"Your parents live here?"

"Yessir."

"What do they do?"

"My mom's a history teacher. My dad's a construction worker."

"They still together?"

"Yessir."

"Where do they live?"

"Here, sir. On the north side."

"What street?"

"*Dad!*" Candace called from the backseat.

"All right," Gerald said and then asked, "I understand you go to school with my daughter. What's your major?"

"I'm pre-med," Tino said with a smile.

Candace thought her father would be proud of that, but Gerald *hmphed*, and Tino's smile faded away.

And that was just the beginning. At the restaurant, things picked up pace.

"What high school did you go to?" Gerald asked Tino.

"Diamond Park."

"*Diamond Park?* Is that a school or a part of town?"

"It's both," Tino said with a curious expression. "I think the school was named after the part of town."

"How'd you know that?" Candace asked her father.

"I did my research," Gerald said. "Diamond Park's on the north side of town, isn't it?" he asked Tino.

Again Candace was taken aback. Tino was equally surprised.

"Um, yeah. It's near the stockyards."

"A lot of gangs up there, aren't there?" Gerald asked.

"Yeah, there are," Tino admitted.

"Mexican gangs," Gerald specified.

"The north side is mostly Hispanic," Tino said. "That's the only reason the gangs there are Mexican. The gangs on the south side are black."

"Are you in a gang?" Gerald asked.

Candace finally got a chance to laugh.

"No," Tino said with a grin. "I'm not in a gang, sir."

"So what's up with the hair?" Gerald asked.

"Mama, make him stop," Candace pleaded.

"Gerald, you're not going to interrogate the boy during the whole meal," Katherine said.

"All right, all right," Gerald said. "Just one more question." He paused to let the magnitude of his final query sink in. "What do you want with my daughter?"

Candace couldn't believe he asked that, but Tino was prepared for the question.

"Your daughter is a great girl," he said. "She's smart. She's nice. She's the most determined person I know.

Everything about her is different from the other girls I go to school with. Candace cares about her future. Everything she does, she does it on her own. I've never met anyone like her."

Candace didn't know Tino felt that way. His words made her warm inside.

"She's pretty, too," Gerald said with a big smile.

Tino stared across the table at his girlfriend and smiled dreamily. "Yeah. She is pretty."

"Hmph," Gerald said.

Tino looked back and saw that he wasn't smiling anymore. Tino's grin went away, too. "But she's pretty inside and out," he said. "Her looks are the last thing I care about. I didn't even bring it up. All that other stuff comes first."

"*All right*," Candace said and picked up her menu. "Can we eat now, Dad?"

Mr. Hendricks gave Tino one last glare and then picked up his menu.

"All right," he said. "What do you want to order, princess?"

◇

With the Q & A over, they went on to enjoy a great meal. For this special dinner, Candace's father took them to one of the nicest Italian restaurants in the city, Chez Panini. Gerald spoke fluent Italian, so he ordered for everyone except Tino. Tino was stuck on *impress-the-parents* mode, so he struggled through the difficult pronunciations himself. And he didn't do a bad job. The waiter knew exactly what he wanted, and Gerald nodded his approval at Tino's meal selection.

With delicious food in their faces, the conversation became more casual, and soon everyone was laughing and enjoying each other's company. Gerald told stories about Candace when she was a child in New York, and Tino began to loosen up. His trademark wit, humor, and innocence kicked in, and Candace knew her parents were starting to like him.

They left the restaurant in great spirits. Gerald let Tino ride in the back with Candace on the way home, and they got a chance to hold hands for the first time that evening. But they had to keep their lovey-dovey eyes to a minimum. Every time Candace looked up, she saw her father staring at her in the rearview mirror. His eyes were still cold and threatening, but at that point Candace knew it was all for show.

When they got back to her apartment, Candace's parents said they were going to turn in for the night rather than visit for a while. Candace hoped she'd have a chance for some alone time with Tino, but he was hesitant. If he waited for her parents to leave, they would know he and Candace were going inside alone. Instead of putting that thought in their heads, Tino was the first to bid a fair adieu. He shook hands with everyone, Candace included, and burned off in his hooptie.

When Candace got upstairs, she put Leila in her crib and breathed a big sigh of relief. The subject of Katherine taking two trips from New York never came up.

Some lies will go away by themselves, Candace decided.

～

The Hendrickses stayed three more days. On Sunday afternoon they packed up their hotel room and drove to Candace's apartment for one last goodbye before their flight back to New York. Candace made sure Tino was there, too.

There were a lot of hugs and kisses and crying from the Hendricks women. In the midst of these emotions, Gerald pulled Tino aside for a little heart-to-heart. Candace watched from a distance. She couldn't tell what was being said, but when it was over Tino didn't look too rattled. Gerald shook his hand one last time and made peace with his daughter's boyfriend.

Candace told her mother she could call anytime she wanted from now on, and she promised to visit them in New York during her Christmas break. When they were gone, Candace went upstairs to her apartment, and Tino followed. It was good to be alone with him again. Candace sat on her couch with Leila in her arms, and Tino cuddled next to her. He wrapped his arms around her waist and laid his head on her shoulder.

"You glad that's over with?" she asked.

"It's not over with," Tino said. "He wants me to call him every week."

"My *dad?*"

"Yeah. He says I can call collect."

Candace was astonished. "Tino, you do not have to call my father."

"I'm just kidding," he said.

She poked an elbow into his ribs. "Quit playing. What did he say for real? I saw y'all talking."

Tino leaned in and kissed her softly on the neck. "He says I shouldn't do that anymore."

Candace grinned. "What else did he tell you not to do?"

Tino scooted up and kissed behind her ear this time. His lips were warm and barely wet. He sucked a little before backing away. A fiery tingle skated down Candace's side.

"I'm not supposed to do that, either."

"*Ooh*," Candace said. She looked down at Leila, who sucked her bottle complacently, totally unaware of the hormones raging around her. "What else can't you do, Tino?"

"You really want to know?" he asked.

She nodded.

He put a hand on her thigh and moved slowly toward those *nether regions*. This was new territory for him.

"I'm definitely not supposed to do this," he said, and stopped abruptly within an inch of her panty line.

Candace's throat was dry. She swallowed roughly. "Why'd you stop?"

Tino took the offensive hand away and put it all the way in his pocket. "I told you, I'm not supposed to do that."

"But you did that other stuff."

"Yeah, but those are minor violations," he said. "That third one will get me shot."

"My dad isn't going to shoot you."

"He shot people before," Tino countered.

"In a *war*," Candace said. "That was different."

"He thinks protecting you is a war."

"Did he really tell you not to touch me?" she asked.

"No."

"What did he say?"

"He told me not to hurt you," Tino said.

That sounded like Gerald.

"So no one told you not to touch me?" she asked.

"No. I do that on my own."

They had only been dating for a few weeks, but Candace knew boys who would have been a lot more aggressive in this same period of time. Especially if they were alone in her apartment.

"All right," Candace said. She turned away and leaned her head to the side, exposing her jugular as if for a vampire. "I like what you did earlier . . ."

"You mean this?" Tino asked, and sucked under her ear again.

"Yeah, that," Candace said. "Do it again."

"Okay," Tino said. "But you're not getting my best until the baby goes to sleep."

Candace looked down and saw that Leila's eyes were already closed. She pulled the bottle from her mouth and the infant didn't react.

"Well, lookey here," she said.

CHAPTER 19

NEWS FROM CELL BLOCK FOUR

Candace was under the impression it would start to cool off after August, but that's not the case in Texas. September crept by like a long blast from a steel mill furnace. October brought much of the same misery. Halfway through the black and orange month, Candace asked Tino why they still had daily highs of ninety degrees or better. It was insane. He promised it would cool off pretty soon, and Candace threatened to go back to New York if it was still this hot on Thanksgiving.

But of course she was kidding.

And of course it wasn't.

On October 31 something weird happened in the skies over Overbrook Meadows. Boreas blew hard from the north and brought with him the first cold front of the season. Leila finally got a chance to wear one of the jackets Candace bought her as the daily high dipped to a treacherous seventy-two degrees.

And it was still like that in November. Candace had Thanksgiving dinner with Trisha and her family, and most of the guests wore shorts and T-shirts.

In December the temperatures finally dropped to a level more worthy of the winter season. Candace bought a pink, New York-style bomber jacket with a furry hoodie. She wore it on the last day of school before Christmas break with a pair of tight jeans and wooly moccasins.

She met with Tino for lunch at the school's cafeteria. Instead of the chips and sandwiches they usually ate, the couple partook in a holiday meal provided by the college. They had a choice of turkey or ham with dressing, mashed potatoes, green beans, sweet potato pie, and a cup of tea. Tino and Candace found a table to themselves and dug in ravenously.

"How do you think you did on your finals?" he asked.

"I did good," she said. "I think history was my worst class this time."

"Don't tell my mom that."

"I won't," Candace said. Tino's mother was an extremely passionate history teacher. Candace had met her a few times in the months they'd been together. She was a nice woman, short and round and as quick as a whip.

"I don't see the point in it," Candace said. "I'm never going to need to know which was the twenty-second state to join the Union."

"Alabama," Tino said.

Candace looked sideways at him. "Why do you know that?"

"It's hard for me to forget stuff I memorized," he said.

"So you've got volumes of useless information up there?" She pointed to his noggin.

"I wouldn't say it's *useless*," he said. "I'm the only one in my family who can get through a game of Trivial

257

Pursuit. And what if you go on *Jeopardy* one day? Alabama might come in handy."

"The twenty-second state, Alabama. I'll try to remember that," Candace said.

Tino smiled. His smile was goofy and cute and sexy at the same time—even with brown gravy in the corner of his mouth.

Candace plucked a napkin from the dispenser. She leaned forward and wiped his face much like she was accustomed to doing for Leila. Tino took it like a man. He seemed to appreciate the gesture. It was interesting how close they'd gotten since August. Yet still so far away . . .

～

After lunch they were both done for the day, and for the semester. Candace looked forward to being off until January. Tino escorted her to her car with his arm around her waist. His hair was down today. He wore faded blue jeans with a white sweater and a black leather coat.

He was very handsome, always the cutest face on campus, in Candace's opinion. She bumped him with her hip as they walked, and he bumped her back.

"Hey, you're not supposed to hit a girl," she teased.

"Ah, but that's not true," he said. "Statistically speaking, forty percent of all men surveyed admitted to hitting a girl within the last month."

Tino was so good at that. It was hard to tell when his facts were fabricated.

"Sixty percent of *those men* have spent six months or more in jail in the last three years," Candace countered.

Tino stopped in mid-stride and turned to face her. Candace stopped, too, but she didn't see anything out of place.

"What?"

He reached out and held both of her hands. His fingers were cold, but the gesture was still comforting. He stared into her eyes and smiled warmly.

"What?" Candace asked again, grinning now.

"Look," he said, jerking his head towards the light pole they were standing next to.

Candace looked and followed it upwards until she saw what he saw: At the top of the pole, an arm extended over the sidewalk with a light fixture affixed to the end of it. This skinny arm was at least ten feet above them, but someone managed to tie a sprig of mistletoe about mid-center. Candace looked back at Tino and smiled eagerly.

"You see everything," she said.

"I never miss an opportunity for a kiss," he said and pulled her to him. She threw her arms over his shoulders and he wrapped his around her waist, and something strange happened when they kissed. Not only did Tino slip her a little tongue, but his hands slipped from her waist, and slid, and slid, and *yes*, Tino had his hands on her butt! He didn't grab or squeeze, but they were there. And this was the first time they'd ever been there in public. The tongue in public was also a rarity. Candace opened one of her eyes to make sure she was kissing the right guy.

It was a nice kiss. It was a sexy kiss. But it was over as quickly as it started. Tino backed away and smiled, then he grabbed her hand and continued their walk to her car as if it never happened. And Candace didn't like that. She wanted him to say *something*. She would call attention to it herself, but how would it look if a female brought up these issues?

How come you don't tongue kiss me a lot in public?

That was only the third time you touched my butt.

In four months it was only the third time.

Why don't you touch my booty more often, Tino?

Why don't you grab it and squeeze it?

Don't you want it?

Don't you want me?

And why don't you attack me when we're alone?

Why don't you pull me into the bedroom and throw me on the bed and rip my panties off like in that movie Fatal Attraction?

Why are we still on second base, Tino?

After four months?

What the hell?

But Candace was much too ladylike to ask those questions. So she walked with him instead. When they reached her car, he gave her a full-body hug that almost lasted forever. And since Candace still got goose bumps whenever Tino touched her, she got lost in the hug and forgot about those other questions, just like she always did.

"Are you staying for Christmas?" he asked.

Candace backed up to her car and pulled Tino close to her, so close their belts touched.

"*Mi mama y mi tias* are making tamales on Christmas Eve," he said.

"*Tamales?*"

"We make tamales every year," he explained. "All the women do. The guys just get drunk and start eating them as soon as the first batch is done."

Candace laughed, but Tino was distracted by something a Hispanic female said as she walked by. She was a pretty girl with long, black hair, dark lips and pencil-thin eyebrows. Candace didn't hear what she said. She wouldn't have understood it anyway because it was Spanish, but Tino stared after the girl for a few seconds. His expression was somewhat somber when he looked back to Candace.

"What happened?" she asked.

"Nothing."

"Tino, you suck at lying. Tell me what happened. What'd she say?"

He shook his head. "You don't want to know."

But that only made her want to know more. "Tell me, Tino."

He sighed. "She asked me what's wrong with me. She said, 'Can't you find a nice *Mexican* girl?' "

Candace looked after the student, but she rounded a corner and was out of sight.

"I didn't know people trip like that," she said.

"What do you mean?"

"In New York, brown and black is like, the same. Where I live, everybody is either black or black mixed with Mexican, or Puerto Rican, or whatever. Blacks and Latinos are in the same boat. We're all brown."

261

"Well, you're down south now," Tino said. "Texas likes racism more than baseball. We get so much racism here, the minorities end up being racist toward each other."

Candace thought about that for a second. But Tino never left her on a sour note.

"So are you going to make tamales with my aunts or what?"

"You sure they want me to?" she asked. "They're not going to get mad because you didn't bring a *Mexican* girl?"

"Naw," Tino said. "My parents love you. My aunts already know I'm going out with a black girl. They don't care, so long as I'm happy."

"Are you happy?" Candace asked.

"Very happy," he said.

"All right. I guess I'll learn how to make tamales then."

"Are you going to come for Christmas, too?" he asked.

"What do y'all do on Christmas?"

"Eat everything they made the day before. We open our gifts and play with our toys and eat some more. We watch TV and fall asleep and wake up and eat some more and get drunk."

"You get drunk?" Candace asked.

Tino smiled. "Not me *personally*, but pretty much everyone else. Even some of my younger cousins. If you've never been around a bunch of drunk Mexicans, then you gotta go. My grandma usually takes her teeth out and throws them at somebody before the day is over with."

Candace laughed. She told him she would go. She looked forward to spending the holidays with him and his intoxicated relatives. She left the campus headed to Trisha's house. She hoped Leila was still awake so she could try on her Christmas outfit.

⌒

When Candace got on the freeway, a terrible thought occurred to her. She just told Tino she'd stay with him for Christmas, but she also promised her parents she would fly home for the holidays. There was no way she could do both.

"*Damn!*" she spat.

It seemed like an awful dilemma, but there was a pretty simple solution: She had to cancel on someone. And that person was sure to be hurt. But who? Candace reached into her purse and found her cell phone close to the top. It didn't take thirty seconds to make a decision.

"Hello?"

Damn! Why couldn't her mom answer?

"Hey, Dad. It's me, Candace."

"Hey, baby! What's going on?"

"Um, is Mama there?"

"She's out back in the garden. You want me to get her?"

Candace sighed. "No. I guess I can talk to you."

"You *guess*? I'm not that bad, am I?"

"No, Dad. It's just that I've got bad news. I'd rather tell Mom than you."

There was a pause.

"What is it, Candace?"

"You, um, you remember when I said I would come home for Christmas?"

"Yes. Your mother's talked about nothing else. We've got a big dinner planned. Everyone's going to be here. *The whole family.* And you will be, too, right?"

He knew how to lay on the guilt.

"Actually, Dad, I'm going to stay down here instead."

"Why?"

"Tino asked me to go with him and his family."

"This is that same shit," Gerald said.

"What do you mean?"

"I mean you running behind that boy the same way you did with that other asshole. When are you gonna get it, Candace? When are you gonna see how they're screwing up your life?"

"Daddy, Tino's different. You know that."

"All I know is you're doing the same thing, Candace. You got a family who loves you, but you're too busy running behind them knuckleheaded boys."

"I love y'all, too," Candace said. "And it's just one Christmas. I can come for spring break if you want. Plus I'm going back to New York next year. Then I'll be there all the time."

"Candace, I'm not going to sit here and beg you to do right. You know right from wrong."

"Dad, it's—"

"Is that it? Is that what you called for?"

"Daddy, don't do that."

"I gotta go, Candace," he said. "I'll tell your mother to call you later."

He hung up on her. That was the first time he ever did that. It hurt just as much as she figured it would.

ᘒ

When she got to Trisha's house, Candace was not surprised to see Delia there. She was, however, surprised to see the hoochie holding her baby. Delia was feeding Leila, and for some reason that was even worse. The contents of Candace's stomach did a flip as she entered the living room.

Delia looked up at her and smiled innocently. "Girl, you got a good baby. She don't cry or nothing."

"Yeah," Candace said. She walked to the couch and took a seat next to CC's girlfriend. Leila immediately began to fuss and reach for her mother.

"I knew she was gonna do that," Delia said. "Here you go, sweetheart. I know you want your mama."

She handed the baby over politely. Candace smiled down at the infant when she had Leila in her arms. Leila always made things okay. She could put a smile on Candace's face with just her presence.

"She got some pretty eyes," Delia said, leaning over Candace's shoulder.

"She does," Candace agreed.

"They look familiar," Delia said. "They remind me of somebody else's."

265

Candace's heart stopped and her mouth went dry. She had long since determined Leila's hazel eyes favored CC's much more than Rilla's dark brown irises. It was a hard thing to accept, but Candace had made peace with it. She wondered if Delia already knew about her and CC. In the months since Delia first saw her baby, she made a lot of comments that came very close to the truth but never quite made it.

She's too cute! You sure that's Rilla's baby?

She got all of your hair, Candace. Her hair don't look like it got no Puerto Rican in it.

How come you didn't give her Rilla's last name?

How come you don't take her up there so Rilla can see her?

If I was Rilla, I'd want to know who you been sleeping around with, 'cause that baby's way too pretty to be his.

And now this: *She got some pretty eyes. They remind me of somebody I know.*

But Delia didn't look suspicious when she said any of that stuff, and she didn't look suspicious now. It was hard to believe, but Delia still didn't know anything. All of those innuendos really were coincidental.

Trisha stepped out of her bathroom, wiping sweat from her face. "Ooh, I'm sorry, girl. Is she still eating? Oh, hey, Candace! I didn't know you were here."

"I just got here," Candace said.

"I had to go to the bathroom," Trisha said. "I would have taken her with me, but the air don't blow good in there."

Candace smiled and nodded. She thought it was respectful how Trisha offered an explanation for leaving the baby with Delia. She knew Candace didn't want just anyone holding her child.

"How was she?" Candace asked.

"She was fine," Trisha said. She lifted Sammy from the love seat and took the chair for herself. Sammy looked around the room until he saw Delia's empty lap. He ran to her, and she scooped him up like a bag of potatoes.

"You off school now, ain't you?" Trisha asked.

"Yeah," Candace said. "I'll only need you to watch her when I go to work."

"Ain't you going home for Christmas?" Trisha asked.

Candace shook her head.

Trisha grinned. "So you're staying with *Celestial*, huh?"

"Yeah, we're making tamales," Candace said with a smile.

"*Tamales?*"

"It's a long story."

"Have you hit that yet?" Delia asked. Candace's bedroom problems were old news.

"No," she said. "Not yet."

"Dang, girl! What the hell you waiting on?"

"It's not me," Candace said. "It's him. He never tries to do . . . those things."

"Why don't you initiate it?" Delia asked.

"I don't want to look like a ho."

"You not a ho just cause you want to have sex," Trisha said.

267

"I don't know how to get it started," Candace said. "What am I supposed to do, throw him on the bed and pull his pants off?"

"That's what I do," Delia said. "When CC be acting all shady with the dick, I be like, 'Fine. Go to sleep.' Bet I be riding him when he wake up, though."

Trisha laughed.

Candace didn't.

Candace had a flashback; she remembered the time she woke up and CC was on top of her.

So that's where he gets it from.

"I can't do that with Tino," she said. "It's our first time. It's supposed to be special. It should be something he wants to do."

"Maybe he thinks you can't have sex," Trisha offered. "He might think you still sore from having the baby."

"Maybe he thinks you don't want to 'cause you already got a baby," Delia said.

"Maybe he's gay," Trisha offered.

Candace was so desperate for answers, she even considered this. Tino was unusually beautiful. But she thought about the way he stared at her, the way he touched her, and the way he kissed her; these were not the actions of a homosexual.

"He's not gay," she said. "I know that much for sure."

"Do y'all be kissing?" Delia asked.

"All the time," Candace said.

"I mean like, *really kissing,*" Delia said. "All hot and heavy, feeling all on each other."

Candace took a moment to reflect. "We kiss a lot," she said. "But it never goes that far. Whenever we start touching too much, he'll stop."

"Why?" Trisha asked.

"I don't know why," Candace said. "That's the problem."

"Maybe he's saving hisself for marriage," Trisha guessed.

"If he is, I wish he would tell me," Candace said.

"Maybe he don't want to tell you," Delia said. "Maybe he thinks you'll leave him."

"Would you leave him?" Trisha asked.

"No," Candace said. "I love him, and I know he loves me. He's the best boyfriend I ever had, except for the sex."

"Listen," Trisha said. "You can drive yourself crazy with this, or you can just ask him. He's the only one who's got the answer to your questions."

"I know," Candace said. "But I don't know how to ask him."

"Like this," Delia said. " 'Nigga, why you ain't giving me no dick?' "

Candace laughed.

"You know Rilla's getting out," Delia said. She threw that in casually, the same way she might ask for directions.

But those words changed Candace's whole demeanor. She felt like someone kicked her in the chest. The room swam. She gripped Leila a little tighter and it stopped. She wanted to scream, but she forced herself to remain calm. Her eyes were as big as dinner plates.

"Wh-who said that?"

"CC told me," Delia said. "He talked to Rilla yesterday."

Candace didn't know if she was going to pass out or vomit. Rilla had been in jail since the end of June. That was almost six months ago. She used to think it was odd that she wasn't called to testify against him, but Candace never cared enough to look into it. When more and more time went by, she figured Detective Judkins took Raul to trial without her.

She had Rilla tucked away and forgotten in one of the far recesses of her mind. She moved on with her life and was doing fine. She was happy. Her baby was happy. Rilla couldn't come back now.

"CC bailed him out?" she asked hoarsely.

"No. I think they're letting him go," Delia said.

"Why?"

"I don't know why, girl. That shit happens."

Candace stood quickly. She felt like she was stuck in someone's twisted dream. Her heart kicked like a mule in her chest.

"I gotta go," she said.

"He ain't gonna mess with you, Candace. He'll probably just want to see his baby, is all."

But Candace didn't hear the second part of that sentence. She was already out the door and halfway down the first flight of stairs.

Back in her apartment, Candace rummaged through her dresser drawers for a card she stashed some four months ago. She hadn't seen the damned thing since she moved, which should have made it that much more difficult to locate, but Candace still had someone praying for her. Detective Judkins's card was in the second drawer she looked in. Her fingers shook so badly, it took three tries to dial the number.

The call went straight to voice mail. Candace left a desperate message.

"Hello, Mr. Judkins, this is Candace, Candace Hendricks. You arrested me back in June when I lived with my boyfriend, Raul Canales. I was supposed to testify against him, but no one ever called me about it. And someone just told me Rilla's getting out of jail. Could you please call me and tell me if that's true?"

Candace gave her cell phone number and called Tino next.

"Hello?"

"Tino, you work tonight?"

"Yeah, baby. What's up?"

"I don't know." Candace chewed on her thumbnail. "I'm scared. I wanted you to come over."

"What's going on?"

"I think Rilla's getting out," she said.

"*Rilla's getting out?*" Tino sounded more spooked than her.

"I don't know. Someone told me he was. I called the police to find out for sure, but I had to leave a message. Rilla might be out right now, for all I know."

"Oh, shit," Tino said. "You think he's coming over there?"

"If he gets out, I know he'll try to find me," Candace said.

"I'm here if you need me. Just tell me what you want to do."

Go back to New York.

"I don't know, Tino. I need to find out for sure if he's out before I do anything."

Candace's phone vibrated, indicating she had another call.

"Tino, let me call you back."

"All right. Do you want me to call in?" he asked.

"No. Go ahead and go to work. If I need to go your place, I can still go while you're at work, can't I?"

"Yeah," he said. "You have to stop by my job to pick up the key."

"All right," Candace said. "If I have to go, we'll do it like that. I gotta go, Tino. I'll call you back."

She disconnected with him and picked up the line her mother was on. She tried her best to sound normal.

"Hey, Mama."

"Hello, Candace. How's it going?"

Candace forced a smile. "I'm okay. Is Dad still mad at me?"

"He's scared, baby. He thinks it's going to end up like it did with that other boy."

"It's not, Mama."

"I know, sweetie. He just loves you, is all."

"You're all right with me staying here for Christmas?"

"It's your choice, Candace. I've been there. Trust me. I know how it is. You should have seen the way I was running after Bernard." Katherine rarely spoke of Candace's biological father. Candace was eager to hear about him, but the story would have to wait. She had another incoming call, this time it was a number she didn't recognize.

"Mama, I have to call you back."

"Miss Busybody."

"I'm sorry, Mom. I'll call you right back. I promise."

"All right, baby."

Candace accepted the other call. It was Detective Judkins this time.

"Hello?"

"Hello. Candace?"

"Yes, sir. It's me."

"What can I do for you?"

Candace took a deep breath and a moment to get her thoughts together. "Um, I was calling to ask about that case. I was supposed to testify against my boyfriend, Rilla, remember?"

"Yes, Candace. I've got Raul's file on my desk now."

"Well, I, um, I never got called to go to court or anything. I was wondering if you still need me to do that."

"Why?" he asked. "You planning on leaving town?"

"No, but someone told me Rilla's getting out of jail."

There was a short pause.

"What's it to you?" he asked. His words made the hairs stand on the back of Candace's neck.

"I want to go back to New York," she bluffed. "If he's getting out, then I want to go home."

"Then go," the detective said.

Candace's heart knocked. "You don't need me to testify anymore?"

"No. We'll be fine without you. If you want to go home, then by all means, please do so."

"So he's out?"

There was another pause.

"No, Candace. Raul is still in jail."

Relief rushed over her like a cold shower. "Are you going to let him out?"

The detective sighed. "No, Candace. I'm not planning on letting him out. But if you're that afraid of him, you need to go home."

"Okay," she said. "Can I . . . can I ask one more question?"

"What is it?" She could tell he was getting irritated.

"Do you think you could call me if you let him out?"

The policeman chuckled. "You're some piece of work, you know that?"

"What do you mean?"

"Candace, I don't know what part of this you don't understand, but you got caught with a duffle bag full of dope. You're in no position to request anything from my department."

"It wasn't mine."

"Yes, you said that. But you were home alone with it, and you knew it was there."

Candace didn't say anything.

"But you know what, hey, it's almost Christmas. Here's my good deed for the day: I will call you if Rilla gets out. Okay? I will take time out of my busy day to give you a heads-up."

Candace didn't like his tone, but she liked what he was saying, and she believed him.

"Okay," she said. "Thank you, sir. I really appreciate it."

"Goodbye, Candace," the detective said and hung up.

Candace called Tino back and told him everything was fine. She told him Rilla was still in jail, and she would know about it if he got out. Tino was happy to hear that, but he still sounded rattled.

Candace called her mother back after that, hoping to hear the story about her real dad. But Gerald was in the room with her then, and Katherine wouldn't dare discuss such things in front of him. Instead she told Candace about the time Gerald abandoned his family on Christmas to be with Katherine and her parents. That turned out to be a pretty good story, too.

Candace told her mother about the ongoing struggle to convince Tino to go to school in New York with her in the fall. He was close to his family and thought the move would be stressful for his mom. Katherine gave her daughter a few helpful tips in the fine art of persuasion, and Candace promised to put them to use in the near future.

CHAPTER 20
A SPECIAL GIFT

Two weeks passed with no further news about Rilla, and Candace was happy to let him take his place as the last thing on her mind again.

❧

On December 24, Tino showed up at Candace's apartment at 8:00 p.m. She thought it was a bit late for a family gathering, but he assured her the festivities would still be underway late into the evening.

Tino wore blue jeans with a red and white Christmas sweater so tacky it had to have come from one of his relatives. He wore his black leather jacket and topped the outfit off with an adorable Santa hat. He was clean-shaven and his hair was tied back with a scrunchy. Even with the hideous sweater Tino was as cute as a button, and he was a gift-bearer on this hallowed evening.

"Hey, sexy," Candace said and stepped aside to let him in. For her night with his family, she wore tan corduroy pants and a white blouse with a red v-neck sweater over it. Her sandals were black with a silver buckle across the toes. She wore her hair in a flip as usual, with auburn highlights she got at the salon just yesterday.

"You look great!" Tino said. He reached into the bag he toted and came out with another Santa hat just like his. "This is going to match your outfit!"

Candace took the cap and closed the door behind him. "I got my hair done, Tino. I don't want to wear a hat."

"C'mon," he said. "We'll look like twins!"

"All right. I'll wear it so we'll look like a *couple*."

Tino set his bag down and wrapped his arms around her. "I got you a present," he said.

"It's not the hat, is it?"

"No, it's in the bag. I got something for Leila, too."

"Can I open it?" Candace asked.

"No! You'll ruin the *mystique*. You have to wait till Christmas. Or at least till we get back from my grandma's house. It'll be after midnight then."

"Okay," she said. "I got you something, too."

"Really?"

"Don't act surprised."

"What is it?"

"It's an ant farm."

Tino knitted his eyebrows. "An ant farm? Why would you get me that?"

"I don't know. It was hard to shop for you. I was walking around the store, and I saw these ant farms, and I thought to myself, 'Tino likes biology!' I knew it would be the perfect gift."

"It's too cold," he said. "I can't get any ants cause they're all hibernating."

"Yes, you can," Candace assured him. "You just have to dig really deep."

He smiled. "Okay. I'm gonna get me some ants then."

Candace shook her head. "Boy, I didn't get you an ant farm."

"Then why'd you say that?"

"Why'd you ask what I got you? You should have known I wasn't going to tell you. And, come on, Tino. You were going to dig for ants in forty-degree weather?"

"I would have," he said. "If that's what you got me, and that's what you wanted me to do. I would do it."

"That's sweet. You'd rather dig for ants than tell me I got you a stupid present."

She kissed him provocatively and went to fetch the baby from her crib. Leila was already dressed in the cutest elf suit Candace had ever seen. It was red and green and had tiny shoes with points on the toes. Leila didn't care much for being awakened, but Candace transferred her directly to the car seat, so there wasn't time to put up much of a fuss.

She was asleep again before they got on the freeway.

"Where'd you get that sweater?" Candace asked shortly into the drive.

Tino rolled his eyes. "My grandmother gave it to me. It's not that ugly, is it?"

"I'm not saying anything bad about your grandmother's sweater."

"Man, I knew it. I'm wearing it tonight so I don't have to wear it on Christmas. If she doesn't see me in it at least once, I'll never hear the end of it."

"It's fine," Candace said. "It's kinda . . . sort of . . . cute, in its own special way."

"All right," Tino said. "I'm going to wear it when we go out on New Year's."

"You'd better not."

～

Tino's grandmother lived on the north side of town. Candace thought the whole area was beautiful like the stockyards, but there was a clear divide.

On one side you had Billy Bob's and the rodeo, with all the glitz and glamour, singing and dancing. On the other side of the tracks, you had the *regular* neighborhood, and much of it was poor, gang-ridden, and tagged with graffiti. There were unkempt parks, liquor stores by the dozen, and sprawling apartment complexes long ago abandoned.

Tino's grandmother lived in the midst of this decay, but her house was nice. Tino pulled into the driveway of a red brick structure and looked over at his girlfriend with a dopey grin.

"This is where *mi abuelita* lives," he said.

"She's done pretty well for herself," Candace noticed.

"Not like you're thinking," he said. "My granddad got run over by an Exxon truck back in '96. He got squashed like a bug."

"That's sad."

"It's okay," Tino said. "The settlement money paid for this house. Plus my grandmother never liked him anyway. She still thinks the whole thing was a blessing."

Candace didn't know how to take that bit of news, but Tino was smiling, so she smiled too.

"All right," she said. "I guess it's time to meet your crazy relatives."

But to Candace's dismay, Tino's family turned out to be well-behaved. Based on his descriptions, Candace expected Spanish-speaking trailer trash fresh off the *Jerry Springer Show*. Instead she got well-dressed, well-spoken, and obviously cultured Mexican-Americans. They greeted her pleasantly, commenting on how pretty she was and how cute the baby looked in her outfit.

Tino's mom scooped Leila from the car seat as soon as they entered. She rushed off to show her sisters one of Santa's littlest helpers. Candace pulled Tino off to the side after they said hello to everyone.

"I thought you said they were drunk and crazy," she whispered.

"The night's still young," he said. "Wait till midnight, and then tell me if they're crazy or not."

He took her to the den, where most of the family was gathered around a huge floor-model television. *The Matrix* was on rather than a holiday program or ballgame. Tino's father was there, as well as a few of his aunts and uncles. There were a lot of wives and girlfriends, too, and most of these women were drop-dead gorgeous.

Tino introduced Candace to everyone individually. Everyone was polite. The whole atmosphere was enjoyable. The house was big and neat and every inch of it smelled like food. Tino found a place for them to sit on the biggest sofa. Candice tried to take her Santa hat off, but Tino took it from her and put it back on.

"How will they know whose girlfriend you are if you don't have that hat?" he asked.

"I don't think anyone else has a black girlfriend," Candace noted.

Tino looked around the room. "You're right, but that's only cause they're not lucky like me."

They watched a few scenes of *The Matrix*, and Tino's mother brought Leila back after a while. The baby was awake, and happy, and licking some sticky substance from her lips. Everyone in the den thought she was adorable. They passed her around like a doobie, and Leila loved the spotlight.

"Who is that?" Candace asked, staring across the room.

"That's Hector," he said. "He just turned twenty. He's Melissa's son."

"Who's Melissa?" she asked.

"That lady over there," Tino said and pointed. "She's my cousin. You just shook her hand, don't you remember?"

"I'm trying to keep track of all these names," Candace said. "There's a lot of people in here."

And they kept coming. Thirty minutes later, the room was stuffed to capacity. Of the twenty-five or so relatives in the den, half of them were under the age of five, so it was quite noisy. There was more family in the kitchen and living room as well.

"Are all of these people coming back tomorrow for Christmas?" Candace asked Tino.

"Some of them," he said. "Most of them will go with their in-laws, though. That's why Christmas Eve is so special. Everybody comes for this."

Candace nodded and someone handed her baby back to her. But she didn't get to keep Leila long. Just then Tino's mom stepped into the doorway with an important announcement.

"Okay ladies, whoever's going to help with the tamales needs to come in here and wash your hands. Come on, Candace."

Candace was a little embarrassed by all the attention, but it was good-natured. She handed Leila to her boyfriend.

"I guess you get to watch her."

"Please," he said. "These women aren't going to let me hold her for too long."

Candace gave Tino a kiss on the cheek and then followed his mom into the kitchen.

⁓

Making tamales turned out to be an interesting experience. Six ladies volunteered for the task, and Candace got to work elbow to elbow with Tino's grandmother. She was a small woman with gray hair and dark lines on her face. She wore thick glasses and had a quick tongue.

It took two grueling hours to get the first batch of tamales in the pot, but things went a lot more smoothly after that. The women situated themselves in an assembly line format: One lady heated up the meat and soaked the corn husks. Another filled bowls on the kitchen table with chicken, beef, or pork. Candace and two other girls spread masa on the corn husks. They passed them off to Grandma, who did the filling and folding. Tino's mom stacked the finished product in the pot and took it to the stove.

When Candace got bored with her task, she asked if she could try her hand at folding. The women were in good moods and eager to teach. After a dozen attempts, Candace could fold a tamale better than Don Pablo's.

At quarter till eleven, the first batch was ready. Candace went to the den to make the announcement and was surprised how quickly the atmosphere changed in there. The television was off and the stereo was bumping. People were dancing and drinking, talking and laughing. Hardly anyone was in their seat anymore.

"Some of the tamales are ready!" Candace yelled, and then moved quickly to let the crowd rush past her. Tino walked up and put an arm around her waist.

"Having fun?" he asked.

"Yeah," Candace said with a big smile. "Your aunts are cool. I learned so much from your mom. I still don't think your grandma's crazy, though."

"Wait till she gets a couple pints in her," Tino said.

"I don't think she drinks," Candace said. "She's got a big glass of tea in there."

Tino laughed. "*Tea*? My grandma hates tea! Get a sip of that *tea* next time you have a chance."

Candace didn't taste Grandma's drink when she went back to the kitchen, but she did take a quick sniff when

283

no one was looking. The stuff was strong enough to start a car.

⌒

The party was still jumping late into the evening, just as Tino said it would be. Things did get a little rowdy towards the end, but it never reached the level of craziness Candace expected. All of the drinkers were the polite drunks you see on TV, not the belligerent boozers you run into at the train station. Tino said everyone was on their best behavior because she was there, but Candace knew it was Tino who had exaggerated about his family's tendencies. Maybe if she expected the worst, nothing they did would surprise or offend her.

And that strategy might have worked, because Candace didn't have any negative experiences during her visit. Everything was charming, new, and exciting. The tamales were the biggest hit, but there were also pies and cakes galore. Candace ate so much, she thought she might have to wear her maternity pants tomorrow. And she didn't drink any alcohol, not even when someone mixed up a batch of margaritas.

At exactly midnight everyone went to the living room and crowded around the Christmas tree. Tino's dad got on his hands and knees and handed out presents to the anxious adults and children. Candace didn't expect anything, but midway through the pile of boxes he held a gift into the air.

"This one's for Candace. Where's *Candace?*"

"She's right here!" Tino yelled. "Go on, girl. Get your present."

"Who got me a present?" she asked.

"Santa Claus, baby."

Candace retrieved her gift and tore it open like everyone else. It was a pair of wool gloves with a matching sweater. Both were pink, Candace's favorite color.

∾

They left Grandma's house at 2:30 a.m.

When they got home, Leila was fast asleep. Candace took her to the bedroom and laid her gently in the crib. When she got back to the living room, Tino was still there, waiting to kiss her good night.

Candace took her stocking cap off and tossed it to the couch.

"Did you have fun?" he asked.

"I did." She stepped to him until their bellies touched. "Our first Christmas."

Tino smiled down at her and kissed her softly. "Are you going to open your gift?"

Candace had forgotten about the present. She picked it up and sat Indian-style on the couch with the decorated bag in her lap. Tino sat next to her and took his hat off. He cradled it nervously.

"Wait," Candace said. She rushed to her room and came back with a small box. "Here's what I got you. And you can see it's too small to be an ant farm."

Tino smiled. They tore their gifts open at the same time and stared in astonishment. Candace had a square can in her hands from the Fossil watch company. Tino had the exact same can in his hands, except his was black and hers was blue.

"No way," she said.

"You got me a watch, too?" he asked.

"Did you follow me to the mall?" Candace wanted to know.

"No. I got that a couple days ago."

Candace shook her head.

"Open yours," Tino said. "If it's the same watch, I'm gonna trip."

They opened their canisters simultaneously. Both contained a brand new watch. Both were silver and shiny. Candace's was smaller, but it looked like the same model as Tino's. Her watch face was pink, his was blue.

"This is weird," he said.

"It's crazy," Candace agreed.

"Or maybe it's not," Tino said. He put a hand over hers and stared into her eyes thoughtfully. "Maybe this is a sign of how close we are."

Candace liked that. Tino leaned in, and she closed her eyes when they kissed, but once again he was poised to ruin the moment.

"I gotta go," Tino said and stood abruptly.

Candace stood, too. She put her arms around his torso and locked her fingers behind his back.

"Kiss me again, Tino."

He did, and he opened his mouth this time. As their tongues danced, Candace felt like she was in a spaceship rocketing toward the moon. Everything about him was awesome.

Tino put his arms around her. She felt his hands on the small of her back. He lowered them to her butt and she moaned in appreciation, but then they were gone.

Tino backed away. "I guess I, uh, I'd better go."

"Why do you have to leave?" she asked.

He shrugged. "It's late. It's three o'clock in the morn—"

"You don't have school tomorrow."

"I know, but I . . ."

She waited, but he didn't come up with anything. "Why can't you stay with me?" she asked. "All night, in bed, with me."

He took another step back, and she followed.

"Wha, you mean *spend the night*? In there?"

Candace nodded.

"Buh-but Leila's in there."

"She's sleep."

"But still. She might wake up."

"We can bring her crib in here."

"In here? There's no room."

"We can put it in front of the couch."

"But you won't hear her if she cries."

"I'll plug in the monitor."

"Buh-but aren't you sleepy?"

"Tino, I want to make love," she said boldly. "Don't you love me?"

287

He took another step back, and she didn't pursue this time.

"You . . . you . . . yes, Candace. You know I love you."

"Then what is it, Tino? We've been together for a long time, and you never come close to making love to me. You don't like touching me?"

He gasped. "I, I duh, I do."

She walked up on him again and pressed her breasts against his chest. "Then touch me."

"Like, like, what?"

"Tino, calm down."

"Okay," he said hoarsely.

"Put your hands on me," she said.

He put his hands on her sides with obvious uncertainty.

She put her lips close to his ear and whispered, "You don't like my ass?"

"Yeah, Candace. You know I do."

"Then grab it."

He palmed it.

"No, Tino. *Grab* it. *Rub* it. *Squeeze* it."

He did as he was told, and the juices began to stir in Candace again.

"Oh, God," Tino said. His whole body shuddered.

Candace looked up and saw that he was scared. His face was as red as his sweater.

"Tino, what's wrong? Are you a—"

"Yes! I'm a Virginian, all right? I'm sorry."

"A *Virginian*?" She smiled. Even in this dire situation he couldn't be serious. "You're a *virgin*?" Candace felt like a whole world of weight lifted from her shoulders. That explained everything.

"I'm sorry," he said.

"Don't apologize. There's nothing wrong with that."

"I feel stupid."

"It's all right," Candace said. "Come sit down." She led him to the couch and they sat together. "You never had sex, Tino?"

"Not with somebody else," he said, and blushed. "Man, I'm stupid."

"No, you're not," she said. "This is just . . . unexpected. And hard to believe. How come you never had sex?"

"I was going to."

"Why didn't you? In high school?"

He grinned at her. "Contrary to what you might think, Candace, I was not a very popular kid in high school. I was a nerd. The girls I went out with, they were weird, too. They were the poets and straight-A chicks. And they weren't interested in sex, so I guess I wasn't, either."

"But—"

"And I wasn't always the awesomely handsome guy you see before you now," Tino said. "I used to have short hair and pimples. I wore glasses. And for a while my dad was injured and couldn't work. I didn't have a good wardrobe back then. You know how they treat kids with Wayless shoes."

Candace did know, but it was hard to see Tino as the target of schoolyard bullies.

"I had big cheeks and big lips," he said. "My mom says I grew into my features. Back then nobody wanted me."

"Aww," Candace said. "But what about when you got to college?"

"Oh, I went through a makeover then," he said brightly. "I got my first job, and got some nice clothes. I let my hair grow out over the summer. When I got to college, you were the first girl I really liked. I wanted to be with you from the moment I saw you."

No one ever made Candace feel the way Tino did. "I wish you would have told me sooner," she said.

"Why?"

" 'Cause I didn't know what was wrong. My friends told me you might be gay."

He chuckled. "I'm nowhere near gay."

"Good," she said. "That's really good, Tino."

He grinned.

"So, um, do you want to do it tonight?" she asked.

"Uh, okay. I think so."

"Tino, if you don't want to, then we're not doing it. I don't want to force you into anything."

"No, Candace. It's not that at all. I do want to do it, I'm just scared."

"Why?"

" 'Cause I never did it before. I don't know what I'm doing, and I don't want to mess it up."

"Tino, there's no way you could mess it up."

"All right," he said.

"All right?"

He nodded.

"Okay," Candace said. "I've got condoms. Do you want to bring the crib in here?"

"Yeah."

"Well, let's go!"

Candace held Leila while Tino hauled her bulky crib to the front room. Leila didn't stir at all during the move. Candace set up the baby monitor and then grabbed a fistful of Tino's sweater and led him to the bedroom. Once there, she pulled the sweater over his head and tossed it to the floor.

"This is gonna be awesome," he said.

"You have no idea," Candace said.

They kissed in the darkness, but there was no hesitation now. All of their animalistic urges had reached the surface, and there was going to be an explosion. One way or another, something had to give.

Candace darted her tongue between his lips. Tino caught a hold of it and sucked it. She put her hand under his T-shirt and rubbed her palms on his flat stomach. Tino had nice definition there. His abs weren't rippling, but he was solid for someone who didn't work out. She fondled his chest and squeezed his nipples.

Tino looked skyward and groaned. Candace took that opportunity to kiss his neck. She sucked his Adam's apple, and he grabbed her ass again. For real this time. He caressed it like he wanted to *do something* with it.

She jerked his T-shirt up towards his head. "Take this off," she whispered.

He did, and this was the first time Candace saw him topless. Tino's body was smooth and creamy. Candace wanted to eat him alive. She ducked her head and sucked his nipple. And she'd been aching to grab his crotch for many, many weeks, so she did it now. She palmed the bulge and squeezed it, and was right away appreciative of the size.

"Oh, *ooh, oh*, God. *Aw, man*," Tino moaned.

Candace didn't think anything of it until she saw his leg shaking. She stopped and looked up at him. Tino stared down at her with a queer expression. His penis throbbed beneath her hand.

"What's going on?" she asked.

His chest rose and fell quickly. His breaths were ragged. "Nuh-*nothing*."

"Tino, you didn't do what I think you did, did you?"

"Do you think I had an *orgasm*?" he asked. " 'Cause I'm pretty sure I *did* do that, if that's what you think."

Candace shook her head and chuckled. "All right, baby. Go clean yourself up. When you come back, I want you naked."

"You're not mad?" he asked.

"No," she said. "It'll be all right."

∽

When Tino returned from the bathroom, Candace lay on top of her sheets completely nude. The sight of her nakedness put Tino in a state of perpetual excitement. Candace stared at his throbbing member from across the room and a rivulet loosened between her legs.

"Tino, you got it going on," she said.

"What do you mean?"

"I mean you're going to make a lot of women happy with that thing."

"I only want to make you happy."

"Good answer."

Candace sat up and scooted to the edge of the bed.

Tino watched in awe. "Oh, my God," he said. "You're awesome. Seriously. Your body, you're like a model. I can't . . . I can't believe this is happening."

"Come here," Candace instructed him.

Tino stepped to her obediently. He stood between her legs, and with his erection in her face, it was hard not to devour it. But Candace couldn't give him all she had. Not tonight, at least. She tore open a condom with her teeth.

"Do you want to do it, or you want me to?" she asked.

"I-I don't know."

"It's not gonna go off again if I touch it, is it?" Candace looked up at him and smiled, but Tino didn't answer.

She caressed him gingerly at first, and then stroked sensually. He looked stable enough, so she grabbed it like a microphone. He pulsated in her hand.

"Oh, *oh, God*. Oh, *man*."

"Tino!"

"*Ahh*, oh, oh."

"Again?"

"No, no, I think I'm all right."

Candace slipped the rubber on quickly. "I think that was close," she said.

293

"Yeah. I think so."

"Are you still nervous?"

He stared down at her like he was hypnotized. "You're beautiful."

Candace scooted back on the bed. His eyes followed her breasts, then her stomach. They settled between her legs.

"You ready?" she asked.

"Hell, yes," he said and crawled on top of her like a Neanderthal.

"Wait," she said, pushing against his chest.

"What's wrong?"

"You want me to teach you right, don't you?"

He nodded.

"I want you to *touch me*, Tino. Kiss me. *Suck me.*"

"Can I touch your breasts?"

"Touch me anywhere," she said. "Kiss me, wherever you want."

Tino may have been a virgin, but titty sucking came as natural to him as a baby fresh out the womb. He squeezed and licked until Candace's nipples were hard and rigid. Then he traced his tongue down her stomach. He licked her belly button and sucked there, too. Every whip of his tongue brought her closer to an eruption. Tino kissed around her panty line and started to go further south, but Candace grabbed his hair and pulled him back up.

"It's okay," she said.

"You don't want me to?"

Candace shook her head. "It's okay. We can do that next time."

She peaked within seconds of penetration, but Tino didn't notice because his eyes were in the back of his head as well. He had to clean up again, but Candace didn't mind that at all.

Tino didn't have the skills of a seasoned pipe-layer, but he made up for it with gentleness, delicacy, and compassion. Candace didn't think she'd ever been handled quite like that.

Everything felt so good.

And Tino was an apt pupil. Making love to him was like making love to a horny robot. Whatever she told him to do, he did. She directed his touches, his kisses, and even the speed and strength of his strokes.

But after his third orgasm, Tino began to find his own groove. He put on yet another condom and rocked her like they'd been married for years.

By the end of the night, Candace wished she could have him, forever.

CHAPTER 21
A BIG DECISON

Leila woke up at 6:46 a.m. Candace squinted at the alarm and then rolled the other way to look at Tino. He was wrapped snugly in the blankets with only the top of his head exposed. He looked like a camper in a sleeping bag.

Candace smiled and slipped quietly out of the bed. She was halfway to the living room when she realized she was still butt naked. That never mattered before, but Tino might wake up. Candace didn't think a *full moon* should be his first sight on Jesus' birthday.

Or maybe it should.

"Waaah!"

Candace ducked into the bathroom and snatched a robe from the towel rack. She put it on and lifted Leila from her crib when she got to the living room. The baby stopped crying immediately. Candace changed her diaper while a bottle warmed in the microwave. She felt guilty, but it wasn't for kicking Leila out of the bedroom last night.

No, Candace knew she was wrong for different reasons. And it didn't take a lot of soul-searching to figure out what it was.

Oh, what a tangled web we weave.

She fed Leila her bottle, and thought about the sacrifice Tino made for her last night. Rather than feel proud of their progress, Candace found herself more and more depressed.

After the baby's breakfast, Candace showered and went to the kitchen to make a meal for her man. The smell of bacon and eggs woke Tino at 8:30 a.m. He walked into the living room with a sheet wrapped around his waist. His hair was messed, and he looked a little drunk, but Tino always looked good to Candace.

He went to Leila and put a comforting hand on the back of her head. He smiled at Candace without speaking.

She grinned back at him and said, "Good morning, *mi amor*."

"*Mi amor*? I like that," Tino said. He stepped behind her and wrapped an arm around her waist. He kissed the side of her neck and sniffed the back of her head. "I love the way you smell."

Candace shuddered. No one could get her hot with one kiss like Tino could.

She turned and wrapped her arms around his naked torso. "Do you know what today is?"

"*Why, 'tis Christmas day, sir!*" Tino said with a British accent, mimicking the kid from *A Christmas Carol*.

Candace laughed. "Tino, you're a trip."

"Check this out," he said. "I've always wanted to ask this, but now I have a reason to . . . Do you know where my pants are?"

Candace laughed again. "They're in the bedroom, sir. I folded them. But your underwear needs to be washed." She had a sly grin. "You're going to have to go commando till you get home."

"What happened to my underwear?" he asked.

"You don't remember?"

"I do, I was hoping you didn't."

"Oh," Candace said. "Well, I guess I don't remember what happened to them then."

"Good," he said and pecked her on the lips. "So we'll never mention that again."

Candace tried, but she couldn't keep a straight face. She snickered, and then giggled. "I'm sorry, Tino. I can't do it. I don't think I can go without talking about that."

"All right," he said. He was smiling, too. "Let's get it out of the way. I had an *accident* last night."

"A sexy accident," Candace said.

"Was it sexy?"

"Mmm, oh yeah," she purred and traced a finger down his chest.

"Has anyone ever had that type of, accident with you before?"

Candace shook her head. "No. Never."

Tino grinned. "So, I guess I'm somewhat of an innovator. A pioneer, if you will."

Candace kissed his chest. "I'll call you whatever you want me to, *papi*."

He grinned.

Candace looked into his eyes. "I love you, Tino. You never have to worry about being embarrassed around me."

"I love you, too," he said. "And I'm glad we talked about this. Now we can we bury it forever."

"*Forever?*" Candace kidded. "I hoped we could talk about it at dinner when we get to your grandma's."

"Or we could talk about it again the next time your dad invites us out," Tino said.

"All right. We'll bury it forever."

Tino showered and put on his jeans and T-shirt from the night before. Candace had breakfast ready by then, but she was not very merry as they ate. Tino devoured half his plate in the time it took her to eat a few layers of her biscuit. He put down his fork and asked what was wrong.

"Nothing," she said.

"You're not hungry?"

"No. Not really."

"Are you sick? You look sick."

"I don't feel well," Candace admitted. "We can talk after you're done."

Tino pushed his plate away. "I'm done now. I can't eat if you're not happy. Tell me what's wrong."

Candace gathered Leila from her swing and led Tino to the living room couch. She cradled the baby like a security blanket, but it didn't work. Her eyes filled with tears as she thought about what she had to tell him.

"Candace, what's wrong?"

"Tino, I'm sorry. I have to tell you something bad." She stared at the dark screen on her television, unable to meet his eyes.

"Are you all right?" he asked. "Are you hurt?"

She shook her head. "I wish it was something like that. The only thing wrong with me is *me*. I'm a liar, Tino. I don't deserve to be with you." The tears fell, and they hit Tino like a slap to the face.

"*Candace!* Candace, please look at me."

She did, and his eyes were watery, too.

"Please," he said. "Tell me what's wrong."

"My parents didn't take Leila to New York," she said.

Tino was supremely confused. "What do you mean?"

"Leila has never been to New York. I told you that because I didn't want to tell you where she was." Candace's tears flowed heavier as the memories of her CPS experience rekindled old fires long since died down.

Tino knitted his eyebrows. "Where was she?"

"They took her from me," Candace bawled. "Tino, I know I should have told you, but I didn't want you to think that way about me. I'm sorry, please don't be mad."

"*Who* took her?"

"CPS. They took her because I went to jail."

Tino's face contorted into an expression Candace recognized as disgust. He shook his head and rubbed his temples with the heels of his hands. "Wha-what? What are you talking about?"

Candace took a deep breath and wiped the tears from her face. If she didn't cry in jail, then she shouldn't cry now. She was a grown woman. She rectified every mistake she made, and if Tino left her over this, she would have to suck it up and move on.

She sighed and managed to look her man in the eyes. "When Rilla got arrested, I didn't have money for the bills. I didn't have a job or anything. He called me from jail and said he still had drugs in our apartment. He told me to give them to his friend, CC, and supposedly CC would give me money for the rent."

Tino listened but didn't speak.

"But CC never came," she went on. "And it got closer and closer to the first, so I pawned some stuff from our apartment and paid the rent on my own. That's when I decided I didn't want to be with Rilla anymore. I knew I could do it by myself."

Tino nodded.

"But CC came on the thirtieth. June thirtieth—"

"That's when Leila was born."

"I know," Candace said. "CC told me to give him Rilla's dope. I don't know why, Tino, but I didn't want to give it to him. I didn't trust him. He was supposed to have money for Rilla, but he didn't have it. He said he was going to bail him out, and he didn't. When I didn't give CC what he wanted, he left, and the next thing I knew, the police were at my door. They broke it down and took me to jail for Rilla's drugs."

"But it wasn't yours."

"I know," Candace said. "But they told me I could still get charged. Plus I told them I knew it was there."

"But still," Tino said, "you could beat that."

"I didn't have to beat it," Candace said. "They said they'd drop the charges if I testified against Rilla."

"You had Leila in jail?"

"No. My water broke while the police were searching my apartment. I had my baby first, and then I went to jail."

"How long did you stay?"

"Two weeks, but CPS took my baby as soon as I had her. When I got out, they wouldn't give her back. It took me two months to get Leila back. I had to get a job and an apartment. I had to show them I could take care of her."

"That's why you stayed in Texas?"

Candace nodded. "I couldn't leave without her."

Tino shook his head. "Candace, that's bad, but none of it's your fault. You should have told me. I would have understood."

"Maybe," Candace said, her eyes watering again, "but that's not all."

Tino waited nervously.

"Before Leila was born, me and Rilla used to party a lot. We used to drink and get high."

"That's okay," Tino said. "You're different now."

"Back then," Candace continued, "Rilla went to jail for tickets one time." Her heart was about to explode from her chest. Her mouth was dry. Candace didn't think she'd have the strength to get through it.

"What happened?" Tino asked, but he didn't want to know. You could see it in his eyes.

Candace began to cry again. Her lips twisted in agony.

That made Tino more apprehensive.

"When Rilla went to jail, his friend CC came by sometimes to check on me, to make sure I was all right. He smoked weed with me, and we got drunk one time."

Tino's eyes watered.

"I got drunk," Candace said, "and I passed out. When I woke up, CC . . . CC had my pants off. He was . . . he was on top of me."

Tino's mouth fell open, but Candace was one sentence away from purging her soul, so she didn't stop.

"I don't think this is Rilla's baby," she blubbered. She looked into Leila's curious eyes. "I mean, I'm pretty sure this is CC's baby."

She looked back to Tino in time to see his face collapse, as if someone had rubbed Novocain all over it. He stood slowly and turned his back on her. He put his hands to his head and took a step towards the bedroom. He then turned and headed for the front door instead.

When he put his hand on the knob, Candace's heart fell into her stomach, but he didn't open it. He let it go and turned back to her. Tears streamed down his cheeks, but she saw more compassion than anger in his eyes.

He stepped to her and fell to his knees. He looked first at Leila, and then to Candace's glistening eyes.

"I'm sorry," he said. "I shouldn't have reacted like that."

Candace wiped her face. "Tino, you have every right to be upset. I lied to you. You don't have to be the nice guy all the time. If you want to leave, you can. I deserve it."

"Don't say that." He wiped the tears from his eyes. "I know you didn't have to tell me. I never would have found out. I think you told me because you love me, and you don't want secrets in our relationship."

Candace nodded. "I'm sorry," she whispered.

Tino looked down at Leila and stroked her head tenderly. "She's been through so much."

Leila looked up at him and smiled.

"Do you feel better?" he asked Candace.

She shrugged. "I don't know, Tino. How do you feel about me now?"

He considered his answer for a few seconds. "Candace, I'm not going to condemn you for something you did before we were together. What happened between you and Rilla's friend, I think . . . I think that was *sick*, but it wasn't something you chose to do. That man raped you." He frowned. "He should go to jail."

Candace studied his features. "Tino, you can't really feel like that. Don't you have any bad feelings about me? I don't know for sure who my baby's father is. Some people think that makes me a ho."

Tino smiled. "If you were a ho, you wouldn't have waited on me for four months. That stuff you did with Rilla, that's not you, Candace. I know the real you, and I love the real you."

❧

Candace didn't think she could tell her story without there being some low-lying resentment, but Tino was true to his word. He loved Candace for who she was now. He never brought up her sins with Rilla or CC again. Candace promised him there would be no more lies, and that was a promise she planned on keeping. Tino was awesome. She knew she was lucky to have him. He was everything she could have wished for.

❧

They left her apartment at ten, and made it to Tino's place thirty minutes later. He showered and dressed again while Candace and Leila watched *Tom and Jerry* reruns on cable. Tino emerged from his bedroom wearing khaki Dockers with a long-sleeved red button-down.

"Look," he said, pulling back one of his sleeves. He had on the watch Candace got him for Christmas.

Candace held up her wrist to show off her new Fossil. They kissed like newlyweds and left his apartment hand in hand.

❧

Tino's grandmother's house wasn't as busy as the night before, but the atmosphere was as warm and cozy as ever. They ate turkey and ham with tamales and menudo. They had sweet potato and pecan pie and were

305

soon stuffed like ticks. There were more presents under the tree, and once again one of them was for Candace. It was a stocking cap with earmuffs, both pink, of course.

Candace called her parents after dinner to see how their Christmas was going. A lot of relatives were there, and her mother passed the phone around to them so they could all say "Hi." Most of her relatives were not too upset about her absence, and even those who were seemed happy to finally hear her voice.

Candace talked to her mom for a while, and then her dad got on the line and came very close to apologizing for his remarks a couple weeks ago. He told Candace he respected her decision and would look forward to seeing her on spring break. He said there was no guarantee her present would still be there then, but Candace knew he was bluffing.

"I love you, Daddy," she said before she got off the phone.

"I love you, too, pumpkin. Merry Christmas."

$$\sim$$

When they got back to Candace's apartment, Leila was ready for her afternoon nap. Candace made her a bottle, but she fell asleep in Tino's arms before the microwave dinged.

Candace had to go to work that evening, so she needed a few winks herself, especially after the night she had with her *former*-virgin boyfriend. Tino said he was sleepy, too, and Candace was glad he wanted to stay. She climbed into bed wearing only panties and a bra, and Tino followed in boxers and a T-shirt.

Candace didn't think he'd go from virgin to horn-dog overnight, but Tino's hands were all over her as soon as they were under the sheets. She giggled when he sucked the back of her neck and smooched behind her ears. He undid her bra and gobbled her breasts like candy. Tino tongue-lashed the small of her back as well.

He climbed on top and they kissed passionately. His hair was down, and it fell in her face, but Candace didn't care. Tino sucked her neck and licked from her throat to her belly button. When he wanted to go further Candace didn't stop him. He pulled her panties off and sucked between her legs like a puppy lapping milk.

Candace was too taken aback to enjoy it at first. She closed her legs, almost squishing his head, but Tino put a hand on each thigh and pushed them apart politely. He looked up at her, his lips moist.

"Am I doing it wrong?"

"Nuh-no, Tino. It's fine."

"Tell me what you like, so I'll know," he said, but that was easier said than done. After a few seconds, Candace couldn't speak at all. She laid her head back on the pillow and moaned, or *screamed*, she wasn't sure which. She grabbed hold of his hair and rocked her hips with his tongue, and when her eyes rolled back this time, she truly believed she was in heaven.

Celestino.

Someone gave this boy the right name.

When he was done, Candace tried to return the favor, but Tino assured her that would not be necessary. He said he was excited enough already, and Candace could see that he was.

"I just want to be inside you," he said.

"I love you, Celestino."

"I love you, too."

She woke up at 4:29 p.m. The alarm clock hadn't gone off yet. Candace sat up rubbed the sleep from her eyes. *What woke me up*, she wondered. But then it hit her: She woke up all by herself, exactly one hour before she had to leave for work. And she did it with inadequate sleep. That was a first for her. Candace took it as a sign of maturity, as evidence she'd become a responsible person.

As if agreeing with her, the alarm went off a few seconds later. Candace shut it off and then rolled over and threw an arm and a leg over her boyfriend.

"Time to get up," she whispered.

"*Nunnnh.*"

"Tino."

"I don't want to go to school today, Mommy."

"Boy, get up, I'm not your mommy."

He rolled to face her. His hair was messed, and he had fresh stubble on his chin. His eyes were dark, and alluring.

"It's time for you to go?" he asked.

"Yeah, sweetie. Some of us have to work on the holidays. Others get to go home and play video games all day."

"I'm sorry," he said. "Do you want me to call your job and demand they let you stay home?"

Candace giggled. "Yeah, right."

"So, how'd I do?" he asked.

"What do you mean?"

"I mean, in bed." He blushed and looked down at the sheets. "How'd I do?"

"Tino, you don't have to impress me. You don't think you're competing with anyone, do you?"

"No," he said. He looked up at her and smiled. "I just want to know if I'm doing a good job. I mean, if I'm passing or not, you know?"

Candace grinned. "Do you hear yourself? Tino, you're such a nerd. You want me to grade your bedroom performance?"

"I just want to know if I'm passing." His coy grin was infectious. It made Candace happy just to see his dimples. She placed a hand on his cheek.

"Well, I would give you an 'A', but you haven't given me a full-body massage yet."

"I can give you a massage," he said eagerly.

"It's too late now. You already turned in your test."

"Where do you like to be touched?" he asked.

Candace was the one who blushed then. "Mmm. *Everywhere.*"

"You have to like some places more than others," Tino said.

"Mmm, I guess my butt, maybe."

"Your booty?"

"Then my breasts."

"I like your booty."

"Are you talking about touching with your hands or lips?" she asked.

"They're different categories?"

"Oh, yeah. *Totally* different."

"I'd better get a notepad."

Candace giggled. "Later. I have to go to work."

"We're going to finish this conversation."

"Okay."

"So what's my grade?"

"I'd give you an 'A'," she said.

His eyes brightened. "No shit? You'd give me an 'A'?"

"There's something you don't understand, Tino."

"What?"

"What you do to me, to my body, that's only about thirty percent of it. How I feel about you and how much I love you, that's what makes our intimacy so special. If I didn't like you, you could do whatever you wanted to me physically, but it wouldn't mean a thing."

"I get it," he said. "Your pleasure variable is directly linked to the emotional bond you develop with your partner."

"You're such a *nerd*," she said, and kissed him on the nose.

⌒

Candace left at 5:30 p.m. She dropped the baby off at Trisha's house but didn't tell her friend about her and Tino. As juicy as the story was, she felt her and Tino's relationship was much more than some locker room sex story. It was more than she could put into words.

CHAPTER 22
RUNNING THE GAUNTLET

Candace didn't get home until ten till midnight. By then the temperature had dipped to a chilly forty-three degrees in the great city of Overbrook Meadows. Candace stepped out of Trisha's apartment and pulled a hoodie over her head. She had Leila totally bundled, lest any devious breezes brush her daughter's face. The baby looked like a larva in a cocoon. Candace held Leila under her jacket, as she made her way down the stairs.

And then she stopped.

Something moved down there. There wasn't much wind, and Candace didn't think what she saw was a floating plastic bag. She was sure that what she saw down there was a shadow. Not a shadow coming, but a shadow leaving, as if someone standing down there suddenly stepped into the darkness.

A ripple of fear tap-danced down her spine, but Candace didn't know why she felt that way. This was a big apartment complex. A lot of people lived there. It was very possible someone simply walked by. And there was nothing wrong with that. People are free to come and go as they please.

But still.

Something didn't feel right. Candace had half a mind to go back up to Trisha's, but what then? Would she ask Trisha to abandon her three boys for a minute so she could walk her down the stairs? Or maybe Trisha could get all of the kids bundled up so they could go as a family.

Candace sighed and started down the stairs again. This time she kept her eyes on the spot where the shadow had been. She was sure she wouldn't see anything, but if someone was hiding around the corner down there, another movement might give them away.

She stopped again.

Are you serious? Do you really believe someone's down there? 'Cause if you do, you need to go back up. But that was just it. All she saw was a shadow. She might not have even seen that.

There is nothing to fear but fear itself.

Candace held onto her baby tighter and calmly made her way down the rest of the steps. At the bottom, she peeked around that suspicious blind spot before heading to her car. There was nothing there. No neighbors, no stray dog, no branch blowing in the wind, and damned sure no boogeyman. But what did she expect?

Candace loosened her tense muscles and stepped quickly to her Nissan. She unlocked the back door and settled Leila in her car seat. Candace jumped into the front seat and locked the doors before anything else.

"Dammit!" She banged her fist on the steering wheel. "What the hell is wrong with me?" Her words bounced around the quiet confines of her vehicle. She hated feeling like this. Fear is worse than physical pain and heartbreak put together.

She put the Sentra in reverse and casually backed out of the parking spot. Even with her headlights shining she couldn't see anything around that damned corner. She put it in drive and left Trisha's apartment complex without incident. Thirty seconds later she pulled into her own parking spot across the street.

Candace got out and unbuckled Leila from her car seat. She didn't feel any of the apprehension she felt across the street.

But then she heard footsteps.

You're supposed to hear footsteps, Candace told herself. *This is a big complex, just like Trisha's. It's late, but it's also Christmas night. A lot of people are off work. Neither shadows nor footsteps should be cause for concern.*

But these footsteps were different.

They weren't the casually walking *oh-la-ti-da-I'm-off-for-Christmas* feet. These feet were moving *fast*, almost jogging, and they were definitely coming towards Candace. She looked in that direction, but could see nothing in the darkness. Just buildings and trees. Bushes and cars.

Candace quit trying to reason with this madness. She positioned Leila in the crook of her arm like a football and slammed the car door closed. She turned and scanned the landscape one last time. Still, there was only darkness. But out of the murk the feet kept coming, faster now.

Candace nearly screamed. She turned and sprinted like an Olympian to her stairway. She was only up two flights, but she felt like she was climbing a downwards escalator. Her heart shot up her throat and rattled there. Beads of sweat blossomed on her forehead despite the frigid temperatures.

Candace made it up the first flight and rounded the corner for home. She took a split-second to look behind her, and she saw him then. But just a glimpse. Her pursuer was tall and dressed in black. Those were the only details that registered.

Candace hopped the final steps three at a time. Leila bounced awkwardly against her body. Candace had never been more afraid in her entire life. She was more than terrified. She didn't know what this man wanted from her, and she really didn't care about her own safety, but Leila was innocent. Her baby didn't deserve anything but love. And the goon behind her hadn't come to spread good cheer.

Candace made it to the top of the stairs. She flipped through her key chain as she bolted to her door. Without looking back, she knew the man was closer now. In addition to his footsteps, Candace could hear his pants rubbing together as he ran. They were made of windbreaker material. It was a sound Candace would never forget.

Zwush.

Zwush.

Zwush.

She found the right key and stabbed it into the hole, but it didn't work. She flipped it over and jabbed again, but still it was a no-go. Her fingers were too shaky. She scratched shiny, bronze lines around the jagged keyhole.

Candace cursed and gave it one more try, but the key definitely didn't fit. She studied it closer and realized it was her old apartment key from when she lived with Rilla. Why the hell did she still have that damned thing, and why did they all look alike? Why didn't she find the right key *before* she got out of the car like they teach on those self-defense videos?

Candace jingled the key chain and found the right one, but it was too late. A large, cold hand grabbed the back of her shoulder. She spun like a tiger, striking out with the only claws she had. The keys glistened in the lamplight, coming very close to the perpetrator's eyes, but CC sidestepped her swing easily. He stared at her and chuckled. His chest rose and fell rapidly.

"Damn, girl. What you . . . what you trying to hit me for?"

Candace's eyes were wide, her breathing ragged. Blood rushed in her ears. She didn't hear what he said, but his presence alone incited a rage in her. Her anger quickly overwhelmed the fear.

CC's hair was braided down in eight shiny cornrows. He wore a black sweater with a black T-shirt underneath. He had on black cargo pants. His sneakers were blue, but not light enough to give him away if he decided to, say, creep through the shadows. He sported a full goatee, and even though Candace loathed everything about him, she couldn't help but see her daughter in his eyes.

"Why are you following me?" she hollered.

CC smiled. His mouth hung open and he took big gulps of air. "I'm not following you, girl." He looked behind her to the apartment number nailed to her door. "This where you stay?" he asked with a snicker.

Candace wasn't an advocate of violence, nor was she accustomed to violence, but for the first time in her life she wished she had a gun. She wished she could reach into her purse and pull out something to make that priggish grin fall right off his face.

"Why are you following me?" she asked again. Her eyebrows bunched. Her nostrils flared.

"All right," CC said. "All right." He put his arms out in a *who me?* gesture. "I *was* trying to find out where you stay. But I wasn't gonna hurt you. Why you so scared?"

"Why do you want to know where I live?"

He stared at Leila, then reached for her. "Is that Rilla's baby? Let me see."

Candace moved her bundle to the arm farthest away from him.

"Don't you ever touch my baby!" she shrieked. Her snarl was real, and her teeth were bared. CC saw something in her eyes that made him back away.

"You still a old *sadity* bitch, ain't you?"

"CC, why can't you leave me alone?" she asked, almost in desperation.

"I'm doing a favor for my nigga. He wanna know where his baby staying at. Delia told me you stayed over here somewhere."

Candace felt like the ground dropped from under her. *Why? Why can't they leave me alone? I don't deserve this.*

"Is Rilla still in jail?" she asked. She hated speaking civilly with this creep, but CC wasn't over here for nothing. He had some kind of information.

"He's getting out," he said. "Maybe tonight. Maybe tomorrow."

A thousand thoughts went through Candace's mind upon hearing those words. She knew she had to move, that was a given. She knew she should go back to New York. It was the end of the semester. This would be the perfect time to go. She could be on a plane tomorrow and have all of her belongings either sold or shipped. She had a million reasons to leave, but only one reason to stay. And though that one reason was important, she couldn't put Tino before her baby.

"I told you, I'm not with Rilla anymore. I don't want him over here."

"I know," CC said. "I heard you got you a *Mexican* now. You stupid. Don't you know Mexicans hate niggas?"

"If Rilla comes over here, I'll call the police," Candace threatened.

CC chuckled. "Bitch, you can't stop him from seeing his baby."

It's not his baby!

But she couldn't say that. The last time she accused CC of fathering this child, he took a swing at her. What would he do now that the baby was here? Candace imagined he would grab Leila by the ankle and throw her down the stairs, screaming, *That's not my baby!*

"He needs to go to court," she said. Her voice hitched, but she tried to be strong. "If he wants to see Leila, he has to go to court and get some paperwork."

CC shook his head. "The hell with court. This the streets. You wanna go to court, then take *yo* fonky ass to court. My nigga ain't gotta go to no judge to see his baby. He coming right *here*."

With that, CC turned and dipped down the stairs. As soon as he was out of sight, Candace put the right key in the door and stormed into her apartment. She slammed it closed and bolted all of the locks. She put Leila on the sofa and unwrapped the blankets. Once free, Leila kicked and giggled at her mother cheerily.

So sweet. So innocent she was.

Candace went through her apartment and checked to make sure all of the windows were locked before she called her boyfriend.

"Hello?"

"Tino, what are you doing?"

"Waiting on you to call."

"CC was over here," she said. Her hands were still shaking.

"*CC?* Rilla's friend?"

"Yeah. I think he followed me from Trisha's house. He says Rilla's getting out tonight, or tomorrow."

"Oh, shit. What are you gonna do?"

"I don't know. I might have to move, Tino. I might have to go back to New York." She was almost crying as she said this.

Tino didn't respond.

"Can you spend the night with me?" Candace asked.

"I'll be there in fifteen minutes."

Tino knocked on her door eleven minutes later. He looked as stressed and haggard as Candace, but at least they were stressed and haggard together. She clung to him like an infant when he walked through the door. Tino made her feel strong again. With him, she knew she wasn't all alone in this.

"Have you called the police?" he asked.

Candace hadn't. She called Detective Judkins, but no one answered. She left a desperate message on his voice mail but wasn't very hopeful for a reply.

Later, she and Tino sat on the couch for most of the night. They listened for sounds at her door or on the stairwell, but these sounds never came. Leila dozed off at 2 a.m. Candace took her to the crib and went back to the living room to cuddle with Tino. She savored his every caress, as their days together appeared to be numbered.

She slept in Celestino's arms that night. They didn't make love, but being close to him was just as intimate. Before they fell asleep, Candace asked again if he would go to New York with her if she had to leave. Tino said he loved her, and he really wanted to, but he was pretty sure he couldn't.

The next morning Candace got up early and fixed a big breakfast. She showered and got Leila dressed for the day. She woke Tino up at nine. They ate together and tried their best to make everything normal, but things could never be the way they were before. They ate quietly, both thinking about the move back to New York. That was a last resort, but there would be stress as long as that option was on the table.

After breakfast, Candace tried to get in touch with Detective Judkins again. The calls kept going straight to voice mail. Candace left another message but had to accept that maybe he didn't want to call her back. He might be on vacation for all she knew. All they could do was wait.

They watched television and played with Leila and talked. Every passing hour was good news in Candace's opinion.

"I don't think he's out," she told Tino at eleven-thirty.

"Why do you say that?"

"Because he hasn't come by."

Tino chewed his thumbnail.

"He hasn't called, either," Candace said.

"He has your number?"

"My cell hasn't changed in a year."

Tino nodded. "You're right. He would call at least."

"He's not coming," Candace said matter-of-factly. "He talked to CC. He knows he has no business over here."

"Unless he wants to beat you up," Tino teased.

"Then he should have beat me up already. I've been waiting on him all day. Either he's gonna put up or shut up."

Tino laughed. "You want to get something to eat?"

"I'd love to."

⁓

Tino took them to The Lotus, an all-you-can-eat Chinese restaurant close to his apartments. Candace thought she wasn't hungry enough for a buffet, but when they got there her stomach had other ideas. She didn't eat at all last night after work, and she had barely gotten anything down at breakfast.

Candace loaded her first plate with pineapple shrimp, sautéed shrimp, and Hunan crispy shrimp. She went back for pan-fried sea bass, spinach fried rice, and salt-and-pepper eggplant. Tino's eyes got big when she still had room for a third helping of yuen-yang spicy beef, with crusted scallops and a little miso soup.

"At least one of us has their appetite back," he said.

Candace smiled. "I think I'm eating so I don't have to think about things."

"Is it working?"

"It was, but now I'm thinking about it again because of you."

Tino grinned and swiped a scallop from her plate. He swallowed it in one bite and smiled up to heaven.

"It works, right?" Candace said.

"Yeah." Tino licked his lips and grinned divinely. "I have no idea who Rilla is now."

"Jerk."

⌒

They got home at two and there was no evil letter propped under Candace's windshield wiper, as she expected. There wasn't one on her front door, either. Candace started to feel more and more comfortable about things, but she didn't tell Tino that. He'd taken kindly to his role as protector, and she liked having him around.

They read Leila a book later in the afternoon and watched a couple movies on cable when the baby took her nap. They snuggled on the couch like newlyweds, and there was some stress, but Rilla wasn't the overwhelming theme of the day. There was a life past Raul Canales, and if Candace could convince herself of that, she might be able to stay with Tino after all.

At five o'clock things got *sticky* again when it was time to go to work. Tino followed Candace to the bedroom and pleaded with her as she got dressed.

"Why would you take her over there? You said CC and Rilla know where Trisha lives."

"They know where I live, too, Tino, but neither one came over here today."

"You're taking a chance."

"What kind of chance? Seriously, Tino, what do you think is going to happen?"

"He might go over there and take your baby."

"Leila's not his baby. That's kidnapping."

"He doesn't know that."

"Tino, Trisha isn't going to give my baby to Rilla. And he sure as hell can't take Leila from her. Trisha's damned near twice his size."

"What if he does?"

"He's not even out, Tino."

"But what if he is?"

"What if the roof falls on us before we leave?" Candace asked. "Tino, we can *what if* ourselves to death. Sometimes you have to go with common sense and hope for the best."

"But what if—"

"Trust me," Candace said. "She'll be okay tonight with Trisha."

"You're sure?"

"I'm one hundred percent positive."

෴

And Candace was sure. She told Trisha what was going on when she dropped Leila off.

"You have to keep the doors locked tonight."

"I will," Trisha said. "But you know I don't like to get up."

"I know," Candace said. "But can you do it tonight?"

"Yeah, girl. You think Rilla's out?"

"I don't," Candace said. "But if he gets out while I'm at work, he only has two places to look for me, my apartment or yours."

"If he come over here messing with me, I'ma kick his ass," Trisha announced.

"You'd have to open the door to kick his ass," Candace noted.

Trisha sighed. "Candace, you know I'll die before I let somebody take your baby." Trisha bounced Leila on her shoulder. Candace grinned at her daughter's big diaper butt.

"I know," Candace said. "That's why I'm here."

"For real," Trisha said. "I'm telling you this before God: He'd have to kill me."

"I trust you," Candace said.

"And if I hear anything about Rilla, I'll go to a neighbor's house and call you at work," Trisha said.

Candace thanked her friend and stepped out of the apartment with a renewed sense of control. She closed the door behind herself but didn't head downstairs right away. She listened, and after a few seconds she heard Trisha slide the deadbolt.

Candace went to work with a smile on her face.

⌒

But that smile was gone when she pulled into the parking lot at Pappadeaux. Candace had a hard lump in her throat instead. She knew she did all she could, but still . . . She and Leila could be on a plane by now. She'd probably be on that plane wondering if Rilla really was out and if she left Tino for nothing, but still, at least she'd be on the plane.

She walked into the restaurant casually, but stopped in the foyer. She couldn't put a finger on it, but something didn't feel right. Candace looked around slowly. People were eating, waiters were serving, and credit cards were being swiped. Nothing was out of order. It was business as usual.

Candace sighed and went to find the manager so she could get her section for the night. She started her shift with a strong sense of foreboding, but after a few tables she relaxed. She served good foods, got nice tips, and her phone didn't vibrate in her pocket. She checked it every so often to make sure, but each time there were no missed calls.

An hour passed.

And then another.

Candace was getting into the groove of her night when the hostess told her she had a new customer, a table for one.

"White or black?" Candace asked. It was sad but true; white people tipped better, especially if they were eating alone. Candace planned to teach her daughter the meaning of the word *gratuity* as soon as Leila could talk.

"He's Mexican," the freckle-faced girl told her. "He's cute, too."

Candace grinned. A cute Mexican guy might be all right. She didn't try to use her looks for monetary gain, but Candace knew she could coax a $20 bill out of any single man, especially if he had enough money to dine at Pappadeaux.

She took the pad from her apron and plucked a pencil from behind her ear. Candace stepped to the table-for-one with the cheesiest grin she could muster. Her customer was already deep in his menu. She couldn't see his face until she was standing over him, and what she saw made Candace's flaky greeting melt away in her mouth.

"Hi! Welcome to Pappadeaux. I'm Candace, I'll be . . ."

Her customer was handsome, there was no denying that. But that's the only thing the hostess was right about. This patron wasn't Mexican, he was Puerto Rican. His skin was darker than most Latinos, the color of coffee with one cream. He had bushy eyebrows and a perfect complexion, not one scar, dimple, or pimple. A neat goatee framed his mouth, but when he smiled, Candace saw that his platinum grill was missing. Maybe he left it at the county jail.

"Damn, baby," Rilla said. "Look at you, Candace. Done got all grown up."

CHAPTER 23
RILLA TIME

Candace's notepad trembled in her hands. Her pencil, poised to jot down tasty delectables like the Oysters Baton Rouge, made a dark, jagged line on the paper.

Candace stared at her ex-boyfriend in awe, and a cold chill enveloped her body. It started at her head and floated down like mist, numbing her chest and arms. Candace's fingertips went white. Her face did as well.

It was hard to get air. Black and gray dots swam before her eyes, and Candace knew she was losing it. It was weird to be aware of that. She thought that if you were *losing it*, you'd have no understanding of what was going on, but that wasn't the case.

Candace felt herself falling. She tried to reach out and grab hold of reality, but reality was elusive. It slipped through her fingers like raindrops.

Her muscles went slack and sleep felt like a wonderful escape. Candace dropped her pad and pencil. She teetered right, then left, willing to land wherever gravity pulled her, but Rilla jumped from his seat and braced her shoulders with his strong hands.

"Candace!"

He stood before her and somehow managed to support her weight, though both of Candace's knees were bent like a stringless puppet. Her eyelids fluttered. She said something, but it was too guttural, more animal than human.

"Candace!"

A waiter rushed forward and supported her limp body from behind. He was a small guy, but with four hands on her, Candace was in no danger of hitting the floor.

The waiter looked quickly from Candace to Rilla. "What's wrong with her?" he asked the customer.

"I don't know, man," Rilla said. "I think she got a little excited. She'll be all right."

"Hey, Candace. Can you hear me? Sit her down." The waiter pulled a chair away from the table, and he and Rilla lowered Candace's butt into it. Her world was starting to settle by then. She shook her head slowly and tried to get a grasp on what was going on. On some *fuzzy* level she understood Rilla had come to her restaurant, but that was illogical. Even if it did happen, it felt like something that happened very long ago.

"*Candace?* Candace, can you hear me?"

She turned to her coworker and nodded weakly. Candace forced her eyes open. The clouds in her head cleared, and she looked around fretfully. She realized this was no dream, and her eyes were not deceiving her. A skinny waiter named Parker held her on the left side, and Rilla supported her on the right. Candace sneered at her ex-boyfriend and jerked away from him roughly, but that only made the syncope come back.

"Calm down," Parker said. "I think you fainted."

"You all right, baby?" Rilla asked.

Candace stared at him and her focus gradually returned, like an old television that took a while to warm up. Rilla wore a short-sleeved golf shirt with a Polo emblem over the left breast. The shirt was solid white, and he looked handsome in it. It was the kind of shirt Candace always wanted him to wear when they were dating, but Rilla thought T-shirts and jerseys were suitable for any occasion back then.

Seeing that his girlfriend had come to her senses, Rilla smiled pleasantly. He stepped away from Candace and casually returned to his seat. He sat right across from her like they were dating again.

Candace shot to her feet and ignored the havoc this move wreaked on her equilibrium. She stumbled forward.

"*Candace!*"

Parker reached to brace her again, but Candace didn't need him. She put her hands flat on the table and supported herself. She kept her eyes fixed on Rilla's and ignored the way the world rolled in her peripheral vision. This seemed to work.

"What are you doing here?" she growled.

Rilla picked up his menu and grinned. "I came to see you, baby. Ain't heard from you in so long . . . I didn't know if you figured I was dead or what." He scanned the appetizers.

Parker looked from Rilla to Candace with obvious concern. "Uh, are you okay, Candace? Do you know this guy?"

Rilla sneered at him. "Get on, *Opie*! You ain't my waiter. This ain't got nothing to do with you."

Parker almost walked away, but he was one of six Pappadeaux staff members who had a crush on Candace. "Huh?"

"You need to leave, Rilla. I don't want to talk to you," Candace said.

Rilla put down his menu and leaned back in the chair. "You ain't seen me in six months, girl. How you gon' act like that? I think we do need to talk. You got my *car*, all my *furniture*. You got my *baby*. You a fool if you think we ain't gon' talk."

Parker was not normally one to confront threatening minority males, but they were in a crowded restaurant. What's the worst that could happen? He wasn't old enough to remember Luby's 1991.

"Um, I think she wants you to leave, sir."

"Man, get the hell away from my table!" Rilla hollered. "This a free country. I can eat wherever I want."

The few customers who weren't already watching because of Candace's fainting spell definitely gave this table their attention now. Parker looked around nervously and dismissed himself discreetly.

"You can have that car," Candace said. "All the furniture, too. I don't need it."

Rilla wasn't surprised by that. "What about my baby?"

Candace was close to telling him about CC, but she considered the impact of her words. Rilla was already teetering on the edge of ignorance. She could either douse or fuel his flames.

"We have to go to court," she said. "We can set up child support and a visitation schedule."

Rilla's smile went away. He stared at her with serious disappointment. "What I do to make you do me like this? I treated you good, Candace. I do six months, and you flipped the script on me. I heard you sleeping with other dudes and everything. You don't want nothing to do with Rilla no more? Won't take my calls from jail. Didn't come see me one time."

"We were already having problems," Candace stalled. "We were going to break up anyway."

"Maybe, but we didn't break up," Rilla said. "We went through our shit, but you was still happy as long as you had some money in your pocket."

Candace knew there was some truth to that. "What was I supposed to do, Raul? You left me with nothing. All that money you were making, you didn't put anything aside. I told you I was pregnant, and you still wanted to live for the day."

"Yeah, you was happy, too."

"*No, I wasn't!* And when you got locked up, I lost my baby because of you! They took my baby!"

"I'm sorry about that," Rilla said. "That's the one thing I do regret."

Candace was incredulous. "*One thing?* That's it? After all you put me through, that's the only thing you're sorry about?"

"You got her back. You make it sound like they still got her."

"I got her back by myself! I got a job and an apartment *by myself*!"

"Then you didn't need me no more."

"That's right, Rilla. I didn't. I asked you to do right. You had a choice. When you chose to stay in the streets, that's when *you* broke up with me. You left me, Rilla!"

He nodded. "So, this cat you with now, what's up with him?"

"What do you mean?"

"I mean, is you serious with him, or is this something you got to hold you over till I got out. I'm willing to let bygones be bygones, Candace. I still love you. You drop that mark, and we can still have a family with our baby. You know he ain't better than me."

Candace couldn't respond to that without making Rilla angry. And luckily, she didn't have to. Parker came back with their manager in tow. The young waiter slowed and let their boss take the lead when they got to Candace's table.

Jesse stood next to Candace and folded his arms over his chest. Candace hadn't noticed before, but her manager had big shoulders and biceps. He stared down at Rilla like a nightclub bouncer.

"Is there a problem here?"

Rilla was not impressed. He wrinkled his nose at the older man. "Who the hell is you?"

"My name is Jesse Fuentes. I'm the manager." He looked to Candace. "Is this guy bothering you?"

"Naw, we just having us a talk," Rilla said. "Me and Candace been knowing each other forever. This my homegirl." Rilla smiled neighborly, but Candace was well past that level of victimization.

"Yes," she said to Jesse. "I want him to leave."

Rilla was floored. His face went blank, but he recovered quickly and filled his eyes with hate.

"You want it like that, Candace? That's how you wanna play it?"

Candace hated to hear those words. The last time she heard them, they came from CC.

This how you wanna play it, ho?

A few hours later the police raided her apartment.

"We don't have anything else to talk about," Candace said to the rapper who brought her to Texas.

"What about my baby?" he asked.

Jesse moved to Rilla's side of the table. "Sir, I'm gonna have to ask you to leave."

But Rilla didn't move. "What about my baby, Candace?"

"You have to go to court," she said. "And set up visi—"

Rilla shot to his feet. "I wanna see my baby *today*! Where is she?"

Jesse grabbed his arm. "Sir, I need you to—"

"She's with my boyfriend," Candace said with a straight face.

"How you gonna leave my baby with some other nigga?"

Jesse tightened his grip. "All right, sir, if you could—"

"Man, get yo hands off me!" Rill jerked his arm away roughly.

Jesse pushed a button on the transponder hooked to his belt and spoke into the headset he always wore. "Josh, send some guys to section four."

Rilla fixed an evil glare on the manager. "You ain't gotta send no guys nowhere. I'll leave!"

"That's fine, sir." Jesse pointed the way to the exit.

Rilla looked back to Candace. He tried to break her will with his scowl, but she glared right back at him.

"Where that fool stay at who got my baby?" Rilla asked.

"Take me to court," Candace said. "If you want to see her, take me to court."

Rilla fumed. "You ain't got no right to treat me like this!"

Jesse's *reinforcement* showed up, and Candace was glad Rilla volunteered to leave on his own. Of the four waiters that came, none were bigger than Parker, and a few of them already had defeat in their eyes.

Rilla pushed his chair in roughly and stepped away from the table. "This ain't over, Candace. You know this shit ain't over, don't you?"

And tragically, she did know that.

"This way, sir."

"This shit ain't over!" Rilla called over the manager's shoulder.

Candace's eyes welled with tears. Again she wished she was on that damned plane.

Jesse took Candace to his office and attempted to get an explanation for the disruption her last customer caused. She tried to explain everything to him, but after three minutes he still had questions; especially about why she had to leave and why she might not be in tomorrow. Candace finally stood and unfastened her apron. A million things ran through her mind, and she couldn't find out about anything from Pappadeaux.

"Jesse, I'm sorry, but I have to go." Candace was near tears. Her hands were shaking. She willed herself to stay strong, just for a little while longer. She went through so much in the last year. There was no way she couldn't get through this, too.

"Candace, I can call the police for you. If that guy's bothering you, I guarantee he won't get back in."

"I have to get my baby," Candace cried. "I'm sorry, Jesse, but I have to go. *Right now.*"

Her manager stood in front of the office's only door, but Candace squeezed by him easily. She rushed through the restaurant at a frantic pace.

"Candace, I can help you!" he called after her.

She stopped and turned. Her face was so different from the first time Jesse saw her. This wasn't the bubbly kid with braces who wowed him with her memorization skills. This was the face of a woman in pain, more pain than he could ever know.

"Walk me to my car," Candace said. "If you want to help, come with me in case he's still out there."

"Sure, Candace. Anything."

He walked her outside, but there was no sign of Rilla by then. Even in the darkness, Candace knew he was nowhere around; he was probably miles away.

She thanked her first boss for everything and told him she'd call when she got things situated.

"I'll see you later," she said as she ducked into her Nissan, knowing full well she would never see the man again.

Candace flew down the highway doing eighty-five in a sixty. She maneuvered past the other motorists recklessly, bouncing from lane to lane without her blinkers. She ignored the many horns blaring at her.

Candace drove without a seatbelt. She gripped the steering wheel at ten and two with sweaty hands. She sat up in her seat like a woman four times her age, her nose just inches from the steering wheel. She stared at the highway and *willed* the road to come to her faster. But no matter how quickly she ate it up, there were still so many streets between her and Leila.

Candace knew everything was all right. She forced herself to believe this, but every time she blinked, she saw terrible things behind her eyelids. *Bloody things.* Trisha said they'd have to take Leila *over her dead body*, and maybe it had come to just that.

But Rilla wasn't crazy, was he? Candace lived with him for over a year. She would have known if he had those kind of tendencies, wouldn't she? Or maybe predicaments like this bring out the worst in anyone.

Candace took her eyes off the road for half a second to dig her cell phone from her purse. There was only one person who might be able to help her, but after five rings Tino didn't answer. Candace left him a desperate message:

"Tino, this is Candace. *Why aren't you answering your phone?* I need you *bad.* Rilla's out. He came up to my job. He just left, and I don't know where he went. I'm scared, Tino. I don't have anyone else. I'm on my way to pick up Leila, and I'm afraid he might be there. Please call me back, Tino. *I need you. I love you.*"

She kept the cellular in her lap in case he called back. Five minutes down the road, the phone vibrated against her bladder. Candace grabbed it anxiously, but it was not a number she recognized. She answered it, fearing Trisha was calling from a neighbor's house.

"Huh-hello?"

"Hello, Candace?"

"Yes. Who's this?"

"As many times as you called, I figured you'd know who I am."

The phone vibrated in her hand, indicating she had another incoming call.

"Detective Judkins?"

"Yes, ma'am. I got your messages, and I'm calling to let you know Rilla *is* getting out of jail."

As frazzled as she was, Candace still found room to get upset.

"Thanks a lot, but he's already out. He just left my job."

"Oh, well, I guess I didn't need to call you after all."

"*Why'd you do that?*" she bawled.

"Excuse me?"

"*Why'd you let him out?* You said you'd call me if you let him out and you didn't call!"

"Jeez, are you . . . are you serious?"

"You arrested me for nothing!" Candace cried. "You knew I didn't do it, but you arrested me anyway. For *two weeks* I stayed in jail till you finally decided to let me go. They took my baby because of you! All I asked is for you to call me when Rilla got out. You said you would, but you lied! *You're a liar!*"

Her phone vibrated again.

"Dammit, Candace, what is your deal? Don't play that *Little Miss Innocent* act with me. You knew what you were getting involved in when you moved in with Raul. You chose to live with a guy who kept dope in the house."

"I *paid* for that!" Candace countered. "I took responsibility for my part. I went to jail. I lost my baby! I took my punishment! But you, you *lied*! You said you'd call—"

"Okay, I'm sorry I didn't call. What's the big deal? Did Raul do something to harm you since he got out? Did he break any laws? If he did, then tell me about it."

"Just tell me why," Candace pleaded. "Why'd you take me to jail? Why'd you let Rilla out?"

"I told you, I arrested you because an informant—"

"*Who?* Who lied on me? I have a right to know!"

The cop didn't answer.

"Was it CC?"

"That information is confidential."

"They're *using* you! Can't you see? It's okay for them to wreck my life, but you won't even tell me who you're listening to. They lied and you know it. Was it CC?"

There was another pause.

"Cordell has been helpful in the past," Judkins admitted.

Candace already believed that for many months now, but it still felt good to have it confirmed.

"Why did you let Rilla out?" she breathed. "He was selling drugs. You caught him red-handed."

"What does that have to do with you?"

Candace exited the freeway and turned onto Trisha's street.

"This thing, this whole thing has caused me more problems than you could ever know, mister. I just want to know the truth." Her voice hitched, and maybe the detective heard her pain and sincerity.

"Raul has been cooperative as well," Judkins said. "That stuff they're doing is small-time to me. I want the guys they get *their* dope from. Raul and Cordell are helping me get him."

Candace couldn't believe it. Two of the hardest thugs she knew were both snitches. She could hear Tino's voice in her head.

Pinche ratas.

"What about me?" Candace asked.

"What about you?"

339

"What about what you did to me?"

"Listen, Miss Hendricks. I apologize for arresting you. I sincerely do. But I have to think about the big picture, and it was a good move at the time."

"I hope you get a *real big* promotion," Candace said. "You're doing a great job out there. Keeping our city all safe and clean. Lock up the good guys and let the bad ones out."

"Okay, goodbye, Miss Hendricks," he said and hung up abruptly.

Candace pulled into a handicapped spot in front of Trisha's apartment building and bolted from her car without taking the keys from the ignition. The crackheads could have that damned Sentra. All she wanted was her baby.

CHAPTER 24
THE FINAL CHAPTER

Candace bounded up the stairs like an antelope, hopping four steps at a time. When she got to the top, she sprinted through Trisha's breezeway and slammed into her friend's front door like a halfback. She wrenched the knob around, but the door didn't open. And although this was the very thing she requested, Candace took it as a sign that things were not good inside.

But Trisha opened the door a moment later, and even more importantly, she cradled precious Leila in her arms. Leila was awake and smiling. She reached for her mother immediately. Trisha stared at her young friend with a look of confusion.

"What you hit my door like that for? And ain't you early? Shouldn't . . ."

With her baby within reach, Candace felt the stress of the last two days ooze from her. It was the best release since she walked out of Gabriella Sands's office for the last time. Candace's legs buckled. The exhaustion from the three flights of stairs suddenly took its toll. She staggered forward, speechless, reaching for her baby.

"*Candace*? What's wrong? You all right?"

Candace shook her head and let the tears go.

"Myah-my baby. Give me. Leila. *Give her* . . ."

"Here, girl." Trisha handed the infant over quickly. Candace cradled her baby like she'd just rescued her from a swimming pool. She stared at Leila's face to make sure she wasn't dreaming. She hugged her tightly, as if this might be the last time.

Candace stumbled into the apartment and fell to her knees in the living room, totally oblivious to the stares she got from Trisha, Willie Jr., and even *Delia*, who sat on Trisha's love seat with Little Sammy in her lap.

"Candace! What the hell is going on, girl? What happened?" Trisha knelt next to her friend and shot an evil eye at Petey, who lounged on the couch. "Get up, boy! Don't you see she needs to sit down?"

"What's wrong with her?" Delia asked. Candace looked up at her for the first time, and immediately felt like a fool. Delia wore a two-piece metallic jumpsuit that probably looked better on her than the Victoria's Secret model. The top was like a sports bra with spaghetti straps. The bottom looked like a pair of spandex biker pants. Both pieces were candy-apple red, with a shine like a brand new Ferrari.

Delia wore her hair down. Her lips were bright red. Her eyes were as alluring as Cleopatra's. She looked down on Candace with an air of superiority that came naturally to her.

Petey moved out of the way, and Candace made it to her feet with Trisha's help. She sat on the couch and wiped the tears from her eyes. Trisha stood before her with both hands on her massive hips.

"Candace? What's going on?"

"Rilla's out," she breathed. "He came to my job."

Trisha shook her head. "I had a feeling he was gonna do that."

Candace looked up at her with a pained expression. "Whuh-what do you mean?"

"Delia said he probably *was* getting out today," Trisha informed her. "I was gonna call you, but she just told me."

"I thought he was coming over here," Candace said.

"I can tell," Trisha said. "You ran up here like you expected to find somebody dead. I heard you stomping all the way up those stairs."

Candace smiled nervously.

"What'd he do?" Trisha asked. "He was starting shit?"

"Talking noise," Candace said. Her heart rate had slowed, and Leila was smiling up at her. She felt better, but Delia's presence still had her upset. Candace was normally fearful of CC's girlfriend, but she'd been through too much in the last couple of days. Candace feared only death now.

"How did he know where I work?" she asked her babysitter.

Trisha didn't answer. Instead she fixed her face with a *not me* expression and darted her eyes in the direction of her love seat.

Candace wiped her face and looked over at Delia with the coldest, driest eyes she could muster. "Why did you do that?" she asked.

The tension in the room was thick enough to spread with a butter knife, but Delia smiled innocently. "Girl, I told CC that a long time ago, when you first started working there. Back then I didn't know Rilla was getting out. I told CC you was doing good by yourself, that's all."

That was a great answer, but Candace wasn't satisfied. "Why'd you tell CC where I live? He followed me to my apartment yesterday."

Trisha's eyes grew wide. Delia rolled hers. "Candace, ain't nobody trying to get you in trouble," she said. "I told CC you stayed across the street from Trisha, but I told him that a long time ago, too. It was just talk. I didn't know he was gonna find out where you stay."

This bitch was good, but Candace was pissed beyond reason.

"So your man's following women around at night? You cool with that?"

"*Hmmp,*" Trisha said. She looked back and forth at the two women like she was at a tennis match.

Delia's mouth fell open, but just for a second. She regained her composure quickly and pulled off a sneer/smile expression that made Candace feel small. "He just did that for Rilla."

"And you helped him," Candace blurted.

Trisha took a step back, her eyes even wider.

Delia cocked her head and worked her neck when she responded. "Well, maybe if you was a real woman, Rilla wouldn't have to find out your address like that. You know you got his baby, and you ain't talked to him *one time* since he got locked up. Honey, you playing childish games, and people ain't got time to play with you. Specially when you playing with they baby."

Candace looked at Trisha, and Trisha begged with her eyes, *Don't do it, Candace,* but Candace was at her wit's end with this heifer. The words flowed from her as if they'd been on the tip of her tongue for years:

"This isn't even Rilla's baby! It's *CC's!* Instead of defending that punk, you need to ask him why he jumped on me when I passed out that night!"

The room went deathly quiet, and Candace's words bounced around the furniture.

passed out that night
that night
that night

Trisha pursed her lips and let out a slight whistle. She looked shocked, but Candace knew she was enjoying every minute of it. She couldn't help it. It was in her busybody blood.

Delia's smile fell for the first time and she stared intently at Candace, trying to find the punch line. Candace stared back at her, assuring there was none. Delia's nostrils flared.

"You lying," she said.

A GOOD DUDE

Candace shook her head. "You know I'm telling the truth. You've seen my baby's eyes. How many times have you told me, '_She doesn't look anything like Rilla. Where'd she get those eyes?_'"

Delia shot fiery arrows from her eyes. All of the muscles in her face went slack. The veins in her neck bulged. "Bitch, you slept with CC?"

Candace cocked her head as if she was talking to a stupid dog. "Naw, _bitch_, CC _raped_ me. Ask him. He'll tell you all about it."

"Uh-oh," Trisha said. She took a step forward, and not a moment too soon.

Delia's eyes narrowed and burned. Her whole face and the tops of her ears turned beet red. Her hands, currently holding Little Sammy, became claws meant to rip and shred until the truth stopped hurting. She stood, dropping the little boy from her lap like a bag of sand. He slammed to the floor with a resounding _thud!_ and bounced slightly.

"_Candace!_" Trisha yelled.

But Candace didn't need the warning. She shot to her feet as quickly as Delia did and was already moving towards the front door. Trisha jumped between the two women and held Delia back like an offensive lineman.

"Candace! _Get out of here!_" Trisha yelled.

"_Bitch, I'ma kill you! I'ma kill you!_" Delia wrestled frantically to reach over or around and even under Trisha's bulk, but there was no gap in that protection.

346

Candace could have stood behind her friend and hurled insults at Delia for a whole five minutes if she wanted. Tony Romo didn't have protection this good.

"Let me go, Trish! *Let me go!*"

Candace opened the front door and then turned back and stared at the women wrestling behind her. Trisha had her feet planted, and though Delia lashed out with every limb, she wasn't making any headway. Little Sammy sat up and giggled at them. Delia caught Candace's eyes and stopped struggling long enough for what was to be her *final decree.*

"I'ma get you, bitch. Best believe, I'ma get you."

Just like an idiot, Candace thought. Attack the problem, rather than the source of the problem.

"Trisha, I'll call you later," she said, forgetting that her friend didn't have a phone.

"*Go*, Candace! Get out of here!" Trisha pleaded.

"Thank you," Candace said. "I love you, Trisha."

"Bitch, *I'ma kill you*! Uhn-uhn! *Let me go*, Trisha!"

"*Go, Candace! Hurry up!*"

Candace took one last look at the apartment, feeling like she'd never see this place again either, and then stepped outside and closed the door behind herself.

Contrary to the madness she had experienced that day, Candace skipped down the stairs with a smile on her face. She heard her cell phone ringing before she reached ground level, but didn't make it to her car quickly enough to answer it. Rather than load Leila in the back, Candace sat in the front seat and plucked her cell phone from her purse. She frowned when she read the display.

Six missed calls.

She pushed the button to make the calls show, and Candace's heart fluttered. All of the calls were from Tino. The last one was less than a minute ago. She called him back hurriedly and let out a pent-up breath when he answered.

"Hello?"

"*Tino! Oh, my God*, I'm glad you called back."

"I called you *six* times!"

"Tino, this has been the craziest day."

"Rilla's out?"

"Yeah. He came up to my job. I was so scared. I thought he was going to take Leila."

"You got her?"

"Yeah, I just did. I almost got in a fight up there."

"Why?"

"I got into it with CC's girlfriend. I'll tell you about it later. I gotta get away from here. I don't know where Rilla is. He could be anywhere."

"Where are you now?" Tino asked.

"I'm still over here at Trisha's apartments."

"Oh. Are you coming home? I'm standing right outside your door."

The hairs stood on Candace's arms. "You're standing right outside *where*?"

"I'm at your apartment."

Candace's head began to pound. "No, I'm not coming home, Tino! What are you doing there?"

"I got your message," he said. "I didn't know what was wrong. I thought you needed me."

"I don't need you *there*, Tino! That's the worst place to be! Was anyone else there? Did you see anybody outside?"

"There's always people here," Tino said.

Candace knitted her eyebrows. She reached up and bit off half her pinkie nail without noticing. "Tino, you need to leave. Head toward your house. I'll call—"

"CC's light-skinned, right?"

Candace's heart stopped altogether. "Tino, please don't do that."

He spoke a little softer now. "No, I'm serious, Candace. There are two guys . . ."

Candace's eyes glossed over again. No way did God hate her this much. She refused to believe that. "Is one of them Puerto Rican?" she asked. "You know what Rilla looks like . . ."

There was a pause.

"Candace, I'm scared."

Her nose filled with moisture. Her bottom lip quivered. "Tino, *please* don't say that. *Please*."

"No, Candace, I'm serious." He still spoke just above a whisper. "When I came up, I *did* see some guys downstairs. I parked right next to them. I didn't think anything about it, but—"

"Tino, leave!"

"I parked right next to them."

"Just run, Tino! Run the other way!"

"Oh, shit, Candace! They're coming up the stairs. Is CC light-skinned? His hair's braided? Please say no."

"*Tino, run! Get off the phone and run! I'll meet you at the front!*"

"Candace—"

"*Run, Tino!*"

"I gotta go."

The phone went dead in her ear.

Candace's keys were still in the ignition. She slammed the door closed and started the car without moving Leila to the back. She backed away from Trisha's building going fast, too fast. She looked up to the rearview mirror in time to see the grill of a Ford F-150 coming at her. Candace stomped on the brakes with both feet, but her Sentra slid on the loose gravel. She came to a stop only after her bumper collided with the parked truck.

Candace's head jerked back and slammed against the headrest. Stars erupted behind her eyes, but she would not pass out again. *Dared not.*

Leila got a much softer cushion against her mother's belly upon impact, and Candace's grip on her baby was true. She looked down, and Leila smiled up at her mother. She giggled as if they were on one hell of a ride.

Candace knew she was lucky but still didn't take the time to put Leila in her car seat. She put the Nissan in drive and peeled off like Jeff Gordon. She made it to the apartment's exit in less than thirty seconds, but her dart across the street was impeded by a string of headlights coming in both directions. She laid on the horn and poked her front end out a little at a time.

"Come on. Come on."

The right lane was finally forced to slow for her. Candace punched the gas as soon as she got a bit of daylight. She shot across the street like a rocket and jumped the next driveway fast enough to soar for a moment. But there were people out, and she had to slam on the brakes again to avoid plowing down a family of four.

The father of the brood snatched one child out of the way and glared at Candace as she flew by them. He might have yelled something, too, but Candace couldn't hear anything over a steady moan that spilled from her own lips. It was a weak, desperate sound.

She saw Rilla's car as soon as she rounded the corner of her building. Candace pulled to an uneven stop next to the Fleetwood and jumped out with little understanding of what she was doing. She heard the sounds of war immediately.

RIIIIP!
WHOMP!
"Aaah!"
"Hold him, cuz!"
"I got him."
HUMPH!

"*Stop!*"

"*Get up, nigga!*"

"*Uhn!*"

"*You got that?*"

"*Hey!*"

WHAP!

"*Watch him, cuz. He trying to—*"

"*Please!*"

"*Stop!*" Candace screamed. She jetted up the steps more quickly than when CC chased her the night before. Her breaths were ragged. Her baby was heavy in her arms.

With all of the flights she had climbed lately, Candace was getting skilled at working those stairs, but her luck gave out just as she reached her floor. A few pebbles tripped her up in full stride, and Candace fell into the concrete steps awkwardly.

She held Leila with her left arm, and broke her fall with the right, but not before her knee smashed into the last step, exploding with a pain almost as vicious as childbirth. Candace's torso never touched the ground, and neither did Leila. Once again she avoided killing her child, and Candace knew God was still with her.

Or maybe He wasn't.

She looked up weakly, and cried out like the mother of a stillborn. At the other end of her breezeway, the scene was much worse than she imagined: Tino was still there. He lay on the concrete balled into a fetal position.

And although this pose left him defenseless, Rilla and CC still bent and punched and kicked and stomped. They tried to pick Tino up by his jacket, but the garment ripped in their hands. The whole sleeve came off. Tino struggled to keep his arms over his face.

Rilla had on the same white shirt as earlier, but it was soiled now with dark stains Candace knew to be blood. CC wore blue jeans with a blue T-shirt. He delivered a devastating kick to the back of Tino's head and then looked up and saw Candace crawling towards them.

"*Stop!*" she screamed, but it felt like she was speaking through the wrong end of a funnel. Her throat squeezed tight, and she could manage little more than a crackling whine.

"*Stop!*"

CC's face was a mask of destruction. He looked from Candace to Rilla quickly, and instead of alerting his friend to her presence, CC reached into his back pocket and produced what Candace thought was a cell phone. But then he flicked the device with his wrist, and a three-inch blade popped out. He looked at Candace again and she knew he was crazed.

CC looked down at Tino. The blade glistened in the lamplight.

Rilla kept punching, with his back to his ex-girlfriend. He reached into the pile of folded flesh and tried to get his hands around Tino's throat.

"*Where my baby, nigga?*"

"Please stop!" Candace croaked.

And Rilla did stop then. He looked around until he saw Candace. They stared at each other solemnly. Rilla stood and took a few steps towards his baby's mother.

CC knelt and plunged his blade deep into Tino's side, all the way to the hilt. Tino let out a scream that was destined to replay in Candace's nightmares for years to come. It bounced around the breezeway like an ambulance stuck in a tunnel.

"AAAAAAAH!"

Tino rolled to his back and groped at his wound with both hands. Candace could see his face now, and she saw that it was twisted in agony. Blood flowed from his nose. His features were knotted and swollen in so many places. Blood leaked from a wound above his hairline. It spilled down past his eyebrows, into his eyes and mouth. His shirt was soiled and ripped. Even his pants were torn. One shoe was missing.

Rilla turned again and stared down at Tino. He saw the fresh spray of blood blossoming on the young man's shirt. Rilla's fists were still balled, but a queer look changed the scowl that was once his face. Rilla looked to CC. His bottom lip hung dumbly and glistened with spittle.

"What'd you do?"

CC didn't respond. His face was stiff like a statue. There was no fear. No remorse. He wiped the knife on his pants legs, his eyes on Candace the whole time.

Candace crawled forward with one arm supporting Leila, the other hand clawing the pavement. Every time she put weight on her bad knee, it felt like she was smashing it all over again, but she kept moving.

"*Please, Rilla. Leave him alone,*" she croaked.

Rilla hesitated, unsure what his next move should be. Tino rolled and writhed at his tormentor's feet.

"Come on, dog. Let's go." CC grabbed Rilla's arm and pulled him towards the opposite stairway.

Rilla looked from Candace to Tino. His look of confusion was real. "What'd you do?" he asked CC again.

"Come on, cuz. We gotta go." CC pulled on his shirt, and then turned and dipped down the stairs by himself when Rilla didn't respond. "We gotta go!" he called from below.

Candace cried and crawled past her ex-boyfriend's feet. Rilla didn't move. He stood stiffly and followed her with his eyes. Sweat dotted his forehead like morning dew.

Candace dragged herself to Tino's broken and bloodied body. She sat next to him and pulled his head into her lap. Tino moaned and cried weakly. His chest rose and fell. He kicked out with his legs and scraped his bare foot across the concrete.

Candace trembled uncontrollably. She sniffled loudly and stroked his hair gently. His wonderful locks were matted and gooey in one spot above his left ear. Her hand was soaked with blood within seconds.

Rilla stared down at them angrily, but his fire was fading. "Thi-this *yo* fault," he said, more for his benefit than hers.

Candace was scarcely aware he was still there. She cried fiercely and brushed her nose with the sleeve of her work shirt.

"Tuh-Tino. Tino, can you hear me?"

One of Tino's eyes was swollen closed. He quieted and squinted with the other one, but it was glossed over with blood.

"Kuh-kuh-Candace?" Blood spilled from his mouth now. Candace knew what that meant, but refused to accept it. She tried to keep her voice steady.

"It's—it's me," she said. She put her maroon-colored hand on the side of his face and brushed his cheek gently.

"I'm—I'm *dying*," Tino said. It was hard to understand him. His lips were misshapen, and there was a gurgling quality to his voice.

Candace's chest shuddered. "No, Tino," she bawled. "No, you're not."

Without any further words, Rilla turned and stepped briskly down the stairs. A moment later Candace heard a car door open and close, but CC didn't peal off like she expected. He drove away slowly and casually as if shanking someone was a misdemeanor nowadays.

"I'm cuh-cold," Tino said.

Candace bit her bottom lip so hard her mouth was soon wet with blood. "It's cold outside, Tino. That's all."

She heard sirens in the distance. They were getting closer.

"They're coming to help you, Tino. Can you hear?"

"Are . . . are you leaving?" he asked.

Candace sniffed loudly. Tears mixed with mucus dribbled past her lips.

"No, Tino. I'll never leave you. *Never.*"

EPILOGUE

Brooklyn, New York
Christmas Eve
One Year Later

Candace sat on the back porch of her parents' home in Prospect Heights and stared out at the many acres of white; wonderful white, beautiful white. The porch was enclosed with solid walls rather than screens, but it was still pretty nippy out there. Candace's lips were cold, and her nose was starting to run a bit.

Leila, on the other hand, was impervious to these frigid temperatures. Gerald said she was part polar bear. Leila pawed through a huge box of toys Grandpa had back there on the porch. Most of the trinkets belonged to Candace many moons ago, but Leila was not one to reject a plaything, even if it was a couple decades old.

The baby was eighteen months now. She wore thick denim jeans with big black boots her grandfather bought for her. The boots had a rubber shell, like galoshes, but the sides were quilted and lined with faux fur. Leila wore a toddler-size bomber jacket. It was pink like Candace's, and had a fur-lined hoodie as well. Leila had fuzzy mittens and a scarf also. She could stand on her own now. She leaned on the large box, but it was almost as tall as her.

"Mama." She pointed with one hand while flashing Candace the most dazzling smile. Leila had a few baby choppers. Her bunny rabbit teeth were the biggest, and they weren't crooked like Candace's were at her age. So far it looked like Leila might be able to avoid braces. Candace had hers taken out just a few weeks ago.

Leila's hood had streaks of brown and tan fur. The tan matched her eyes, and the brown matched her skin, which had gotten a little darker over the last twelve months.

Candace smiled at her daughter. "What is it?" she asked.

Leila tried to climb into the box, but the rim was chest-high. She stood on her tiny tippy toes and reached with both hands, still unable to claim her prize. She looked back to her mother and smiled eagerly.

"Puppy," she said. "*Mine.*"

Candace stood from the padded rocking chair she was so fond of and peered into the cardboard box. There really was a puppy in there. It was the Laugh and Learn Puppy. Candace hadn't seen the thing since she moved back to New York, but she recognized it immediately. She bent and retrieved it for her daughter.

This was the doll Tino bought for Leila when Candace first regained her from the CPS network. Back then the stuffed animal could sing songs and teach baby her colors, 123's and ABC's. Candace was sure it wouldn't work after all this time, but when she squeezed its paw, the dog began to sing again.

Sort of.

It sounded like an old record spinning with extra slow RPMs. The noise stopped altogether after only a couple seconds, and the oversized puppy went mute again, possibly forevermore.

"Uh-uh!" Leila pulled on Candace's pants leg, reaching up with both hands.

Candace handed over the old toy, and Leila held it out at arms length and studied the puppy's goofy face. Candace remembered when the dog was just as big as her daughter. Now Leila was twice as big as the dog. She giggled and hugged it like it was a long-lost friend.

The back door swung open and Candace's mom stepped out.

"*Ooh, child!* It's freezing out here, Candace! What are you doing? And I know you don't have Leila out here! What's wrong with you, girl?"

"There's no wind," Candace said. She walked back to the rocking chair and took a seat. Candace wore jeans with her fluffy bomber. She also wore Isotoner gloves and had a thermal under all of that. Katherine Hendricks wore only thin slacks and a sweater. Of course *she* was cold.

Grandma scooped up Leila, and Leila held on to her dog. Katherine kissed her grandchild and frowned at her daughter.

"Candace, this girl's face is *cold*."

"She likes it out here."

"She likes anything you like," Katherine said good-naturedly. "What are you doing out here, anyway?"

361

"Just looking at the snow," Candace replied.

"You didn't get any snow last year," Katherine remembered.

Candace smiled and stared out as if in a daze. "No. I didn't."

"I'm taking the baby in," Katherine said. "Gerald has some more outfits he wants her to try on." Candace's mom turned to go inside, but she stopped and stared at her daughter. "What are you thinking about?"

"As soon as it got close to Christmas," Candace said, "I started thinking about what happened."

Katherine nodded. "You probably will for many Christmases to come."

"I want to have a Christmas without thinking about that stuff," Candace said.

"My mother died on her birthday thirteen years ago," Katherine said. "Every April I still think about her."

Candace nodded. Her mother took Leila inside and left Candace alone with her thoughts, but the solitude didn't last long. Candace's favorite cousin stepped out onto the porch a few minutes later.

"Hey, girl!" she said, and took a seat in the other rocker.

"Hey," Candace said, still looking out onto the barren landscape.

Gerald's sister, Aunt Betty, came down from Staten Island every Christmas. She was a single mother, very successful in pharmaceuticals. Her daughter, Toya, was raised much like Candace. The two girls both went to private schools, both made excellent marks, and both lost out on what they considered regular kid experiences; they never saw fights or had friends who were potheads or anything cool like that.

Candace rebelled against her storybook life by running halfway across the country with Rilla. Toya might have done something similar, but the opportunity never presented itself. Toya was now a freshman at Long Island University. She was thinking about transferring to Columbia with Candace.

"What you doing out here in the cold by yourself?" Toya asked. She was thin and attractive. Her complexion was darker than Candace's, and she was also prettier, in Candace's opinion.

"Just thinking," Candace said.

"You thinking about what happened in Texas, ain't you?" Toya asked.

Candace looked over at her and grinned. "Why would you say that?"

"Your mama says you're out here thinking about last year and you're all depressed."

Candace shook her head. "I'm not depressed."

"But you are thinking about it?" Toya asked.

Candace sighed. "Yes, *Miss Nosey*, I'm thinking about it."

Toya sat up in her seat. "You wanna talk about it?"

Candace smirked. "Are you asking because you want to help me get through something, or do you only want to hear a bloody story?"

Toya grinned unabashedly. "Was it really bloody?"

Candace closed her eyes and she could see it all. She shook her head and vanquished the memories. "Sorry, Dr. Phil. I don't think I'll be sharing today."

Toya stomped her foot. "Come on, Candace! You know I don't get to see you that much."

"If you come to Columbia, you can see me all the time."

"Mama won't let me," Toya pouted. "I wish I could run away like you."

"That's your problem," Candace said. "You think I had it easy out there on my own."

"You won't never talk about it," Toya said. "What am I supposed to think?"

Candace knew this was yet another ploy to get the story out of her. "You heard about the fight and cops. You know I lost my baby. You know I went to jail. What part of that sounds cool to you?"

Toya grinned. "*All of it.*"

Candace rolled her eyes.

"I'm serious," Toya said. "You the only person I know who went to jail. And you're the only person I know who had their own apartment and a baby all by themselves. I told my friends about you. You're like a queen to them."

"I know how it is," Candace said. "I went to private schools, too."

"So you'll tell me a story?"

Candace leaned back in the rocker. "How about I tell you what your mom would want you to know," she offered. "I'll tell you about the consequences of negative behavior."

"That's boring."

Candace chuckled. "That's all I'm giving you."

Toya listened intently.

"Did you know," Candace began, "that if you're with someone who tries to kill someone else, they can charge you with attempted murder?"

"I know if you do a drive-by they'll charge you with it, even if you were just driving," Toya said.

"Even if you're in the back and you don't even have a gun," Candace said. "Even if you just got picked up and you had no idea they were going to do a drive-by."

"That's what happened to Rilla?" Toya asked.

Candace nodded. "He didn't know CC was going to stab Tino. I was there. I saw the whole thing."

"But he did beat him up," Toya noted.

"That's what got him," Candace said. "He attacked Tino on his own accord. So everything CC did was Rilla's fault, too."

"What'd they charge him with?"

"They both got charged with attempted murder," Candace said. "I thought they were going to beat it because CC had connections with the police, but they were found guilty. Twenty years apiece."

"Damn," Toya said. "That's a long time."

"It is," Candace agreed.

"But they'll get out one day," Toya said.

Candace smiled. "I don't think CC's ever getting out. He was working with the drug police to turn in a big-time supplier, but the deal fell through when he stabbed Tino. CC has to do twenty years for the fight, plus a life sentence for the drug charges. They run concurrent, but that's still forty years before he gets paroled."

"*Dang*," Toya said. "How can they give you life for dope?"

"I used to think like that, too," Candace said. "But CC's a creep. He might have got life for selling drugs, but there's more stuff he never got arrested for. Like when he raped me. It doesn't say it on paper, but I'd like to think some of the time he's serving is for what he did to me. Trust me, he deserves a lot worse."

Toya nodded. "But why can't you talk about Tino? It's not like he's dead or nothing."

Candace laughed. "He'll be here any minute."

"He's already here," Toya said. "He was in there talking to your dad when I came out here."

Candace shot to her feet. "Tino's here?"

Toya nodded. "Yeah."

"Why didn't you tell me?"

"He'll be here all day," Toya said. "I figured you'd see him sooner or later."

Candace rushed to the back door. She kicked her cousin on the shin on the way by.

"Ow!"

But the door opened on its own when Candace got to it. This time it was Tino. The last twelve months hadn't changed him much, except his hair was an inch longer and his eyebrows were fuller. Tino wore black jeans with dark brown boots. He had on a white turtleneck sweater and a full-length black trench coat. He looked dashing and daring, fresh off the cover of *GQ* magazine. He was clean-shaven, but it was by choice these days. Tino could grow a full moustache in forty-eight hours if he wanted to.

Candace squealed and threw her arms around him. Tino stepped down onto the porch and embraced her fully. He smelled holiday fresh, like Aspen cologne. His cheek was smooth against Candace's, and his body was warm.

"Tino! Oh, baby, I missed you! Why didn't you tell me you were here? I've been sitting out here with *this heifer* for ten minutes."

"I'm sorry," he said into her neck. "I just got here. Your dad cornered me as soon as I walked in the door."

"What y'all so excited for?" Toya asked. "It ain't like y'all don't see each other all the time."

And that was true. Tino's infamous stab wound one year ago turned out to be one of his least serious injuries. CC's blade slipped in just below Tino's ribs, neatly slicing through muscle and fatty tissue, but the knife did not puncture his liver, stomach, or even his intestines. Contrary to the blood loss, no vital organ or artery was damaged.

It took only a week to recover from his other bumps, cuts and bruises, and Tino walked out of the hospital before their holiday break from school was over. Candace completed the spring semester with him at the community college, and over the summer she was finally able to convince him to move to New York with her. They both began their junior year at Columbia University four months ago.

"I haven't seen him since school let out on the fifteenth," Candace said. "I miss my baby."

That was the one hard part about the migration. They both lived on campus, but Tino didn't have any nearby relatives to live with during the holidays. He had to stay in the dorm, while Candace only had to cross the Manhattan Bridge to spend Christmas break with her family.

"Tino, will you tell me about when you got stabbed?" Toya asked.

He laughed.

"Get out of here!" Candace shouted.

Toya got up obediently. She opened the back door but paused in the doorway.

"Tino, can you get her to come inside?" she asked. "She's been out here for like an hour."

"I'll be there in a minute," Candace said. Toya gave her a wicked grin and closed the door behind herself.

Candace took a step away from her boyfriend so she could look at him.

"Your nose is red," Tino said.

"I know. I am getting cold now," Candace admitted. "You ready to go inside?"

"Hold on," Tino said. He reached down and held both of her gloved hands. "I have a present for you. I want to give it to you while we're alone."

Candace smiled expectantly. "Okay."

Tino reached into his breast pocket and pulled out a small box. From the size of it, Candace knew only a ring could fit in there. Her heart fluttered, and she felt warm all of a sudden.

"Before you get excited," Tino said, "I have to tell you my mom wouldn't let me propose to you."

Candace's smile grew bigger rather than fade with this revelation. "You wanted to propose to me?" she asked.

Tino opened the box to reveal a silver ring with a small diamond. "I did want to propose," he said. "I was going to do it today. This is the best ring I could afford."

Candace stared at the band, but she could barely see it twinkle because of the tears in her eyes. "That sure looks like an engagement ring to me," she said.

"It is an engagement ring," Tino said. "It was. I have to call it a *promise ring*. I'm sorry. I wanted it to be more special, but my mom says I have to wait until I get my bachelor's before I can ask you to marry me."

Candace wiped a warm tear from her eye.

"Is it okay?" Tino asked.

Candace nodded wistfully. "It's perfect."

He smiled. "Can I put it on you?"

Candace pulled her left glove off with her teeth and let it fall where it may. Tino plucked the ring from the box and slid it over her third finger. It fit perfectly.

"How'd you know my size?" she asked.

"I measured your finger while you slept," Tino said. Candace didn't know if he was kidding or not, and she didn't care. The gift was wonderful.

Tino pulled a folded sheet from his coat pocket. "This is a promise ring," he said as he read from the paper. "This ring means the following things: I will be faithful to you. I will keep you in my heart always, and we are best friends. This ring means I will always be there for you. It means I love you, and my intentions are to marry you one day."

Candace took the paper and read it for herself. "Tino, you're such a nerd," she said affectionately.

"I wanted to make sure I presented it correctly," he said. "I looked it up on the Internet."

Candace smiled. "I accept your promise ring," she said, "and all the promises that come with it. Especially the," she looked back to the sheet, " *'My intentions are to marry you one day'* part. I really like that."

"I'd marry you right now if I could," Tino said.

Candace nodded. "I know you would."

"Man, screw that," Tino said. He took the promise ring paper and balled it up.

"I'm gonna do it," he said.

"Do what?"

"I'm gonna propose like I wanted to. Gimme my ring back."

Fiery butterflies danced in Candace's belly. She returned his gift reluctantly.

"What about your mother?" she asked.

Tino dropped to one knee like a proper gentleman and cradled Candace's hand in his. "She got married when she was seventeen," he said. "She's not one to talk."

Candace's legs felt prickly. She squirmed like she had to go to the bathroom.

"*Oh, my God*," she breathed.

"Candace, we've been through so much together . . ."

"*Oh, Tino*," she said, bouncing now.

"I've never met a woman as beautiful as you," he said. "I've never met anyone as wonderful as you, and as smart. No one makes me feel like you do . . ."

"*Yes!*" Candace said.

"Wait, I haven't asked you anything yet."

"Hurry up!" she whined.

"You cold?"

"No, I'm *anxious*."

"Okay. Okay." He cleared his throat. "Candace Hendricks, will you marry me?"

"Yes, Celestino! Yes, I will!"

He slipped the ring on again, and it was an even better fit this time. He stood, and Candace threw her arms around his neck and lifted her feet in the air.

"*I'm so excited!*" she squealed.

Tino wrapped his arms around her waist and held her close. "Me, too. This is the best day of my life."

They kissed to seal their engagement and then stared into each other's eyes longingly.

"Let's go inside," Tino finally said.

"Oh, my God, I can't believe we're engaged. You brought your luggage, didn't you?" Candace asked.

"Yeah. But I don't know about staying here until school starts back," Tino said.

"Why not? I got the guest room ready for you."

"Because your dad says I have to be in there *all by myself*," he said with a grin. "He says you can't come visit me past 8 p.m."

Candace giggled. "Did he say anything about you coming to my room?"

Tino shook his head with a sly smile. "No. He didn't say anything about that."

"I can have visitors as late as 3 a.m.," Candace said.

"That's risky."

"Not really," Candace replied. "After a few eggnogs, my dad usually passes out around midnight."

They grinned conspiratorially and walked through the back door hand in hand. Candace's parents had a huge kitchen. It was warm and filled with the smells of the season.

"So you finally got her to come in?" Gerald called from the refrigerator.

"Yes, sir," Tino said. "She's seen enough snow today."

"Great!" Gerald said. He emerged from the fridge with a fresh glass of eggnog in hand. He took it to the counter and added hard liquor to his drink.

Candace squeezed her boyfriend's hand.

Tino looked over at her.

"See?" she whispered. "One down, two to go."

Tino smiled.

Candace winked at him and let go of his hand for a second to brush a few hairs away from her eyes. That simple move was all it took.

"What's that on your finger?" Katherine asked.

THE END

ABOUT THE AUTHOR

Keith Walker is the author of *Fixin' Tyrone* and *How to Kill Your Husband*. He is a graduate of Texas Wesleyan University, where he earned a bachelor's degree in English with a specification in education. Keith started writing in fifth grade and has won many awards. He is an avid poet who performs at various venues throughout his hometown and neighboring cities. He lives in Fort Worth, Texas, with his wife and two children. You can visit him at www.keithwalkerbooks.com.

2010 Mass Market Titles

January

Show Me The Sun
Miriam Shumba
ISBN: 978-158571-405-6
$6.99

Promises of Forever
Celya Bowers
ISBN: 978-1-58571-380-6
$6.99

February

Love Out Of Order
Nicole Green
ISBN: 978-1-58571-381-3
$6.99

Unclear and Present Danger
Michele Cameron
ISBN: 978-158571-408-7
$6.99

March

Stolen Jewels
Michele Sudler
ISBN: 978-158571-409-4
$6.99

Not Quite Right
Tammy Williams
ISBN: 978-158571-410-0
$6.99

April

Oak Bluffs
Joan Early
ISBN: 978-1-58571-379-0
$6.99

Crossing The Line
Bernice Layton
ISBN: 978-158571-412-4
$6.99

How To Kill Your Husband
Keith Walker
ISBN: 978-158571-421-6
$6.99

May

The Business of Love
Cheris F. Hodges
ISBN: 978-158571-373-8
$6.99

Wayward Dreams
Gail McFarland
ISBN: 978-158571-422-3
$6.99

June

The Doctor's Wife
Mildred Riley
ISBN: 978-158571-424-7
$6.99

Mixed Reality
Chamein Canton
ISBN: 978-158571-423-0
$6.99

2010 Mass Market Titles (continued)

July

Blue Interlude
Keisha Mennefee
ISBN: 978-158571-378-3
$6.99

Always You
Crystal Hubbard
ISBN: 978-158571-371-4
$6.99

Unbeweavable
Katrina Spencer
ISBN: 978-158571-426-1
$6.99

August

Small Sensations
Crystal V. Rhodes
ISBN: 978-158571-376-9
$6.99

Let's Get It On
Dyanne Davis
ISBN: 978-158571-416-2
$6.99

September

Unconditional
A.C. Arthur
ISBN: 978-158571-413-1
$6.99

Swan
Africa Fire
ISBN: 978-158571-377-6
$6.99$6.99

October

Friends in Need
Joan Early
ISBN:978-1-58571-428-5
$6.99

Against the Wind
Gwynne Forster
ISBN:978-158571-429-2
$6.99

That Which Has Horns
Miriam Shumba
ISBN:978-1-58571-430-8
$6.99

November

A Good Dude
Keith Walker
ISBN:978-1-58571-431-5
$6.99

Reye's Gold
Ruthie Robinson
ISBN:978-1-58571-432-2
$6.99

December

Still Waters...
Crystal V. Rhodes
ISBN:978-1-58571-433-9
$6.99

Burn
Crystal Hubbard
ISBN: 978-1-58571-406-3
$6.99

Other Genesis Press, Inc. Titles

Other Genesis Press, Inc. Titles (continued)

Other Genesis Press, Inc. Titles (continued)

Other Genesis Press, Inc. Titles (continued)

Other Genesis Press, Inc. Titles (continued)

Other Genesis Press, Inc. Titles (continued)

Other Genesis Press, Inc. Titles (continued)

Order Form

Mail to: Genesis Press, Inc.
P.O. Box 101
Columbus, MS 39703

Name _____
Address _____
City/State _____ Zip _____
Telephone _____

Ship to (if different from above)
Name _____
Address _____
City/State _____ Zip _____
Telephone _____

Credit Card Information
Credit Card # _____ ☐ Visa   ☐ Mastercard
Expiration Date (mm/yy) _____ ☐ AmEx ☐ Discover

Qty.	Author	Title	Price	Total

Use this order form, or call

1-888-INDIGO-1

Total for books _____
Shipping and handling:
  $5 first two books,
  $1 each additional book _____
Total S & H _____
Total amount enclosed _____

Mississippi residents add 7% sales tax